During the wait in the dark, he was so close to her, that Justine felt strands of his silken hair brush against her face. Yet she kept quiet, not wanting him to know the mere thought of him was consuming her.

Darrius could hardly stand being that close to her in the dark and not think about her naked and lying on his bed in air conditioning. He imagined how her body would react to him joining her on the bed, the taste of her lips against his, the feel of her breasts in his large hands.

Tasting one nipple after the other began to control him to the point where he could actually taste them. His mouth watered, his body stiffened, his breathing became shallow. What on earth was the woman doing to him? Was she even real, or a figment of something the stars really did bring? Whatever the case, he wanted her. Screw being a gentleman, he wanted her raw, pulsing against him. Now.

Thoughts became actions and he bent to the nape of her neck, kissing the tender flesh. He knew he'd probably get slapped and possibly lose the one woman who had taken his mind off everything in the real world. She was sweet to the taste, gentle to the tongue, and his erection pulled tight against his jeans. His only thought: *She isn't pulling away from me.*

RED SKY

RENEÉ ALEXIS

Genesis Press, Inc.

INDIGO LOVE SPECTRUM

An imprint of Genesis Press, Inc.
Publishing Company

Genesis Press, Inc.
P.O. Box 101
Columbus, MS 39703

Copyright © 2009 by Reneé Alexis

ISBN: 13 DIGIT : 978-158571-286-1
ISBN: 10 DIGIT : 1-58571-286-8
Manufactured in the United States of America

First Edition 2009

Visit us at www.genesis-press.com
or call at 1-888-Indigo-1

DEDICATION

First, I dedicate this novel to God. Without His help every day of my life, I wouldn't have made it this far. Also, to Pumpkin, my new puppy, who was so good and patient while I edited my manuscript. To my family and friends—what a big help all of you have been throughout my writing career. Lastly, to my fans. I love and appreciate all of you. You are the reason I do this. I love to entertain and take people to places and times that everyday life can't supply. My sincerest gratitude.

1

THE LAND OF ENCHANTMENT

Monday Afternoon

Justine Roberts-Paretti had finally found the perfect bracelet, one she had been searching for far and wide. She was a photojournalist and had traveled throughout the United States on assignments, and wherever she had gone she would look for that special bracelet. Turns out it wasn't that far away after all. It was right here in Gallup, New Mexico, where she'd come on assignment for the *San Francisco Examiner* to photograph the annual Intertribal Indian Ceremonial. Another side benefit of the trip was the distance it placed between her and a gone-astray love life.

And so here she was in Red Sky Jewelers viewing the long-coveted bracelet up close. The shop's website was what had drawn her here. The site was beautifully designed, displaying paintings of Acoma basket weavers, Native American pottery, carvings, jewelry and clothing against a turquoise and desert sand backdrop—everything she loved. Justine had grown up around Native American children in her San Francisco neighborhood and had developed an abiding interest in their culture as exhibited by their arts and handicrafts, as well as expressed in dance, song and legends.

Now she was facing the bracelet that promised to take her bank account straight to the cleaners. She took a closer look at the price. She looked at the cost again: nine hundred dollars. So what; it was magnificent, with brilliant hues of turquoise, silver and coral, and was exactly what she had been looking for. She hadn't expected it to cost quite that much, but damn it was awesome! Sure, she made a good living as a photojournalist for a major newspaper, but not enough to splurge on a single piece of jewelry—no matter how glorious.

Looking in the showcase for less expensive bracelets that were just as glorious, she finally found one. The one with spiny oyster and turquoise-linked hearts got her attention. It was a terrific second choice at about a third of the cost of the other. Much better. She looked around for help, but saw no one. Sounds coming from the back meant someone was around. As she scanned the area, she saw that the store was as lovely as the web site, with desert-pink walls on one side showcasing animal skins and native rattles. The other side featured turquoise walls with a variety of masks and headdresses. To one side was a rack of boxed teas, another side featured shelves of T-shirts, dresses, cowboy boots and other attire. Everything was so fascinating and beautiful. But then her attention went back to the jewelry display at the front counter. Again, she looked to where she heard background noises. She wanted to see whoever was back there so she could make this purchase—one she would never regret. *Where the heck is the sales person?* she wondered.

Justine was a gemstone connoisseur, having studied precious stones for years at her family's gem store. Inlay and the intricacies of wire-wrapped jewelry, multi-stone arrangements and alternating patterns briefly took her mind from the lack of sales help.

Then she heard someone ask, "Ma'am, is there anything I can show you?"

Justine turned from the showcase and came face to face with a tall, slender version of—perfection. His bronze face and hip-length jet black hair had to be an illusion; in reality, no mere mortal could be that beautiful. He reminded her of the character Wind in His Hair from *Dances With Wolves,* only so much better! She was momentarily at a loss for words, but then she recovered her senses. Remembering that she was finished with men, she decided this pretty one before her was probably no better than any of the others—bent on getting whatever he could from a woman. At least, that had been her unhappy experience with past lovers. Justine also knew there was another side to the male-female saga, but where did she have to go to find it? Gallup? No way!

Her gaze returned to his rich caramel eyes, and all the while having to try to remember her own thoughts: *You're done with men, remember? You* are *done with them, aren't you? Well?* Definitely! She was finally able to muster a reasonably sane reply. "I, uh, I'd like to see the turquoise and spiny oyster bracelet. The one with—"

"Yes, I know the one, and I think it'll be perfect for you."

Either he was psychic, an unusually perceptive salesman, or a wolf on the prowl. In truth, though, he truly didn't look like the last. The young man unlocked the showcase, took out the exact item she wanted and placed it on a black velvet display pad.

"This is the one you had in mind, isn't it?"

"Exactly, but how did you know? There's several turquoise heart and spiny oyster bracelets in there."

"It's my personal favorite, and this style sells well. Beyond that, it fits you, matches your aura. If you don't mind my saying so. I've been watching you from the moment you entered, but wanted to give you time to discover your heart's desire."

"Really?" *Beginning to sound more and more like wolf material to me.* "I did look for sales help, although not very hard. I was that dazzled by your jewelry display."

"Easy to get sidetracked in a place like this, I suppose, since I have so much merchandise here. Would have been hard to hear me anyway. I have a quiet step."

Justine looked down at his moccasin-clad feet. Even his footwear, white shell, jet and turquoise-beaded moccasins, was beautiful. "Do you sell moccasins here, too?"

"Ma'am, I sell just about everything Western and Native American. Give me your wrist."

His directness was unexpected. "What?"

"The bracelet."

"Oh." She had been so entranced with his silken voice and striking, finely defined Native American features she had forgotten everything else, even her own internal warnings to not be sucked into the looks-to-kill-for vortex. The man projected both tranquility and a restless kind of sexual energy. She was finding it hard not to stare at his tight light-blue worn jeans over which he wore a buckskin poncho with a deep V. Hints of feathery dark chest hair glistened against his skin. A single strand of red shell hung around his neck, along with a jeweler's loupe. Justine cautiously raised her wrist to him.

Skin brushed skin as he fastened the bracelet around her delicate wrist. His fingers even felt soft, smooth, rich—luxurious. Justine wondered just what else on him felt rich, and then realized her mind was galloping away. She moved her wrist back and forth. "I like the heft of it."

Turning on a small display lamp, he said, "It looks better when light is on it. See?"

Justine agreed. The bracelet sparkled, casting shades of reds, oranges and blues against the counter and walls. "It's even prettier than I thought. At first I wanted the turquoise nugget bracelet, but nine hundred dollars kind of threw me for a loop."

He took that bracelet out, holding it to the light and inspecting its rounder, heftier stones. "This isn't the right piece for you. It doesn't bring out your mystique as much as the spiny oyster does. It's not delicate enough. You need something with elegance and grace, which this piece doesn't have. The heftier piece is for every day; you know, casual."

"Can't the heart bracelet be worn casually as well?"

"Sure, get as fancy or as free as you like with it." He held her wrist to the light again, appreciating the delicacy of the bracelet against her skin. "This one definitely is the better choice. It looks wonderful against your complexion. The cinnamon of your skin blends well with the oyster. Your long, dark hair is also compatible with these colors." He paused. "Pardon me for asking, but do you have any Italian in your background?"

"Some. My paternal grandfather was Italian—from Salerno, to be specific."

"And the other part, again, if you don't mind the questions. You look very different from a lot of women—but I think that's a good thing." Her rich caramel complexion, along with long reddish-brown hair, mesmerized him. He'd seen many a beautiful customer, but this one with her slender frame and charming personality was one he wouldn't soon forget. His eyes lingered on her as she spoke.

"Of course I don't mind." His naturalness began to seem genuine by the second. However, she had been fooled before, the memory of which made her pull her hand free of his. "I'm mostly African American."

"Feisty cultures. I like feistiness; it makes for good character."

"Definitely makes for interesting company."

"African Americans and Indians have a long history, probably dating back to before the seventeenth century."

"I know. Actually some of my ancestors escaped slavery and were accepted into native tribes." She tapped her fingers against the countertop. "I'm also a history buff."

"I see. Considering my heritage and yours, we'd probably get along quite well." He extended his hand. "By the way, I'm Hopi."

"I know that's a tribe, and I seriously hope that's not your given name as well."

He smiled seductively. "I like your sense of humor. Yes, I'm a member of the Hopi nation. My given name is Darrius Red Sky. I own this store and a few others."

"This is amazing! You're the man?"

"The man?"

"Yes, the man behind the legend."

"Sorry, but, ah, I haven't any idea what—"

"What I'm talking about? I know you don't, but this store and your website are a favorite of mine and of my friends. Probably others, too."

"Legend, huh? Glad to know I'm so popular—well, at least in certain areas."

"Very popular. I've pulled up your site many times to marvel at your very beautiful merchandise. But I've never seen this piece." She jingled her newly acquired bracelet.

"It's new, just suddenly came in one day without a purchase order." Pausing, he added, "Maybe it was destined to be here just for you."

"That's a good way to think of it. By the way, why isn't your picture on your site? I've seen the name Darrius, but when I saw you I didn't associate your name with the face."

"Why not?"

"I just didn't is all. You look too much like a male model who should be out on a photo shoot instead of selling jewelry to strange young women with loads of questions."

"That's a great compliment, but as far as being in a photo shoot—it'll never happen. I'm camera shy."

"Why? I think you'd be doing the camera a favor—not to mention the women I know who log on all the time."

"Really? That's awfully kind, and I do get in a lot of Internet orders. Tell your friends thanks."

Their eyes lingered on one another in the silence of the moment. They definitely liked each other, but that was exactly what she didn't want to happen again. Men were on the back burner, even this handsome one. Somehow, he was different from any man she had known; not only heritage-wise, but he had a way of making her seem special from the way he looked at her. Feeling special wasn't on her agenda. She was there to take pictures of great dancers and to capture the color and interactions and mysticism of a powwow. His voice drew her back to the present.

"My brother Derrick scours the entire Southwest and beyond for fabulous one-of-a-kind pieces that would make a customer remember her experiences in Gallup for many moons to come."

"No wife to help you with the stores?"

"Nope! No wife." As if not to dwell on his single status, he tapped her wrist. "How about the bracelet? Do you like it?"

"I love it, but can I wear it a little longer? You know, to get used to it before you wrap it and bag it."

"Of course. Is there anything else I can show you?"

"I'd love to walk through the rest of your store and see your collections."

"Great." He looked down at her hobo purse and large backpack. "You may want to take those along, or I can put them behind my counter."

"I'll take them. My digital cameras are in the backpack, and I never go anywhere without those. Been a shutterbug since entering Brooks Institute—even before that."

"That's impressive. The Ventura or Santa Barbara location?"

She smiled. "Santa Barbara. You know something about photography?"

"I dabble around a bit, mostly armature shots of landscapes. I don't use those digital cameras—just my old standby cameras."

"I like to use those sometimes."

"You here for the ceremonial?"

"Yes, sir. Thanks to *The San Francisco Examiner*. Flew into Albuquerque, spent two days there and then took the train into Gallup."

"Then you should have great shots to take back home. Well, grab your stuff because I've got lots to show you."

"Wonderful." As they walked down the hallway, she remembered to ask about her favorite kachina. "Do you have any of the Koshari?"

"Ah, the Hano clowns. You like them?"

"I do indeed. I know a little about the history of the Hano clowns and some other kachinas, but not nearly enough."

"Really? What interests you about the Koshari?"

"The trickster part of him. I also know he serves as a guard at some functions, but mostly I love how they're painted in the alternating black and white paint; kind of reminds me of some of my African sculptures."

"Really? You collect those as well?"

"An entire wall in my loft is dedicated to West African tribal art. Now I'd like to begin building my Native American collection. Native American culture has always fascinated me, and I would love to know more."

"We're an interesting people as a whole—every tribe has aspects relative to them alone. I do have some Koshari clowns, but if you're interested in more knowledge of the kachinas, you have your pick of hundreds. Many people, myself included, believe the Crow Mother is the originator of all kachinas. I would be glad to give you more info on them one day before you leave, if you have time."

"I would love that."

"I have an entire collection of the Koshari clowns from paintings to carvings. Would you like to see them?"

"Sure. In fact, since I'm on a photo assignment, would you mind terribly if I photographed your store one day this week?"

"I'd be honored. My long nights are Wednesdays and Thursdays. Let me know if either of those nights would be good for you."

"So far either night would be just fine."

"Great, then it's a plan, so long as I don't have to be in the pictures."

"You're safe, but it would be nice if you could be; you know, to give you exposure."

"I don't need it."

"Sure you do. Every great store could use more exposure. Well, think about it. Even if I can't photograph you on film, I hope to get some great shots of the dancers at the ceremonial."

"Maybe. It's always a good idea to get permission before taking pictures of the performers. It's the custom of the ceremonial, and some tribes are more camera shy than others. You're here for the ceremonial only?"

"Mostly. I've always wanted to visit New Mexico but never got the chance until now. I hope they'll allow me to bring my cameras into a few of the ceremonies."

"Some shows allow cameras. Ask and see what they say. Actually, my brother is a dancer at the main event Saturday night at Red Rock State Park. He's a Koshari dancer."

"Awesome! You think he'll let me photograph him?"

"If the performance managers will allow it." They stopped before a large, open set of carved oak doors and he held his hand before him, ushering her inside. "This is a nice room here. If you like native art, this room will impress."

Darrius walked her past turquoise painted walls that housed a collage of metal wall art, from shaman to highly sculpted bison, antelope, Kokopelli and other legendary petroglyph figures. They passed by stucco walls of the basket section loaded with woven items from the Navajo to the Anasazi, and in all shapes, sizes and colors. Then he walked her straight into a room filled with giant paintings of the Koshari clowns and stopped right in front of one.

Darrius continued. "I think this is the place you want to see—your famous Koshari. I'll ask Derrick in advance about getting permission to photograph the ceremony since he's one of the managers of the show. But you may want to think about it, as Koshari is a known trickster by nature, according to legend. They take unsuspecting onlookers and pull them into the ceremony by harassing them, aiming water and fruit at them. You'd get soaked to the bone. If you get too close, Derrick may get you. I'd hate to see that happen." He stopped when a suggestive image entered his head.

Justine saw budding interest in his eyes, and hoped he hadn't seen the same in hers. She blushed at the thought of Darrius Red Sky being attracted to her. Being made to blush by the intentions of a man was absolutely the last thing Justine wanted to happen. These days, she would prefer blushing at a beautiful setting sun or breathtaking landscape. Another man. God, no!

Once again, his voice drew her back to the real. "What's your name? I forgot to ask with all the talking we've done."

Justine held out her hand. "I forgot as well. I'm Justine Roberts-Paretti."

"What a beautiful name. It fits you, much like the bracelet. Married? You do have two names."

"No. I joined my mother's maiden name to my father's Italian one. It looks more professional in photo credit lines and on business cards."

"I agree. I like the sound of it."

His eyes had a hypnotic effect on her, and she felt herself falling into a dream-like state. She lacked the will to fight what was happening to her. It was like being struck by lightning, and so damn quickly at that! *This just can't be!* She was desperate for a diversion, so she looked down at the bracelet still adorning her wrist. "Oh! Don't forget to remove the bracelet. Something this gorgeous can tempt a girl."

"Can't have that, now can we?"

She delivered a shy smile. "Well, Darrius, I suppose not."

He got her drift, smiled and turned to the Koshari clown painting he had singled out. The black and white clown, wearing only a breechcloth and a funny matching hat with tassels, had been painted against a bluish-gray background. He held a watermelon half in his hands, and one foot was raised in a dance movement. A funny smile was on his highly decorated face. "This is one of my best pieces; it was modeled after my brother during one of his dances."

Justine studied the painting, admiring the muscle tone of the dancer. She lightly touched the raised oil paint strokes. "It's beautiful. How much?"

"This one's five thousand, but I can sell it to you for three point five. Here's another one on the back wall. It's more expensive, though, close to seven thousand dollars."

Justine knew instantly why the price was higher; turquoise and other precious stones embedded in the oil paint. Blocks of jet were mixed in with the black paint on sections of the dancer's legs, arms and chest. They shone against the paint, making it look almost surreal. "Wow, this is gorgeous!" she exclaimed.

Justine went from painting to painting of the Koshari. Darrius loved her enthusiasm, loved how her expression changed from happy to almost ecstatic just from the sight of a dancing trickster. Mostly, he was intrigued by her beauty, her questions, her desire to know a culture so different from her own. He couldn't recall when he'd seen a woman who made a faded pair of jeans, a dusty orange-and-blue peasant blouse, hobo bag and backpack look mind-blowingly sexy. She filled out everything in provocative, desert-heat ways. And he loved it. The thickness in his groin was a sign that it was time to move on and show her other things, because he, too, had to remember he was done with relationships. Explaining more merchandise from his collection would divert attention from a female body he'd love to stroke.

"I have Koshari clowns carved of the highest quality cottonwood."

"Where?" Her excitement overflowed at the sight of seeing so many beautiful things in one store. And that included the owner. She could see Darrius Red Sky dancing nude in black and white paint, his shiny black hair whipping fiercely across his face, carrying her to an erotic high. She wondered if he ever danced, but she hadn't the nerve to ask. She wasn't supposed to like him, anyway, yet the cards were tumbling in his direction.

Darrius walked her to a corner of the same room to a set displaying the funny clowns, handing her one. "This one is by an exceptional carver, Frederic K. I love his detail. Feel how light the wood is. He uses real fur on his pieces."

Their hands touched again, and erotic images invaded Justine's mind: she saw him dancing with just a breechcloth covering the juice and girth of everything she knew he had. She took the clown, checked it out, and then handed it back to him. "I like it," she said simply.

"I have cheaper ones." He handed her another beautiful clown, which cost sixty dollars.

Her smile lit his world. It was apparent she liked the smaller cottonwood Koshari with suede and leather accents. "You like him, huh?"

"Yeah! He kind of reminds me of you in some way. I need a memento of my visit here other than my photographs and this bracelet." *Right! As if you won't have images of Darrius embedded in the deepest recesses of your mind for the rest of your life!*

Darrius cradled the doll in his hand. "You'll be back, won't you—just to look around, I mean?"

"Love to, but what I have on tap for today will take all day, believe me."

"I mean back to New Mexico."

"Every chance I get. What I've seen so far is . . . miraculous."

"Good then. What *is* planned for today?"

"I don't have a hotel room yet, Mr. Red Sky."

"Call me Darrius."

"Good, I will. Anyway, my train was late from Albuquerque, where I had been helping with the mission schools."

"You did that? You've really been a busy girl. Was it for the article?"

"Partly. I love children, though. I love showing them new things, bringing them into another world other than the limited ones they're accustomed to in certain low-income areas. I even gave a photography lesson or two. At home, I volunteer in very impoverished areas. Those children deserve chances to see another side of life, too. Don't you agree?"

"Of course." Darrius smiled approvingly. A woman who loved children had to have a heart of gold. Yes, Justine Roberts-Paretti was definitely an enigma, and he was beginning to like her more and more with each passing minute. "We have mission schools in the area if you have time on your hands to help out more children."

"That would be great if I can find the time. Anyway, the Super-8 gave my room away when I called to tell them my train was late. When I arrived in Gallup, I rented a car, had something to eat and then came to see your store."

"I'm flattered you think so much of the place."

"Right. The store." *What is it about this man that makes me act like such a fool?*

Darrius got the hint, and it made him feel good. "I've got an idea. A friend of mine is the manager of the Best Western Red Rock. They may have something, like suites or something. This ceremonial really packs people in, and they take the less expensive rooms very quickly. José's been known to pull strings before."

"I sure hope so. Sleeping on the streets wouldn't exactly be the highlight of my trip."

"I'd let you sleep here before letting that happen. It's down the street from Red Rock State Park, where most of the ceremonial events will take place. Easy access, so let's try it."

"That would be great."

"Just let me get Bob to watch the counter and then we can go."

"You could call the hotel instead of leaving your store. I'm sure you have other things to do besides taking some silly girl to a hotel." *That didn't exactly come out right.*

"That sounds like a good idea, but no, let me take you and introduce you to José. Besides, there are only a few minutes before closing time. I won't start my ceremonial store hours until Tuesday or Wednesday."

"Ceremonial hours?"

"Staying open later due to the Intertribal Ceremonial."

"Oh, I see." She pointed to the doll. "I have to pay for him."

"Right."

They walked back into the main showroom and to the register; Darrius rang up the Koshari purchase and handed her the bag.

Darrius left the showroom when Bob, his assistant, came in. He'd decided he had better call José before all the rooms at the Best Western were booked. Holding his cell at the entrance to the stockroom, he couldn't help but thinking about Justine. He had not thought about a woman since he and his last girlfriend had broken up nine months ago. The breakup had been a healthy dose of good riddance to her!

His mind on a woman was not what he needed in his life now—even the beautiful young temptress who had come into his store from nowhere. The last thing he needed was to be swayed by a customer simply because she was beautiful. He had done that way too many times in the past, and it had gotten him nowhere. He then decided that Justine was just a sale—hopefully, a major one before the ceremonial ended on Sunday.

2

TURQUOISE DREAMS

Justine climbed into her rented black-on-black Neon and Darrius got into a beat-up Ford truck parked next to her. Historic Route 66 took center stage now. She had heard of the famous stretch of highway and had been dying to see it from the New Mexico side. It brought to mind the Nat King Cole song, "Get Your Kicks on Route 66." Justine sang the song aloud instead of the usual hip-hop music she liked.

She stopped when Darrius abruptly turned into the parking lot of the Best Western without benefit of a traffic signal. She wiped the sweat from her brow, hoping it was more from the heat than from his deplorable driving. "He's beautiful, all right, but he drives like a madman."

Twenty minutes later Darrius had a luxury suite for her, but at the price of a single. Yes, it was good to know people, and she definitely had thoughts of *maybe* wanting to know Darrius for more than just hotel rooms and Koshari clowns. *Maybe!* No matter, she was in New Mexico to work, not mix interpersonally with handsome storeowners. She looked around the spacious room. "I love it, Darrius; it has almost all the luxuries of home. The only thing missing is the Jacuzzi."

"For a little more money, I can swing a room with one of those, too. But you'd have to cut me a little piece of the pie."

"Meaning?"

"I get the chance to use it, too; alone, of course."

"Of course." Thinking all the wrong things made her feel a little foolish. She smiled sheepishly. "I'll let you know when I'm done using our proverbial Jacuzzi. Deal?"

"Deal. Enjoy your room, Ms. Paretti. Glad to have been of assistance to you in the Land of Enchantment. If there's anything else I can do—"

"I'll call. I do have your business card somewhere in my garbage bag of a purse. Oh, there is something."

"Anything."

"You can take payment for the bracelet. I still have it on."

"That you do. Why not wear it a little longer, as if on loan for the evening."

"You trust me that much?"

"Sure. Besides, I know where you work. I sometimes do that for special customers; let them get the feel of the jewelry and, if they are 100 percent satisfied, they bring the money back."

"You're too trusting, Darrius."

"Every item is insured—heavily."

"Smart man, but I know I want it, so—"

"But, you may change your mind. Live with it a little while. I'll see you again."

She looked at her bracelet again. "Sure are right about that."

Before leaving, Darrius made her promise not to leave without stopping back in the store to see him and do her interview. She quickly agreed.

Finally, Justine's weary body could rest on a comfortable bed. She put off unpacking, just wanting a few minutes of shut-eye to calm her nerves and dream turquoise dreams—dreams of Darrius Red Sky. What an impression the man had made, and in a short amount of time. He had gotten her to thinking there were still some good men left in the world.

After unloading her cameras, she plopped onto the bed and heard a jingling sound. Darrius's heart bracelet was still on her wrist, and she smiled knowing she would definitely see him again.

There was nothing she could do about the bracelet until the morning, so she decided to take her catnap and then go scope out Red Rock State Park. Tomorrow was the start of a busy week. She planned to attend nearly all the ceremonies before she left for home. There would be no rest after tonight.

Justine awakened with a vivid memory of a dream she had of Darrius dancing the dance of the Koshari. It was a sexy, wild dream where she ended up in his arms as onlookers chanted and called to them. Her fingers tangled in his long dark hair as he whirled her around the arena. Soon everything vanished, and the two of them were left alone in her world. Justine looked into his eyes;

they were different, but the face was the same. It was as if he had changed into another man. And he had; he was no longer Darrius Red Sky. But who was he? That was what jolted her awake.

Thinking it must have been later than it actually was, she looked at the alarm clock. Only 7:00, and there was still plenty of daylight. Never having been one to sit around and do nothing, she immediately freshened up, grabbed her camera bag and was off to Red Rock State Park, the heart of the Land of Enchantment.

The desert heat was still so stifling by 7:00 that evening, and she thanked God for her sun visor and shades. A long stretch of Route 66 unfolded before her as she drove in the direction of Red Rock. It was a little overwhelming at first with its long, narrow stretch of highway that passed through several states. She simply said to herself: *This is what you asked for, Justine; the famous Route 66. Now go and explore, make it yours—represent it well.* With her mission in mind, she started the car and drove into the sun.

Heading west would take her to the entrance of Red Rock State Park. Still reveling about her dream, she looked north of the highway and saw Darrius's store sitting on a stretch of desert land. She wanted to find him; travel to where he lived, see how he lived . . . where he slept. Nothing doing. He was a memory, at least until morning, and Red Rock was waiting to be explored. The bracelet served to remind her of him in the meantime— as if her mind would let her forget.

Red Rock State Park was everything a woman seated next to Justine in the Albuquerque train station told her it would be. Huge brick red slabs of volcanic rock walls stretched to the sky, surrounding the entire park. She had never seen anything that majestic, that beautiful, other than the flat lands of the Arizona mesas she saw two years ago at the Phoenix Powwow. That had been only her second large assignment since graduation and getting assignments from *The Examiner.*

Justine pulled onto the road that led to Red Rock and felt almost giddy. Countless times she had dreamed of being exactly where she was now. And now that she had arrived, she could hardly believe it. Standing before her were the looming reddish slabs of rock that was Red Rock's signature. She parked, paid for her ticket and followed the crowd to the arena for the rodeo. Along the way, she saw alcoves, smaller arenas and bandstands situated all around the park. In the center was the large arena, and she figured that was where the main dances would take place. There were trees and grassy areas throughout, along with food stands of all kinds that featured a wealth of different kinds of native dishes along with burgers and fries and other types of fast foods.

As she walked down the main strip toward the main arena, there was a large museum on the left side. On the front of the building was a lifelike painting of Olla Maidens from the Zuni Pueblo. The women looked real enough to talk to. The pottery on their heads looked so real she almost believed she could reach out and touch it. She photographed it with the thought of possibly making the photo the feature picture. Enchanting.

She entered the museum, seeing all kinds of encased artifacts, from clothing to tools and jewelry. Minutes later, she looked at her watch and noticed the rodeo would be starting soon. She walked back outside and followed the pathway to the main arena. It was a large sectioned-off area with trees and grass all around. Lights hung on lines and circled the entire area. It looked to be large enough to hold the rodeo in there, but it was mainly for the dancing.

She looked at her map that she had received at the entrance and saw where the rodeo was being held in area C, so she walked in that direction. Area C was a large, circular arena toward the back of the park. There were lots of cement seats in circular formation. It was a very attractive place. Everything she had seen thus far, from the schools and scenery in Albuquerque to Darrius's store and a small stretch of Route 66, had been so rich and real, a marvel. Now actually looking at Red Rock State Park, she could definitely add this to the list of outstanding sights.

According to the schedule, it was just minutes away from the All Indian Rodeo. She had loved rodeos ever since learning that some of her relatives on her mother's side had been among the first black cowboys to ride in rodeos. Who knows? Some of her own relatives may be there riding. Capturing black and Indian cultures interacting should make for dramatic photographs.

The fading sun provided welcome shade for the attendees. Several highly decorated ponies delighted the crowd, and Justine moved to the first row to shoot the first of many photographs. She faced the galloping ponies, admiring their rich colors and the designs painted on by their owners. White ponies had black and red handprints all over their bodies. Black ones had red lightening streaks, but her favorite was a gray pony with turquoise circles of life tattooed in a connecting formation around its body. The rider wore a matching silver and turquoise hat and a fringed cowboy-style shirt. He had long black hair and wore tight jeans.

She aimed her camera at the rider and zoomed in, but then she pulled back. Was her mind playing tricks on her, or did every man in Gallup suddenly start looking like Darrius Red Sky? She aimed the camera again, knowing for sure her mind was on Darrius. She took several photographs of the Darrius look-alike and the beautiful ponies that actually were the opening act for the rodeo. She could hardly shoot the pictures for watching their performance. The riders galloped around the arena in style and with such perfection. The ponies jumped into rings, hurtled around obstacle courses and even stood on parade just before their show ended.

Rodeo clowns wearing baggy cowboy outfits and floppy hats performed for the crowd doing rope tricks and other cutups. They made her think about the Koshari clowns; she could hardly wait for the main powwow so she could see the Koshari truly perform.

Though Justine had enjoyed the clowns and other rodeo performers, she had kept her eye on the rider on the silver horse. It was amazing how much he looked like Darrius. Was it he? That she didn't know, but each time he and the pony moved, she moved as well, following him until she could prove to herself that the rider was not Darrius. The man was probably at home wondering if he had, indeed, made the perfect jewelry sale. She looked down at the stunning bracelet. Yes, it was a keeper, and her money was as good as in Darrius's cash resister.

From a distance, she saw the rider walk his pony into the assigned parking lot, put him into the trailer and then get into a large white F150. She photographed that as well, but never took a face shot. If it was Darrius, he would object to having been photographed. That she was careful of.

The rodeo ended just before 9:30, which gave her time to grab a quick bite and head over to the night parade on Route 66 by 10 o'clock. She needed a break anyway, and was beginning to feel the weight of the backpack of cameras. She lugged the black camera bag over to a fry bread stand.

For once, it was a relief to sit back, eat and do absolutely nothing for the few minutes she had to herself. Being the second of five children hardly ever afforded her the luxury of having time alone whenever she wanted it; she was always on the go for or with someone. Her photography afforded her the opportunity to be alone, quiet, concentrating on landscapes, cityscapes and other beautiful things that caught her eye. She thought back on when she got her first camera. She was nine years old and her parents had given her the camera for her birthday. She had been hooked since then, becoming the shutterbug of the family. She toted the camera everywhere, probably pissed off everyone with her never-ending group pictures. Then one day she discovered landscapes and, as she got older, her and her friends traveled all around California—she was in photo heaven. Her interest in photography continued to grow and soon landed her in photography school. Upon graduation, she had local jobs and then the *Oakland Piquet* called, landing her pretty decent-sized assignments. When *The San Francisco Examiner* pulled her away from her photography assistant's job with the *Piquet,* she went running.

Her education and experience were paying off now; this was her second major assignment for the *Examiner.* The Gallup powwow was growing in popularity but pictures in other magazines generally did not do it justice, with exception of *New Mexico Magazine.* She had wanted this assignment very badly and had campaigned for it. Her boss almost gave the job to Wilfred Sands. Wilfred's photography was good, but not like hers was. She remembered her boss saying how much he liked her pictures from the Arizona powwows and her local work assignments with area craft shows and sporting events. She never shied away from dangerous situations. Just a few minutes ago at the rodeo, a charging bull was turned around and headed for the crowd. Instead of thinking of saving her own neck, she stayed put and was able to get a couple of shots before a clown corralled him. She was scared, but she got her shot!

The sun had finally disappeared. It was now a cloudless, star-filled sky with streaks of pink, red and orange—the only clues left behind by a robust sun. As she drove down Route 66 on her way to the night parade in midtown Gallup, she looked at what seemed to be millions of stars in the sky. It was a perfect sky for a night parade, the perfect atmosphere, and she and her cameras were ready.

She picked a place on the sidewalk near one of the many storefront jewelry shops and waited for the start of the parade.

Several native children dressed in traditional ceremonial costumes led the parade. Feathers were attached to practically every inch of their gemstone-studded, multicolored outfits. This was something Justine had wanted to see ever since hearing about the ceremonial years ago. The lifestyle of Native Americans had always fascinated her, and she had read a few books on their customs and way of life on reservations from early eighteenth century to the present. She was not, however, as familiar with the different kachinas and what they symbolized. She had read about some of them, but there were over three hundred. If at all possible, she would ask Darrius to give her more insight into the kachina stories. But for now, here she was watching real ones, performing traditional dances from the wolf dance, jingle dress dance to the warrior dance—all fascinating, and all being photographed to become a lasting memory in the minds of anyone who would read her article.

Justine's last round of photographs were of the male hoop dancers. She was amazed by their precision and dexterity as they maneuvered the hoops into intricate designs and danced in and out of them. The hoop dance, as she remembered reading, meant that all things were related, designed to be part of a whole—one people, one world. A good philosophy, one everyone should adhere to.

The dancers' jumps and spins transformed their decorative costumes into colorful blurs. Watching, she wished she were part of the custom. Of course, her African American and Italian customs had their own dynamic traditions, but she'd always had an affinity to the Native American culture. Could it be she was destined to be a part of it? Could this destiny also include a man—Darrius Red Sky? Realizing her imagination was running amok, she shook herself and returned to the dancing.

The combination of dance, enticing foods and the festive night atmosphere had relaxed her, put her on another plane. She liked it.

Her cameras were becoming tiresome after being carried around for hours. She couldn't wait to dump the bag on her nice luxurious bed and drift off into another turquoise dream. She packed up and went looking for her car, but the departing crowd made it hard to see where she had parked.

She stood in the middle of a side street off Route 66 and finally spotted it near a sign advertising the Ranch Kitchen Restaurant. She had parked there because she wanted to remember its location. She planned to eat there before leaving town, having read great reviews about it in *New Mexico Magazine*. Walking toward her car, she spotted a tall and slender figure with long dark hair. It could have been any Native American man in New Mexico, but even in the dark, this one had Darrius's profile. She realized her mind had been so fixed on seeing Darrius that she would see him in any man until she came face to face with him. Even so, she followed the man, calling at the top of her lungs, "Darrius! Darrius! Stop! It's me, Justine, from your store."

But he kept walking as if he hadn't heard her. What with the crowd noise, it was entirely possible he hadn't. She called out again, and followed until she lost sight of him in the crowd. That didn't stop her. She had to find him, look into his eyes again—and, of course, pay him for the bracelet.

She saw him emerge from the crowd and keep walking until he unlocked a white Ford F150. With all of her might, she called his name again. To her surprise, he heard her this time—at least he heard something, and he turned around.

Justine grabbed a hold of her camera bag and ran in his direction, still calling to him. When he recognized her emerging from the crowd, he smiled and that let her know that, yes, the man had seen her and was willing to wait.

Panting and out of breath, she stood before him. "I've been calling you for almost a block."

"For that long? You know I would have stopped sooner had I heard. You here photographing the night parade, I see. Take any good shots?" he added, moving closer to her.

"Lots. Probably more than my editor can use."

"I saw you snapping away, getting in the middle of the action. It was exciting to see you at work."

She stood next to him, leaning against his truck. "Should have seen me at the rodeo. Almost got nailed by a bull."

"I saw it, and my heart skipped a few beats. I relaxed once you were safe behind the row of seats." He turned and faced her. "Now my heart is skipping beats again."

"There's no danger around, Darrius."

"Exactly my point."

His meaning was well understood, and Justine didn't quite know how to take it, so she turned to her profession as a safe space. "So, you were at the rodeo?"

"Indeed. I love rodeos."

"Were you riding?"

He leaned in a little closer. "I may have been. Why? Did you see someone there who looked like me?"

"Maybe. I took pictures of a silver pony with rings of life on his sides."

"He sounds beautiful."

In a dream-like tone, she responded. "He sure is—was."

Darrius definitely got her meaning and smiled to himself. To elude any further comments on their apparent attraction, he took her wrist. "How's the bracelet holding up?"

"Wonderful. You should let me pay you for it now, while I have you here. Though I'd have to pay by check."

"Save your checks. There's an ATM near your hotel. You can come by tomorrow and pay if you like. Then again, you may just change your mind and go for the nugget bracelet instead."

Christ! The man's hands on her made her weak in the knees. No man had done that to her since—since never! What was it about Darrius Red Sky? Everything! She slowly withdrew her hand. "I'd better get back and upload these pictures to my editor. My laptop is in the room."

"You could use mine. But you would have to come to my house to use it. I do have some pictures I would like to show you—some taken of Red Rock."

"Though I'd love to, maybe another time. It is getting late."

"I'll hold you to that. Where are you parked?"

She smiled. "At least a block away thanks to you."

"Then I should walk you back. Can't have you walking in the dark alone, can I?"

"I'd like the company, and thanks."

Minutes later, they arrived at her car. "This is my stop. I'll find you tomorrow and bring cash. I don't carry much on me at any given time."

"That's smart."

He moved in front of her and, though it was dark, she saw his outline; hair blowing in the wind like wisps of silk. She wanted to reach up and stroke the magnificent mane, but decided Darrius was better off being a sexy storeowner and nothing more to her. Yeah, like she could believe that!

She reached inside her purse for her keys and he took her by surprise by kissing her forehead. She stood in place, barely able to comprehend what had just happened. Her mouth parted. "What . . . what was that for?

"No reason. I'm sorry if that offended you."

"It . . . it didn't. But I really should leave."

"I should leave, too. It's late and I have to open early. Lots of things on the agenda for tomorrow." He held her door open and watched her slide inside. "You have a great evening, Justine."

She looked up and smiled. "I will, and thanks for walking me back."

"My pleasure."

And mine. The giddy feeling returned, and it had been brought on by one simple kiss. She hadn't been turned on so much by an innocent little kiss since Ernest Boyer kissed her in the sixth grade. She put a cap on her emotions long enough to start the engine and ride off.

3

BLUE CORN HEAVEN

"Ma'am? I have your complimentary breakfast here."

The voice at the door awakened Justine from a wild dream about everything she had done the day before, including meeting Darrius, who was now the highlight of this photo assignment.

Complimentary breakfast? I didn't know they did that at the Best Western. She quickly put on her robe and opened the door. A petite Native American woman wearing a traditional morning-dance costume, complete with jingle dress and ponytail wrapped in binding, smiled and held a tray out to her.

Justine opened the door wider and the woman entered and set the tray down. "I didn't know they did this here."

The beautiful young woman turned and smiled pleasantly. "We don't. This was a special request."

"From whom?"

The woman picked up the note from the tray and handed it to her. "No tip is required. The customer already took care of it."

"You can't tell me who hired you?"

She turned without answering, leaving Justine in the center of the room, holding the note and smelling fresh wild sage bread, blue corn crepes and a traditional Native American breakfast drink called blue corn atole.

Who in New Mexico knew her well enough to send her breakfast? No one. But one particular young gentleman she had met had obviously been impressed. The thought made her smile, and she couldn't wait to taste everything. She had come to New Mexico fully intending to dine strictly on Native American foods. She opened the envelope on the tray and read: "I hope your day will be as pleasant as you are. Enjoy. Darrius Red Sky."

"I knew it!" Of course it would be he. Darrius Red Sky had single-handedly jump-started her day, and in the best possible way. Justine decided to shower; the aroma from the crepes was making her stomach rumble.

One taste of the blue corn crepes and she couldn't help thinking how sweet and kind he was to think of her when his day was probably so full. She couldn't wait to thank him in person.

The salmon-and-turquoise-hued stucco exterior of Darrius's store seemed even brighter in early daylight. Justine was anxious to see Darrius and thank him for the wonderful breakfast, and to pay for the bracelet that she now saw as a constant reminder of Darrius and of the kind treatment she had so far received while visiting Gallup. What she had encountered from her first step on to native land was . . . enchantment, kindness and a rich culture, and she wanted more of it.

There Darrius was behind his counter in the front of the store setting up a display of assorted boxes of tea. A little bell above the door announced her arrival. "Good morning. I hope I'm not too early, but I wanted to take care of business before you got busy. I love the bracelet, and I'm giving you the money instead of a check or credit card."

He smiled but looked perplexed. Justine saw this and got to the point, thinking he was too busy to sit and chat. She marched up to the counter and plopped the money down. "Here ya go. Ring me up for a legitimate sale, Mr. Red Sky. Can't have you getting into trouble over little ol' me."

He, again, looked puzzled. Justine looked into his eyes, visible confusion on her face. *He couldn't have forgotten about me so soon after that sweet kiss last night and then having delivered such a marvelous breakfast.* She was a little worried now. "I, uh, yesterday when I came in, I forgot to pay for the bracelet. Don't you remember? I also looked at the Koshari dolls . . ."

Still no recognition.

Whatever! Her voice became a tad more serious, hating that she had been forgotten, and so quickly. "Anyway, I'm here to pay for the bracelet now."

"The bracelet?"

"Sure, don't you remember?" She held it up to his face.

"Ma'am, there isn't paperwork for a missing bracelet. I've redone the books and everything is in order. All purchases have been paid for and their proper documentation filed."

She couldn't understand his professed lack of knowledge, his polite but distant business-like attitude. "I—I made a mistake and walked out wearing it."

"That's impossible. All of our merchandise is coded and then de-coded once payment is made. I'll check again." He smiled into her lovely face. *Never had a beautiful woman, or any woman for that matter, come in to give money for no reason.* "May I see the bracelet please?"

"Sure, but I'm trying to pay for it. And don't you remember this morning—"

"Just give me a minute."

His abruptness took her aback; she didn't know what to think of his current disposition. Yet she stood there, impatiently tapping her foot.

He scanned the applicable code on the register's minicomputer. "Ma'am, this bracelet has already been paid for."

That definitely took her by surprise. Her mouth opened, but nothing came out.

"Ma'am, are you okay?"

"No! No, I'm not okay. Don't you remember anything? I came in yesterday and bought the bracelet and the Koshari. You took me to the Best Western, got me a room and then sent me breakfast—"

"Will you hold on a minute? I never did any of those things, miss. And I certainly didn't take you to the Best Western."

"Am I going crazy here? Darrius, you did take me to the—"

"Ah, this explains everything. I'm not Darrius. I'm Derrick, his twin. And believe me, had I taken you to the Best Western I'd have stayed there with you, if you'll pardon my boldness."

Then she remembered. *He did mention having a brother.* "Oh, my God, I'm so sorry. I've all but accused you of being a cad. You must think I'm so weird."

"Not at all. I'm Derrick Red Sky, and you must be Justine."

"Yeah! He told you about me?"

"He told me he had purchased some jewelry and had left the money in the register with the receipt. I had no idea it was the same bracelet; I thought it was something he had bought for himself. Sorry. He described you, but didn't do you the least bit of justice. I'm sorry to have confused you."

Whew! What a relief! "No, it was all me," she said, taking his outstretched hand. "I'm so pleased to meet you. Boy, you two are totally identical, except Darrius has lighter eyes." That would explain the different colored eyes in her dream. *Damn! I dreamed of his brother! How weird is that?*

"That's the only difference," he said.

"So I guess it's safe to say you weren't the one who sent me breakfast?"

"I'd like to take credit for it, but my brother found you first. He has quite a thing for you."

"Really? So soon?"

"He doesn't fall easily for women, but I think you may have snagged him. Why else would a man pay $393 for a bracelet unless it was a gift for someone?"

"He really did pay for it?"

"Yes, ma'am. The best I can do is offer you a few bags of these." He gave her a handful of Native American tea bags. "These are really good. I like the Warrior's Brew best."

She accepted the bags, saying, "Thanks. I'll have to find Darrius and give him his money back for the bracelet."

"Why? Don't you like it?"

"I love it," she said, fingering the precious spiny oyster.

"It was a gift. Believe me, he can afford it. He owns this place, and a few others. I'm just taking over for him today until he comes back from his golf outing."

Flustered that the sexiest man in the universe had given her an expensive bracelet, she barely heard a thing Derrick said, other than the golf part. "Where is he? I'd like to thank him in person for everything."

"Municipal Golf Course on Susan Street. Do you know how to get there?"

"I passed it last night on my way to the night parade."

"How was it? I missed it."

"Beautiful. I took loads of pictures. I think the *Examiner* will be happy."

"Yeah, he told me you were a photojournalist."

"That reminds me. He said you're a Koshari dancer. You think I could take pictures of you in your costume Saturday night?"

"Maybe before the ceremony starts. They won't allow cameras after that."

"I'd love to. That's such an amazing deity."

"He is, indeed."

Slinging her hobo bag over her shoulder, she said, "I'd better go, but if it's any consolation for me weirding you out a few minutes ago, you're just as sexy as Darrius."

"Best compliment a fellow can get. Darrius is a big man around here, and being seen as anything like him is worth hearing."

"Then he's a cool guy?"

"The best. I know he's my brother, but I like the person he is."

"That's a nice thing to say."

He walked her to the door, hating to see her leave, but knowing duty called in *other* places. He saw how the mere mention of Darrius lit her face and was actually jealous of his brother for the first time. "Here, take my business card. I work the family tea business in Los Alamos. It was in Taos, but I moved it closer to the family."

"I'll enjoy these tea bags, and thanks. It was nice to meet you. Sorry for thinking you were Darrius."

"How would you have known? We're identical."

Walking out, her only thought was, *Wow! Two of them.*

Municipal Golf Course was beautiful with its rolling hills of green grass like carpet and finely detailed designs.

After a search, she saw the true wonder of the area—Darrius. He was playing a round of golf with two other men. He hadn't seen her, so she took a few shots of him swinging the club.

His stance was perfect. He twisted his body to make the shot, exposing every sinewy muscle through his stark white polo shirt; rippling, taut, smooth. She took as many shots as she could while he was still unaware of her presence. But she was acutely aware of *his* as she zoomed in for some headshots, admiring how his black hair shone so brightly in the sun, making it look wet, but with such luster. He wore a single feather in it—his style, his tradition. Suddenly, she felt a compulsion to run her fingers through it—feel it in her hands, feel him in her arms.

After teeing off on the eighteenth hole, Darrius looked up and saw Justine photographing him from the closest hill. He waved at her, and then quickly hit the ball to the hole. She had been the only thing on his mind that day, and was the reason he was about to lose the game to his friends. After having the breakfast delivered, he began wondering if she even liked Native American food; if not, what had she thought of him being forward enough to send it? But mostly, he wondered how she would take to having a stranger buy her an expensive piece of jewelry. The last thing he wanted to do was scare her off. Normally, he didn't buy gifts for women right off the bat, but there was something about Justine that took him to places he had never been; had made him do things that were uncharacteristic for him—like worrying. He didn't have to worry long, because before he knew it, his golf ball had rolled right over the hole. Game over. As expected, he lost, but hoped he would be the winner of a certain lady's attention for a little while.

He returned his club to the golf bag and walked up the small hill, going right up to her, perhaps closer than he should have. She smelled so good, like a fresh rain shower on an early summer morning. And she looked incredible in a pair of gaucho jeans and a mint green lace blouse. Her dark hair was pulled back into a loose ponytail with ringlets framing her face. Her caramel brown face was simply dazzling. He knew and had even dated African American women, but Justine was different, special. She could be Native American, although her features were predominantly African American: sumptuous, almost thick lips, big, dark eyes and a small nose. Simply beautiful. She was wearing the bracelet that he had boldly paid for, and in the light of day, it made her shine and sparkle more—and his mouth water. She was the first woman to make the powerful Darrius Red Sky shake, rattle his nerves, cause the tenting erection in his jeans to actually hurt him. She was a natural beauty, and he had to try to steal a part of her day.

"You didn't actually see me miss that shot, did you?"

"Saw it all, and photographed it to add insult to injury. I hope you don't mind. I forgot what you said about having your picture taken."

"I don't mind—this one time. You play golf?"

"Badly. I'm better at bowling."

"We should play sometime. There are lots of bowling alleys here."

"If there's time. There is so much to do today, with the activities at Red Rock and the day parade in an hour. Lots to get ready for. But I'm here to thank you for the breakfast and this gorgeous bracelet."

"You're very welcome, Miss Justine. I'm glad I made your day better."

"Brighter. No one has ever bought me anything this expensive, aside from my newspaper, that is. One of these cameras costs eight hundred dollars."

"You're worth that and more. I was happy to buy it. It looks incredible on you, especially with the mint green of your blouse. That's beautiful, too." Before he caught himself, his eyes lingered on her breasts. "I just hope I wasn't being too forward with my gifts—and the kiss. I hope I didn't embarrass you last night."

"It was wonderful—a perfect end to an enchanted evening. You're treating me like a queen, and you don't even know me. There aren't a lot of men around who would have done that."

"You mean there's no man in your life showering you with praise and gifts?"

"Can't say there is." She looked down at her sandals. "Well, not anymore."

Instinct told him not to pursue the subject. Instead, he took her heavy backpack from her shoulders and started down the hill. "Why don't we go to the day parade together, and then get lunch. I know of a great place—"

"I'd love to. I mean, I'm hungry again." *Damn!* She hated sounding so eager, and tried to tone down her too-obvious elation. "Oh, I'm sorry to cut you off, but I'm just so glad you'll come to the parade with me. Be a kind of tour guide."

"Love to. It was interesting last night watching you photograph the dancers. You were crouching on your knees almost in the middle of the street taking your pictures. You looked fabulous . . . sexy, if you don't mind me saying."

Mind? Get real! You could say that to me all day long, Mr. Red Sky.

Justine could feel herself blushing, her heart pounding, her mouth becoming dry from wanting to kiss this incredible man.

He led her down the hill. "We can talk at the Eagle Café. They have wonderful food there. By the way, did you like the blue corn crepes?"

"Ate them all up and looked around for more."

"Good, because I made them, put them in a food warmer and had my cousin Wendy bring them over."

"You should have brought them yourself and had some with me." *Good idea, stupid, being in a hotel room with him . . . and a bed. How long would you have stayed out of his pants?*

His voice returned her to reality. "No, you had things to do. Besides, I would have caught up with you later. After all, I know where you're staying."

"And thanks to you I'm not staying on the street."

He took her hand and led her to his truck, saying, "Seriously, do you think I'd let a visitor to my land sleep in the elements?"

"You have been quite the host, and I'm grateful for everything you've helped me with. Also grateful for the kiss. I know it was a simple gesture of friendship, but it was something a lonely woman needed after such a hectic trip."

"I'm glad to be of service anytime, Justine. Anytime."

She caught the hint, but still, she and men were finished—at least for a while. Another thing she had to remember was that Darrius was a host, not a lover. Too soon for that anyway, she thought.

She looked back at her car. "Shouldn't I trail you? I could get ticketed or towed away."

"We won't be gone long enough for that. Besides, there's many cars here. How would the police know the driver isn't here?"

"True. I suppose it's okay, so long as you don't try to keep me for too long."

He smiled an innocent smile. "That *could* be arranged."

"It could, but not today. Work. Remember?"

"Yes, ma'am."

Once inside the cab, Darrius saw Justine still worriedly looking back at her car. "Still worried?"

"A little."

"Don't. It'll be nice and safe until I bring you back to it."

She smiled. "How did you know I was still concerned about the car? I could have been looking out at the range."

"But you weren't."

"You're right, but how did you know?"

"The wind told me."

She playfully brushed against him. "Come on!"

"I can't explain it. I just knew. I guess it was one of those things called vibes."

"Could be." *Maybe I have them, too.*

The interior of Darrius's truck was sparkling clean, just like his store. A dream catcher and small bone-carved coyote hung from the rearview mirror. The seat covers were of a woven native design—from what tribe, she didn't know.

"They're actually Navajo, despite the fact that I'm Hopi."

"There you go again. How did you know—?"

"That you were thinking about the seat covers? Honestly, I saw you looking at them, but I'm in tune to you, anyway. I think it started with the kiss on the forehead last night."

"For me, it started the minute I entered your store."

"That soon?"

"Is that good or bad?"

"It's very good, Justine."

Darrius felt he should pace himself, not rush things, but he could hardly avoid touching her. Her hand felt good in his, but again, that wasn't where he wanted to go. Better he should change topics, he thought. "Do you know much about the tradition of the parades?"

"I've done some reading in the past, actually own a few books on Native American cultures. I know that the dances interpret various aspects of Native American traditions."

"Yes, the dances are important to our lives. They don't do a lot of the religious ceremonial dances at the day parade. Most of those are performed at the night parade at Red Rock, the powwow's official kick-off. The day and night parades are mostly ceremonial, mostly. They showcase many of the tribes and dancers who will be performing in the grand arena on Friday and Saturday nights for the powwow."

"So, I can expect to see some amazing dance movements."

"Yes, and you should be able to get some incredible photographs."

"That's my plan. Actually, Dana and José, members of the research department at the paper, filled me in on a few things to expect while attending the dances. They named several types of dances like the grass, the hoop, those I knew about. But they mentioned others, like the different types of traditional dances."

"There are a lot, but I hope you do more than work while here. You should have some fun. I can tell you about a lot of things to do in the area. Or, better yet, show you."

"So, does this mean you'll be my official tour guide?"

"I thought we established that already."

"So, now that you're my guide, does this mean one of the stops on your route includes seeing your photographs?"

"You remember that?"

"I would love to see them."

"Then let's see them. But don't be alarmed. I'm not as good at photography as you are."

"I'll be the judge of that, Darrius."

They soon pulled into a parking lot near historic Route 66. Darrius parked and grabbed her camera bag. "Next to the Amoco station on Route 66 will be a good place to stand. The actual parade and banner will come from the east. You'll get a good view of the banner here that represents the theme of the powwow. It changes every year and has some of the most interesting designs."

"That could be a candidate for the lead photo."

"Good. I know you will do us proud here."

Holding her hand, he pushed through a few spectators who were also early for the Grand Entry. He watched her set up the tripod and position her camera and decided she was the most spectacular woman he'd ever seen—the complete woman. She was also the complete professional, handling the heavy cameras with ease and total assurance. And he saw something in her he liked in a woman—fearlessness. Yes, she was definitely the entity he felt she was—endearing, yet so together with everything she did.

When the parade kicked off, Justine was already in position, crouched almost in the center of Route 66, capturing the essence of the Comanche dancers, Cheyenne Scalp Dancer representatives and Olla Maidens with their pots. Darrius was awed by her dexterity and determination to get the perfect shot—no matter what it took. And she was strong for a woman. He saw her muscles ripple while aiming the camera. Sometimes she would let the camera rest on the tripod, catching shots of full-length costumes swirling around her. She looked good in that milieu, natural—as if she were a natural part of the Indian heritage. That was her endearing side; the other side was all sexual, and he wanted to experience more than just her ability to take the perfect picture.

While her camera's eye saw only the dancers, her mind's eye saw only Darrius Red Sky. She turned her camera on the spectators, and there he was looking perfect in his white polo and tight jeans. Having changed his golf shoes in the truck, he now wore a pair of dusty brown cowboy boots with contrasting brown engravings in the shape of desert cacti. The sunglasses he wore added an aura of mystery to this man she knew so little about. He was looking away from her and was thus unaware of the camera on him. She seized the chance to take a few shots of him—raw and unsuspecting.

4

GOOD VIBRATIONS

The Eagle Café was little more than a hole in the wall, "But the food is superb, the best in Gallup," Darrius said, handing her the small menu. "They may not offer a lot of dishes here, but take my word for it, the enchiladas will take you to another world."

"I'll just have to take your word for it. After all, you're quite the man to know around these parts, aren't you?"

"I try." He delivered that perfect smile for both her benefit and his, loving her sense of humor. "You're some girl, Ms. Paretti. How did you become so fascinating in only twenty-eight years of living?"

"How did you know I was twenty-eight? Oh, let me guess, the wind told you."

"It did. Well, I did kind of cheat. Yesterday while you paid for the kachina with your credit card, I took a look at your driver's license; born September 10, 1980, in San Francisco to Vinchinzo and Bernadette Paretti."

"What? Come on now. Certainly my driver's license didn't tell you all of that."

"No, it was the trees this time. They told me you were coming."

"Darrius!"

"I'm so serious. Nights before I met you, I stood outside my store before closing. Something told me of a visitor. The trees were moving funny that night."

"Do you have visions?"

"I think I do sometimes. All I know is that I've always known things for some reason. I knew about you coming. I just didn't know exactly when, but I knew you would be lovely."

Her cheeks reddened, and her hunger to kiss him set her ablaze, but she tried to ignore it. "You really are too kind; paying me compliments; giving me bracelets, photo opportunities, breakfast."

"And now lunch."

"Right. And to think I accused your poor brother of being the culprit. I went into the store to pay for the bracelet, and I thought he was you. He gave me tea bags and thanked me for complimenting him on being you."

"No way!"

"Seriously! He holds you in high regard. Maybe he thought the Warrior's Brew would calm me down, because he gave me a big stack of them."

Darrius's brow piqued. "Well, he's always been good at promoting the business."

"I was quite insistent that the bracelet hadn't been paid for. I know he thinks I'm crazy."

"Not from what I've told him. I mentioned meeting the most amazing lady, and that she had been sent here."

"Yeah, by *The San Francisco Examiner*."

"No, it's deeper than that, Justine. You don't believe me?"

The waitress arrived, and Justine decided to wait before trying to disprove his claim. "Maybe I'll try your enchiladas, Darrius, since you're so big on them."

"Best in the Southwest. Right, Rita?"

The lanky woman with obviously dyed blonde hair pinched his cheek. "Right again, Red Sky."

"I'll have what the lady is having, and a Coke."

After Rita left, Justine couldn't resist asking, "What have you been right about with her?"

"I told her that her son would come back alive from Iraq. He came back on a disability two months ago. Other than a leg injury, he's fine."

"Handy man to have around to deliver good news, aren't you?"

"I'd like to be. There's a lot in Gallup and the surrounding cities I could show a girl from California."

"You may just get the chance. I still have so much to do, though. There's the queen contest tonight at five, the arts and crafts exhibit by three. I also need to send some photos over to my editor. I have more good shots, like those at the day parade."

Rita placed their Cokes on the table, and Justine quickly took a thirsty sip. "Umm, this is so good and cold; a good thing to have on such a hot day."

"You're going to be very busy, so take a lot of liquids with you because this heat can be stifling. If you like, just to save you some time, I could always take your film to my darkroom and develop them, bring them to your room later—if you trust me with them."

"Remember, I have digital cameras."

"That's right. Seems I'm the only one still in the dark ages."

"Don't say that. I still like those old ones, too. Though I haven't actually developed photos like that in a while now, I still like to."

"Then maybe you can help me develop mine. That is, if you have the time."

"I could probably find a few minutes. Are you talking about today?"

"Sure. Why not? The Queen's Parade is hours from now."

Being huddled in a dark room with the likes of Darrius Red Sky could get her body and emotions in a peck of trouble. She was finished with men. Right? "Um, I don't know. I really wouldn't want to be late to the contest."

"And you wouldn't be. I promise to have you back at Red Rock way before time."

"What kind of pictures did you say you take?"

"Amateur ones. I like to piddle around with scenery. I have pretty good shots of Ship Rock."

"I've heard the name but don't exactly know what Ship Rock is."

Their food arrived and the scent of enchiladas wafted through the air. The scenery he was describing sparked interest, and she listened as he spoke of the mystic rock formations.

"It's the core of a basaltic ancient volcano, considered sacred by the Navajo. Its real name is Tse Bit'a'i—The Rock With Wings. I go there sometimes to cool off, do some thinking and get my head on straight."

53

"Kind of like what some of the ancient priests and hunters did before ceremonies or major hunts?"

"Kind of, but I go there to get away from the real world, the world of work, bills, family." He cut into his enchilada and stuck a heaping forkful into his mouth.

Justine watched him enjoying the meal as if he hadn't had enchiladas before. But his story was so interesting that she pressed for more, wanting as much information from this spectacle of a man as she could get.

"To get away from family, huh? Who else is there besides you and your brother?" she asked as she cut into her enchilada.

"We're just two pieces of the puzzle. Everyone participating in this ceremony is my family—we are all natives. The intertribal festivities represent what it means to be a native family."

"I've always found that so fascinating. I only wish other nationalities had the kind of cohesiveness I see with the Native Americans. Others do have togetherness as well, but it seems to be more pronounced in this culture."

"Oh, we have our issues. Don't get me wrong and don't romanticize us so much. We have everyday problems with family and everything else. It just seems that most of us put our differences aside this time of year to celebrate what is truly important to us. This ceremonial represents our heritage, our way of life, now and traditionally. Our belief systems are derived from our life source, which is Mother Earth, the wind, the sky, rain; we see value in everything. The word *intertribal* means 'related in some way.' Sure, there are over eighty different tribes in this area, but this is our way of celebrating a heritage we all share throughout the Americas and elsewhere. This may sound like a cliché, but it is true. The intertribal ceremonial also allows non Indians to join us, celebrate."

"Where would the deities come in?"

"The deities must be your favorite part of our traditions."

"They are. I like the sacredness of them, the different gifts they offered, the way they served as protectors in a lot of cases. I'll admit to needing more schooling to know the entire story of the deities. Would you be willing to help me with that?"

"I'd love to, but it's a long story. I'll just give you a snippet for now, and then if you have more time a few days from now, I can go in deep, answer all lingering questions. They come from everywhere, literally."

She swallowed the last of her enchilada. Darrius Red Sky was not only a storehouse of information, but the absolute best source to get it from. He, apparently, was a man who loved his culture, and she admired him for that. She would have one hell of a memory to take back home with her.

"Whatever I can do to make your stay here more enjoyable and knowledgeable, you tell me. I can be at your disposal, Justine. We *are* the land, and loving it is like loving ourselves. You understand that? This is my home. I love it here. My brother and I were actually born in Zuni, but the family moved to Gallup when Derrick and I were four years old. Now, you wanted to know about my traditional family, right?"

"I would like to know more about you."

"Right. For the story?"

"No. For my own personal knowledge. Believe me, someone else is going to write the text. I'm just giving them a hell of a lot to go by with my photographs. Really though, I like you, find you interesting, kind, so helpful to a girl in need of the best shots."

"To show up my people and my home, I'd gladly write my autograph across your skin—that is, if it would please you."

"Why, Darrius Red Sky! I do believe you're a bit of a flirt."

"Only when it's important."

"Is it?"

"I'm still sitting here with you, aren't I? I could be relieving my brother at the cash register instead. The minute I saw you looking at the bracelets, I knew you were something to behold. The sky told me of your arrival, remember?"

"I do, and I find it fascinating that you have such broad knowledge. Is this typical of your family?"

"Oh, that's right, my family. You see what you do? You draw a man's attention away from everything but you. My parents live near Farmingdale. My father retired from the family business, which, as you know, is producing tea."

"Warrior's Brew?"

"That and more. I have a sister who is fifteen and living with my parents."

"What's her name?"

"Her name is strictly Indian, created way before *Native American* was the so-called politically correct thing to call us."

"Before it was fashionable to be Native American?"

"That's a good way to put it, although we've always been proud people. My sister's name is Asinka. It's the Hopi name for youngest daughter. She was born with a twin as well, but he died at birth. His name was Honovi, kind of a play on words. He was a weak baby, had bad lungs, but his name means strong deer, meaning he would be strong in life and in death."

"So, twins run in your family?"

"Rampantly, except for my youngest brother, Jemez. Who would want to be born with him? He's a trickster who should have been named after the Koshari."

"Much younger?"

"He's twenty-two." Darrius could see her making mental calculations, and beat her to the punch. "Derrick and I will be thirty-two on October 31."

"You're kidding! You two were born on Halloween?"

"And you're thinking that explains my mysticism?"

"That had crossed my mind."

"I know it had."

"Halloween is my favorite holiday, well, next to Christmas. I love all those scary movies, decorating, taking kids out trick-or-treating."

"Really? What kids?"

"My nephews. I also take the kids at one of the local Boys and Girls Clubs I volunteer at in San Francisco. They love going out with me since I'm such a big kid, anyway. We usually eat all the candy I've checked out before I get them back home."

"What do you do with them at the club?" Darrius asked, finding her generous spirit especially appealing.

"I teach photography. You know, show them camera and lens angles, how to operate cameras, things like that. It's fun, and it gives kids an alternative to getting into trouble on the streets."

"That's really incredible. I knew you were someone with a soft heart."

Twiddling her thumbs, she hesitated before meeting his gaze, and then carefully stated, "I have that kind heart with children. As for adults, I rarely get the chance to show them my softer side. It's either work all the time or helping to organize family functions. I suppose that can bring out the bear in someone."

"A bear is not what I see when I look at you. I see the softness. I knew you had it the day we met."

"How?"

"I just do, is all."

"Has to be something else."

He leaned against the back cushion of the chair, smiling. "You're right. It is something else. I googled your name, and your bio from *The Examiner* came up, along with some family information."

"That's how you knew my parents' names. Do you know my brothers' and sisters' names, too?"

"Yep. There's a Justin, Miranda, Selena and Vinchinzo—after your father."

"Right, but you forgot Patrick, my oldest brother. I guess you're not so perfect after all, are you?"

He smiled. "But I do know you're a pretty hot prospect in the photography world. The site mainly highlighted your photography. Seems I'm in good company."

"You are, but you cheated! Weren't you *supposed* to know these things about me already?"

"Well, the wind can't tell me everything, but I like what I see so far. Besides, you haven't told me a lot about yourself. What makes Justine Roberts-Paretti tick? What do you like to do, other than help children at missions and children's clubs? That's very admirable."

"True, I love children very much."

"Enough to have some of your own one day?"

"I'd love to, but my past with men hasn't been great. You see, I'm looking for what my parents have—a forever kind of relationship. Men find it hard to deal with me for some reason."

"Is it your inquisitive nature?"

"Maybe, but I can't help it. It's in my blood, probably came from my father's side. He wouldn't stop until he had his own business. Working for The Man was never for him. I'm like that in a way."

"I think it's a good trait. You're making a name for yourself, but I can't see why that would turn guys off."

"Has it turned you off?"

"As I said before, I'm still here, aren't I?"

Justine smiled. "Right. You're okay, Darrius. I think I'll keep you. Just don't run off. I have that way about myself for some reason. And I'm bullheaded, never listening to advice until reality slaps me in the face."

"I'll stay around. Besides, you're on my side of the country."

"True."

"Then I guess it's safe to say you're not dating anyone presently."

"Very safe. I have only dated sporadically, and only one man for any decent length of time—my high school sweetheart. We parted before college, promising to get back together one way or another, but it never happened. He's married and has a daughter now."

"Then he's the unlucky one by missing out on you."

"Maybe, but my aggressive side can be a turnoff. The other few relationships weren't that intense. Maybe I wasn't meant to settle down with the man of my dreams."

"Why would you believe that? I think anything is possible. Besides, I like aggressive women. They make for interesting conversation."

"I'm glad. There is more to me than taking pictures and scaring away boyfriends. I love to ballroom dance, believe it or not. I know a lot of people can't visualize black women ballroom dancing. I also enjoy the usual African American dances—soul, rhythm and blues. I love hip hop, soul music, blues—all kinds of music, basically."

"That's good to know; I have a lot of Indian CDs you may enjoy. What else do you like?"

"Bowling, most sports. Maybe that's because I have brothers. All of us played together, and I can throw a football pretty darn far."

"Now, there's my sport. I love a good football game. I like bowling, too, so maybe we can go if you have time."

"Depends on work. Other than that, I'd love to go. I also like going on picnics, staying late and stargazing before returning home. I live alone in a loft, and sometimes my girlfriends and I stay up late, make popcorn, drink a little booze on occasion and watch Mel Gibson and Denzel Washington movies. Oh, another thing I like doing is having enchiladas with handsome Native American men. Are those good interests?"

"They sound pretty good as far as I'm concerned."

"Well, that's me, but what about you? What else do you like, and do for recreation?"

"Sports, alone time, time to think. I'm a pretty reserved man. I don't do crowds much unless it's like events such as the powwows; the ballroom dancing, no way! My thing is action movies and golf, eating out with pretty young photojournalists and taking pictures."

"What about women? Is there one in your life?"

"Wow! You are on the information trail, aren't you?"

"You asked me."

"Fair enough. No, no women lately."

"Surely there are many who would like to be."

"Maybe." He looked at his watch, purposely avoiding the subject. The last thing he wanted to do was scare her off. In the past he and relationships hadn't mixed well, but there was always the possibility of starting over—he hoped. He took a deep breath and let it out slowly. "We should get your pictures developed at my place before I ship you off to the market at Red Rock. I'll show you my amateur pictures of Ship Rock."

She noted his reluctance to touch the subject of women, and glanced at the clock as well. "Okay, that'll give us a couple of hours."

"Good!"

Justine loved the way his eyes narrowed seductively. Yes, he was definitely a flirt, but she was beginning to love it. "Your house, huh? I don't know. Far be it for me to go to a man's house so soon after meeting him. You may be a little too swift for me, and the stars may tell you to take advantage of me."

"The stars won't be out, and I promise to have you safely away from me by the time they do shine tonight. Really, though, you won't have to worry about being alone with me. I'll be a perfect host while you and I develop my pictures. I swear. But I am like a werewolf; once the moon appears I'm liable to turn on you, but in all the best possible ways. C'mon, give it a shot."

"I'm kidding, Darrius. You have good vibes. I felt safe with you yesterday while I tried to steal the bracelet."

"It worked. You got the prize."

Her voice rose an octave. "Well, not yet."

Darrius left a twenty on the table, wrapped his arm around Justine's and led her back to his truck.

The scenery on the route to his house in the upper-most hills of western Gallup was simply gorgeous.

Salmon pink, desert beige, and shadow brown mountains were dazzling. The mountain's quiet wind songs made her imagine the old ones of long ago, as Darrius called them, harvesting their crops, constructing homes, worshipping the earth with all the splendor of the plains as their backdrop. The people had to know the way of the world, as did all societies before the living became easier. They had to have incredible intuition. Apparently, some of it passed down to Darrius.

Darrius made a point of not driving like a coyote for her benefit, and for that, she was grateful. He was so aware, so knowledgeable in showing her points of interest, so—perfect, from his hair to his cowboy boots. Normally, after knowing a man only one day, any thought of going to his house was a non-happening event. But with Darrius, she felt she would belong anywhere he took her, that he would guide and protect her as well as entertain her. She felt safe with him.

After a mile or so of the mountains, they came to an adobe house, desert beige with accents of turquoise and dark brown trim. It was beautiful, its features including an enclosed deck on top and a wraparound porch. It was almost as awesome as its owner. "Is this your house?" she asked.

"Home sweet home."

"And only you live in such a huge place?"

"Just me. I love space. Do you see the large lawn and garden? There's an even larger backyard."

"Your closest neighbor is more than a city block away."

"I like my space." He pulled into the circular driveway, parked and popped the automatic locks. "You get to see where I have my dreams, create my schemes, cook you breakfast and develop photographs of Ship Rock."

"You really love Ship Rock, don't you?"

"I do." He helped her from the truck and led her into his personal paradise—only this time there was a perfect sunflower of a woman latched on to his arm.

5

PICTURE PERFECT

The large oak double doors with carved panels of desert flower designs took Justine's breath away. She touched the fine engravings, relishing the feel of the raised wood felt against her fingers. The blue corn ristra hanging from it added to the appeal. "Are these here for a specific reason?"

Standing directly behind her, Darrius managed to take his attention off the flowery scent of her hair and skin to answer. "Ears of blue corn have aesthetic, nutritional and spiritual values. I try to make my home as tranquil as possible. You'll see when we walk inside. The place is filled with totems from my ancestry. It all helps me to maintain peace in my life."

She touched the carved flowers again. "I've never met a man with flowers on his door."

"Does it make me seem less masculine?"

"Nothing could do that. Besides, I like a man who has a sensitive side. Men shouldn't always be about the brawn, right?"

When he didn't answer immediately, she turned and saw a slight weariness in his eyes. "Is something wrong, Darrius?"

"No, it's just that sometimes the life of Indians in a non-native world can be hard—flowers or brawn. No offense to anyone non-native, of course," he added unlocking the door.

"None taken. I understand perfectly. Your people's land was taken over for reasons of greed. A lot of my people were forcibly brought here for the same reasons."

"I knew you would understand. But I want you to feel at home here despite what I just said."

Justine walked in, through the foyer and into a Native American version of Eden, with stained wood floors so shiny they looked wet. An off-white partitioned wall with a fireplace in the middle of the huge living room separated it from the open kitchen. "This is spectacular. I've never seen a place so, so full of custom and—"

"Heritage?"

"Exactly! May I explore?"

"Only if I can follow; I'd like to explain a few things."

Justine gladly took his arm again. "You lead the way, master."

As she walked through the living room, she saw metal wall hangings similar to the ones in his showroom at the store. The steer skull hanging above the tiled rust-and-red fireplace was her favorite. "Do you use the fireplace often?"

"Only on cool nights, and sometimes for effect when company is here. Don't you have one at home?"

"My loft at home doesn't have one—some do, but not mine."

Richly designed Hopi and Navajo rugs in all sizes, shapes and colors lay on the hall floor and in areas in the living room. There were quivers of arrows on walls of his living room and hall; baskets and pots decorated corners. A large cherry wood island was apparently used for both food preparation and casual dining. "Is this where you cooked my crepes?"

"Yes. I love to cook. Mother taught all of us."

"Even Derrick?"

"Yes, why?"

"I don't know, he just doesn't strike me as the cooking type."

He took a fruit drink from the wood-framed refrigerator and handed it to her. "Derrick made this. It's a blend of natural fruit, coconut milk and spices. Tell me how you like it."

"Umm, this is delicious."

"Derrick made it when he was here the other night. He's actually a chef at La Carouas when he's not overseeing the tea factory, dancing in ceremonies and finding rare gems."

"A chef, huh? Well, that's impressive. What does Jemez do for a living?"

"Landscaping and designing. He designed my home. Good, isn't he?"

"Clearly a master."

"Come, let me show you one of my favorite places."

They walked through a hallway as wide as a gallery, its walls covered with Native American art by masters such as Ernest Franklin, Roger Deal Jr. and Tony Abeyta. Justine lingered at a painting of a warrior by JD Challenger, fascinated by its details: the feather headband, multi-patterned robe and steer-skull shield. She was quite intrigued by the red outline of a buffalo skull painted across the warrior's mouth.

She had been so absorbed in the painting she had become lost in time until Darrius came up behind her, taking her hand and kissing it. She was quickly brought back to reality. His warm hand covering hers made him want to touch her in other, more intimate places. She looked up at him in the stillness of the hallway and swallowed hard. "Where is your darkroom? Do you still want me to help you develop your pictures?"

"There's time. Just one more place to show you."

I hope it's not the bedroom. But her mind *was* on seeing the bed on which his naked, sculpted body slept. His bed would hold his scent, his sweat—memories of the pounding he gave it as he made love to someone. The image racing through her mind was so vivid she had to close her eyes to drive it away. She felt him pulling her along, heard him speaking of something of minor interest to her. How he *felt* next to her was what interested her. *He's just a man, not a god. He's flesh and blood. He's . . . he's intoxicating.* The sound of his voice startled her.

"This is where I downloaded your bio. It's my favorite place, next to the darkroom."

There were large windows on all sides of his study. Intricately woven bear and deer symbol rugs hung from the walls and Pueblo pots were on either side of a wicker ottoman chair. A basket sitting on a coffee table caught her eye.

"It's a Hopi basket from second Mesa in Arizona." Darrius handed it to her. "I knew you'd like it. Here. Take it."

The basket was so light it felt like cotton in her hands. She examined it, ran her fingers across the fine straw. "It's lovely. I love the colors, the way the weave is patterned in star and moon designs."

"Then it's yours."

"Oh, Darrius, I can't. You've given me so much already."

"Please. That's how we do things sometimes. If a visitor likes something, we make a gift of it to show kindness and respect."

"This looks very expensive."

"Aren't you worth it?"

"Yes, but—"

He took the basket and went into the living room where he placed it next to her purse. When he returned, she was smiling. "You're the most amazing man I've ever met."

"Not really. Looks and actions can be deceiving. Come on, let's get your pictures developed before you change your mind about accepting my gift."

"I wouldn't do that. A gift is a gift, right?"

"You got it," he said, leading her into the darkroom.

As soon as Darrius switched on the lights in the darkroom, Justine noticed photographs of mountain ranges pinned to a line. Justine went over for a closer look at the now dry shots.

"What place is this?"

"It's Ship Rock."

"You took these?"

"I know they're not very good, but—"

"They're great! I love them. Waiting until almost dusk to snap these was a nice added touch. That time of day enhances the beauty of the mountain peaks against the royal blue sky. During my endless train ride here, I saw how beautiful New Mexico sunsets are. It's truly a photographer's paradise."

"Well, I guess it takes a professional to know what makes a photographic image unique. I guess I really didn't do so badly with these after all, but I'm not nearly as good as you are, Justine. I have seen your work."

"Worthy of hanging in *your* darkroom?"

He moved closer. "From where I'm standing, the view is fantastic. I'd love anything of yours in here."

This was just too much for the overwhelmed Justine. She was so close to standing on tiptoes and kissing his full lips it was pathetic. The last thing she wanted was to get tangled up with him after only one full day of knowing him. Then again, maybe getting in a tangle with Darrius was just the thing she needed—but later. She had to somehow pull her eyes away from his before their lips really did touch. If that happened, there would be no turning back for her.

"I have pictures of Red Rock, if you want to see them." He opened a drawer and pulled out three more large pictures of the fabulous place. "I took these last year during the ceremonial, just before the Grand Entrance."

"You really are good. These bring out some of the smaller caverns."

"How do you know about the caverns there?"

"When I was there yesterday I looked up the winding road near the park's entrance. Red Rock is higher than I thought. It was kind of overwhelming, a little scary, so I didn't go any higher. Besides, I think I would have needed an off-road vehicle to survive going that high up."

"You would have because it's dangerous. I can take you some time soon and show you parts that aren't sacred if you like, since you're intrigued by it."

"You should submit your photographs to *New Mexico Magazine* and see what happens."

"Maybe." He walked her over to the photographic paper and solutions. "Let's get started. I want you to see a few of the shots I took, get your expert advice on them. Before you know it, it'll be time to get you to the open-market crafts."

Darrius unloaded his 35mm camera, filled the three developing tanks with the different solutions and turned out the lights. He was almost ready.

"Did you do your contact prints yet, Darrius?" Justine asked.

"Nope! See, had you not been here I would not have remembered that. Want to help?"

"Sure, where's your photo paper?" He turned the light back, handed her a few sheets and they both worked together. After a few more procedures, they were ready to put his photographs in the solutions.

Justine nudged his shoulder. "From what I can see, I think you took more pictures of those caves at Red Rock. Is that what you did?"

"Guilty. I'm as intrigued by them as you are. Always have been, even though I've seen them up close. I also have one of the hill you looked up near the entrance. That intrigues me, too and I do know what's on the other side of the hill, Justine."

"What?"

"Danger, like I said before. I don't want you going up there. You don't have the right type of vehicle and experience."

"The vehicle, you're right about, but the experience—I think I might. I've been in dangerous situations before, like with the bull. Remember."

"You could always get away from him. He was one of the older bulls, anyway. The other side is not a good place to be unless you're an experienced rock climber or someone who goes on digs and expeditions in hilly territories."

"Why are you telling me this?"

"Because I saw how you looked at the negative. That's why I brought it up."

"Save your worries. I've got too much to do to go up there anyway. Even though I'm sure there are great photos up there."

"There would be, but they're not worth the risk." He moved in behind her. "Now, let's see what we come up with so you can get to work."

During the wait in the darkness, he was still so near, so close to her, that she felt strands of his silken hair brush against her face. Yet she kept quiet, not wanting him to know the mere thought of him was consuming her.

Darrius could hardly stand being that close to her in the dark and not think about her naked and lying on his bed in air conditioning. He imagined how her body would react to him joining her on the bed, the taste of her lips against his, the feel of her breasts in his large hands. Tasting one nipple after the other began to control him to the point where he could actually taste them. His mouth watered, his body stiffened, his breathing became shallow. What on earth was the woman doing to him? Was she even real, or a figment of something the stars really did bring? Whatever the case, he wanted her. Screw being a gentleman, he wanted her raw, pulsing against him. Now.

Thoughts became actions and he bent to the nape of her neck, kissing the tender flesh. He knew he'd probably get slapped and possibly lose the one woman who had taken his mind off everything in the real world. She was sweet to the taste, gentle on the tongue, and his erection pulled tighter against his jeans. His only thought: *She isn't moving away from me.*

Moving away from Darrius Red Sky would have killed her. All she wanted was more of him, more kisses, more flicks of his tongue against her moist skin. And she let him. Her body backed against his, feeling the tightness in his jeans, feeling his erection squirm for want of release. He was hard, pulsing, racing, feverish against her, and he felt good, great, undeniably alive. Everything in her ached for him, wanting to turn and face the man of a thousand rushes. That's what he gave her, a thousand tingles and chills.

He supported her wobbly legs with his own as he turned her around. And then they were face-to-face, lips barely inches apart. Her arms reached across his shoulders, flushing her body closer to his, feeling her breasts press against him. The tight nipples ached for his lips and, at the same moment, his hair was in her hands. Since meeting him, she had wanted to play in his river of hair. The heft of his silky hair drew her closer to him, and they kissed, hard, lazily, lavishly. Tongues searched, hands caressed with ease and greed at the same time. His long fingers enclosed her derrière, forcing more of him into her.

The feel of it against her stomach set off a chain reaction of sensations. Without letting go of him, her body spiraled in sexual hunger, quivering against him, seeing rockets behind her eyes. It had been the best orgasm a woman could have possibly experienced. It was the epitome of sexual encounters in all her years of living.

Realizing what she had done, and who with, she stepped back despite the fact that he was still holding on to her blouse. "Darrius . . . what have I done?"

He stroked her blushing face. "It wasn't you. It was me. I started this because I couldn't help it."

"What about your photographs?"

He looked in the tray. "They're fine. Kissing you felt as though it were longer than it actually was. It felt so right, Justine."

"But we shouldn't have. I barely know you, and I let you master me."

He took a few steps back. "I'm sorry." He looked down, feeling bad for taking advantage of a situation he should have backed away from. In his heart, what he felt was real, natural, and he would never *truly* feel sorry for it.

Justine saw the anguish on his face, and stroked his cheek. "Don't be sorry, Darrius. I could have pulled away—"

"Yet you didn't. Why?"

"Because I wanted it; wanted what I shouldn't have had."

"Is the idea of me kissing you such a terrible one?"

Her smile lit the darkness. "The kiss was amazing, Darrius, but I'm here to work. My story has to come first."

"And so it will." He stepped to the photographs, took the tongs and lifted each one. Together they put the rest of the pictures into the solutions, but in dead silence.

He hung several and stepped back, looking at them. "The cave ones turned out great. Better than I expected them to."

"You're a good photographer, Darrius. I see that in work you think is so mediocre. You're good with more than just pictures, and that's what has taken me away from my work. No one has ever done that before."

"And it would take a mere store owner to capture you."

"Yes. Why do you think I didn't pull back from you and slap you across the face a few minutes ago? Because you do something to me, Darrius. I've never admitted that to a man before; never had the occasion to. My camera simply aims at you without my help." She looked at him, and then down at her sandaled feet. "My work must still come first. I'm not here to be romanced, unfortunately." Her eyes met his in a sorrowful, heartfelt gaze. "I can't come back here."

"You can. I promise I'll never touch you again unless you say so."

"That's just the problem. I would say so." The neon hands on the clock caught her attention. "It's after three. I should soon be on the way to the arts and crafts exhibits by now. I may have enough time to use your laptop to send a few photos to my editor. Would that be okay with you?"

"Sure, or you could come to the store this evening and do it. I have several laptops. The one at work is more sophisticated," he added with the sly smile that he was so good at using. "Would that be good? Seeing as though you're running out of time."

Now comfortably eye-to-eye with him, she spoke. "It's all good. Maybe I can come by and take a few shots of your store. Would that be okay with you?"

"When it involves you, everything is okay."

6

UNCHARTED TERRITORY

They drove in silence, and they both knew why. There was no denying that what they had shared had been powerful, maybe more powerful than either of them could handle. Someone had to break the silence. Hers was the voice that eventually echoed in the stillness of the truck. "I left my basket at your house."

"I can bring it to the store. Do you still want it?"

"Of course I want it."

"I'll bring it."

That was all he said, and he barely looked at her. She knew why and understood. Desperate for him to feel good again, she touched his arm. "Darrius?"

"Yes?"

"Will you be able to meet me at the outdoor market-place at six?"

"Well, I still have to rescue Derrick, who is probably wondering what happened to me. And then I have to check on things at my other store in Taos, but I'll try."

The car was still intact in the now more crowded golf course lot. Pulling up beside it, Darrius said, "I guess this is it. Take good pictures; capture the spirit. I know you will." He moved a strand of hair from her face and looked into her eyes briefly, as if a permanent goodbye was in his thoughts. "I'll get your camera bag and help you out."

Justine didn't know what to say to him. She sensed he wasn't mad—but maybe a little hurt, but that was the last thing she had wanted to do to someone so incredible. She sat behind the wheel looking up at Darrius. "Is there still a possibility of me taking shots of you in one of your stores? I think it'll be great business for you."

"My business already does quite well."

Her heart sank. "Oh."

"But more is always better."

"Really? Is Wednesday night still good?"

"It's your schedule, your time. You tell me."

That told her he was detaching himself, letting her make the moves if any were to be made. The best thing was to let it ride, see where the situation took her if any-where. A single kiss may have ruined everything. All along, she knew she should have made him stop instead of indulging him, but what an indulgence. It was one she'd never forget even if she never saw Darrius Red Sky again.

"I'll set up a time and tell you tonight if I see you. If not, I'll call you. I still have your card."

"Sounds good." With a tap on the hood, he sent her off to dwell deeper into that desperate no-man's land he knew she was thinking about, beyond the entrance of Red Rock.

Red Rock's peaks seemed higher than the Transamerica Building in the heart of San Francisco. She had heard that its elevation was over six thousand feet.

In the sun, the peaks looked like giant dark entities—mysterious. She knew the story associated with Red Rock, how it got its name, where it led to, who lived there years ago, but not having Darrius around to tell her things no textbook or magazine could tell her seemed rather dismal now.

The winding road she had been driving on had ended. Another winding road off to the side led to the other side of Red Rock, the dangerous side that Darrius had spoken of. She was curious to see exactly where this road went, but when she drove closer to the foot of the hill and looked up, it was scary; the peaks appeared even more shadowy. The tricky turns she was encountering were not meant for a car like hers; a vehicle like what Darrius had was more suitable. Darrius! He was the only thing that could take her mind off venturing into the shadow lands.

Still, her mind returned to the peaks, wondering what was behind them. What was drawing, pulling her in, taking her to where the old ones worshipped, cured their sick, smoked their peyote. Yes! A good dose of peyote right about now would rid her mind completely of Darrius . . . and going up the forbidden hill.

Ceremonial activities awaited her, so she had to put aside her passion for Red Rock's peaks and Red Sky for the moment. Funny that red had become her new favorite color. It had always been blue. Blue was now the color of her mood.

The outdoor festivities, such as the gem show and craft shows took place at Convention C, the same place the main portion of the powwow would be on Saturday night. It's where she hoped to see and photograph Derrick doing his dance of the trickster.

There were plenty of tables and stands displaying a dazzling assortment of Native American arts and crafts. The Hopi baskets made her think about the basket left at Darrius's house. It *would* have been a good memento to take back and display on one of her tables at home. Too bad. It, along with her emotions, was probably lost in translation. She shrugged. *Hyperactive hormones are not a girl's best friend.*

There was an abundance of events and activities to photograph, and that would have to suffice. Her editor would be happy nonetheless; her photographs always spoke for themselves.

Waving her press card, Justine received permission to take pictures of the baskets. Many artisans gladly opened their booths to her, eager to have their wares photographed, hoping this would help business. Others didn't care whether pictures were taken or not, so long as their crafts sold. There *were* children to feed, and Justine understood. To help, she purchased a silver heart charm from Big Buffalo Jewels.

She visited many booths and collected many business cards, some of which she planned on using to pull up some of the vendors' websites on her laptop while alone in her room later; she was sure she would, unfortunately, be alone. She also planned to visit other stores before leaving New Mexico.

Many stands offered a variety of kachina dolls, but she saw none of the Koshari. Thus far, she hadn't seen anything like what Darrius had displayed in his showroom; there were no Frederic K clowns, the Navajo carver who most impressed him. But she took many shots of the other kachinas. Unfortunately, very little paperwork accompanied them. There was a world of kachinas to discover, but who would be her guide? Darrius was gone, probably in more ways than one. No one could tell the story better than a Native American. Or, as Darrius might say, Indian.

By sunset, the cameras were heavy on her shoulder. Several trips back to the car to be rid of them had been her only remedy. On a trip to a water stand, she saw male traditional dancers outside a fenced-off tepee practicing for a ceremony. As she had learned from some of the Arizona powwows, teepees were changing quarters and restricted to outsiders. The teepee before her had paintings of a buffalo hunt. The images were very descriptive in appearance, with a single hunter with arrow chasing a running animal. The painting had been exquisite, so unlike how movies and television made native art out to be so archaic.

She wanted to get closer, touch it, feel the buck or doeskin it was made of, but had to keep her distance. The dancers' costumes consisted of eagle feathers, bone breastplates, breechcloths and moccasins. Cameras were never allowed during practice and she would have been escorted out of Red Rock if she were caught photographing, so she just listened and watched. There were chants, step dancing, painted faces. One face stood out among the dancers.

It was Darrius's face, yet it wasn't. He never danced at the powwows. It was Derrick, or even another relative who danced. Whatever the case, their performance kept her there, enlightened by the rhythmic dance steps, the chants, the calls. It all reminded her of the local and other powwow shows she had been so entranced with in her journeys as a photographer. The chants had a way of relaxing her, setting everything on an even keel—at least for a few minutes.

The practice ceremony ended, and some members headed for the food stands, while others went in the area of the crafts. Two walked in the direction of the main arena where a beer stand stood. The Darrius look-alike held a tall, cold plastic cup of something gold in color, and then he and his buddy walked to a patch of grass and sat down. Justine wanted to approach, but stayed back, not wanting to disturb their moment. But after watching him laugh and drink, seeing another side of him, she regained her nerve.

The friend soon departed and Derrick was alone. The grass was quiet under her sandals. Another good thing.

All she needed was for him to see her approach and stop her dead in her tracks. Without even being a whisper in the wind, her quiet steps landed her next to him, but without a word. She would let him feel her presence.

Her presence was indeed felt, and he smiled at her standing there so quiet. "Where the heck did you come from? You make it a habit of sneaking up on guys like this?"

"Wasn't sure you wanted company."

"Your company is always welcome. But why aren't you with my brother? The way the guy has been ranting and raving about you, I'd have thought the two of you were huddled in some close space together."

"As much as I would like to huddle in a small space with Darrius, I do have work to do." Images of being with Darrius in the darkroom filtered in and she smiled. Indeed, he and Darrius could easily have their way with women and no one would be the wiser. How many women liked Darrius, she wondered; and does he always use the line about the wind on them?

"Darrius and I parted around three this afternoon. He had work to do at the store."

"He did, but I thought you would be with him."

"I have my work. That's why I'm here, to get pictures."

He looked around her, halfway scoping her slender frame. "How many cameras you got in the big book bag?"

"Three."

"All digital, I assume."

"You assumed right. Who has time for cameras? Besides, digital cameras are so much faster, and that's a good thing if you're on a deadline—which I am. I was headed back up the hill when I heard your song and dance, you and the others near the tepee. What was that, anyway?"

"Practice for the grass dance. Did you shoot us?"

That scared her. What if she had? Lie and save your neck. "No, I know some ceremonies prohibit it, so I—"

"It would have been cool. That way, even I could be in your newspaper for you to remember me."

"Like I could forget. What woman could forget two sexy men who look just alike?"

"That could be exciting. Know what I mean?" He wriggled his brow.

"Darrius did tell me you're a card—a wild card."

"His actual words?"

"Not really. I like you, though. You're fun, different. How can two totally different people live in the same womb together for nine months?"

"I ignored him and stuck to my side of the womb. We had different embryonic sacs."

"Too much info, Derrick!"

"Just kidding. He's a great brother, though I'm older by eight minutes. He'd never do the threesome thing, anyway; too private for that."

What a thought. One on each side, taking turns with me, filling me with joy and surrender that only belonged in romance novels. I could never do that to Darrius, though, so

*get your mind back on track, girl! You're losing it out here.
Think fast.* "What's the grass dance all about?"

"The Ponca say it originated on the plains. People
went to an isolated spot on the prairie to give thanks. It's
a pretty simple story, actually, but very important to our
culture."

"What I saw of it was engaging; wild, vivid. Does
Darrius participate in any of the dancing?" she asked,
hoping to find out if Darrius danced at all.

"Not really. He used to."

"Why did he stop?"

"He just stopped is all. His soul is as deep and raging
as a flowing stream. Maybe deeper. He keeps a lot of
things to himself—other than talking about you. The
minute he stepped into the store, he couldn't wait to tell
me he had seen you again. You two developed pictures
and went to the day parade, huh?"

"Is that all he told you?"

"Basically. Why?"

"No reason." *Don't divulge a thing, sister!* "You must
have just gotten here, because it seems I left Darrius only
a little while ago."

"We caught each other in passing; he was coming
into the store as I was leaving it. He knew I needed to be
here by a certain time to practice with my troupe, so I left
Joe in charge for a while."

She looked into Derrick's face, seeing shadows from
nearby flames from pits, from trees and the looming rock
wall behind him. His features were crisp and angled,
square-jawed, beautiful, just like Darrius's, and could

possibly stir her body in much the same way. This twin may have had the same face, but his spirit seemed different, swifter, more commonplace. He was kind, funny, and seemingly just as knowledgeable. Something told her to leave, just leave and find Darrius, make up for shying away from his affections, because from what she was feeling, apparently they were meant to share more than a darkroom.

Justine said her goodbyes and headed to her car. It was getting dark, and it had been a long day. She was ready to sleep, be fresh and ready for more work and exciting scenes the next day. Wednesday was to be very busy for her, returning to Red Rock for more of the pre-festivities. Her laptop sat next to her on the bed and she was happy that she had the chance to send more photos to her editor. The issue would be a late September release, and she and her photos were always ready weeks in advance. This time would be no different.

After showering and relaxing on her bed, she thought back on the day's events and realized she had not made contact with Darrius. They were supposed to meet at Red Rock earlier that day. Maybe he had gotten too busy with inventory or store hours. Before long, fatigue took over and Justine fell into a restless sleep. Even then, Darrius invaded her dreams.

7

MOONLIGHT SERENADE

Darrius's message machine at home and work came on, so Justine was reduced to leaving a mechanized version of herself. She hoped he would get it. Wednesday had been a long day, and maybe a nice refreshing shower was what she needed more than a face-to-face with Darrius.

The shower jets pounded her body, relaxing her, clearing her mind. The trail leading to the upper hills came to mind. Going up there and photographing whatever was there challenged her. But, would she be brave enough? She needed an off-road vehicle. Darrius had one. He had two, in fact, but she didn't want to dismiss his warning, despite how photogenic the other side of the mountain probably was.

It seemed that no matter where her thoughts wandered, they eventually came back to Darrius. He filled her mind as her soapy hands traveled over her body—to her breasts, pinching the heightened buds, wishing her fingers were his. She remembered how she felt pressed against him in the darkroom, how tight his body was, how warm, smooth. She had sensed his blood rushing, his fire starting. Remembering the length and thickness of his erection as it pressed firmly against her consumed her. Her hand moved past her stomach and into warmer territories.

Water and flesh joined, making her sex tingle and rush with thoughts of Darrius touching her there. His nimble fingers moved like a swift wind inside her, thrashing against her clit, massaging the soft outer folds of her womanhood—making her peak. Her eyes closed as the pounding within stampeded over her. She held her breath as her stomach contracted and her back arched. Her body constricted around her fingers, and in the distance, she heard herself calling his name.

After the hurricane that swallowed her body ceased, her eyes slowly opened. There she was leaning against the shower wall, hair dripping across her shoulders and breasts, her heart racing, her mind on the man who had taken over her body. *Weak!*

How could I let the mere thought of him invade me like that?

Easy. It was Darrius Red Sky, and he had conquered, claimed his territory—at least until yesterday in his dark room. Before then, she could practically see him willing her into a storm of an orgasm, smiling at her rush as she delivered to him. Hell, his smile was on everything she saw. Who was to say he couldn't actually see her in his thoughts? He had apparently done so before.

Hearing the room phone, she ran back into the bedroom just in time to pick it up before it stopped ringing. The display read: Red Sky Jewelers. Thank God. Then she wondered: *Does he know what I just did in the shower?* "Darrius?"

"Hi, beautiful. How was your shower?"

Christ! "It was relaxing. How did you know I was taking a shower?"

"I'm sure you had a long and tiring day at Red Rock, and that's why I didn't disturb you. Isn't a nice, long shower the next logical step?"

"Usually."

"I'm sorry I couldn't make it last night. How did things go? Take any good pictures?"

"Everything I photographed was beautiful, of course, and I did take some great shots. I ran into your brother last night. Almost thought he was you, but then I remembered you were at the store all day yesterday."

"Just remember this, his eyes are darker. That's the only difference."

The only one? "Is that all?" The tightness of his crotch came screaming back into her mind.

"Well, he's taller by half an inch. How were the events there today?"

"Fabulous; wish you had been able to make it."

"I got really busy with inventory. Sorry."

"That's okay. We can get together another time." Then she thought about the main reason he may not have been there. *The darkroom affair!* "Darrius, about yesterday in your lab—"

"I know what you're about to say, and I'm really sorry."

"No, don't be. I may have been a little, well, rude pushing away from you like that." She debated whether to say more, but decided she had to at least try to make him feel better. "The kiss was . . . the only word for it is delicious."

"It gets better with time. And what makes you think I would ever shy away from you?"

"You were awfully quiet in the truck yesterday." She suddenly realized she was stark naked while talking to him. Instead of getting dressed, she slipped between the bed sheets and let Darrius's voice and the cool, crisp cotton lull her.

"I was quiet because I felt like a cad taking advantage of you."

"You're not a cad, Darrius; you're wonderful. It may be bold to admit this, but you felt natural in my arms, made me feel like a woman all over, and in all the right places."

"You're definitely all woman, Justine, and I liked how you felt in my arms."

Justine felt the rise in body temperature within her sex as he seduced her with words. Her back arched against the sheets and her body trembled when she heard him call her name . . .

"Justine? Are you still there?"

"Definitely. I seemed to have zoned out."

"Did you go somewhere nice?"

"Real nice!"

He wanted so badly to comment, to say other seductive words just so he could listen to her climax. He could tell what a woman's body was doing just by listening intensely. What he wouldn't have done to see her come.

Instead, he stuck to the *typical*, the *normal*, not wanting to get into trouble with his thoughts. "Are you hungry? I know I am. I can bring over—"

God, it was hard saying no to this man, but she was tired and figured her rendezvous yesterday was enough. In the past, she had hardly been the woman to fall for a man so soon, and she surely didn't want to start now. But it was the way Darrius reacted to her, treated her that made her want to release the wild side she had been adamant about keeping hidden. Surely, if she let him in her room again, there would be no saying no to him. "You're sweet, but it's late; besides, I ate a buffalo burger at the campgrounds. You haven't finished work for the evening yet?"

"I still haven't finished inventory. There's a lot to do when you own your own business. Besides, I had customers, you know, late ceremonial hours."

"I forgot about that. Which store are you calling from?"

"The one where I met the most amazing woman."

She curled up, loving how his voice calmed her. "Yeah? What's her name?"

"Let's just say you know her well."

"Ah, not committing to anything, huh?"

"I won't say that. However, you were supposed to come over and take pictures of the store. You still can."

"It really is late, Darrius."

"Yes, it is, and you should rest. But are you still interested in taking pictures of me and my store?"

"Of course. I didn't think you wanted to be in them."

"Can't a guy change his mind?"

She beamed with pure joy. "He sure can. You set a time?"

"I think tomorrow would be good, say about two?"

"That's perfect, Darrius. How long will you be working tonight?"

"Probably another hour or so."

"Don't wear yourself out. There are others who would gladly do that for you."

"Would that be you?"

"I'm not committing, either. Thanks for everything yesterday, Darrius, even the little pleasures you don't know about," she said mysteriously.

"Oh, I know about those, too."

"I'm sure. You go home soon, okay?"

"I'll try. Sweet dreams."

Darrius hung up. He had missed seeing her, but knew she had work to do. Thoughts of her made his manhood so stiff and hard, and it hurt brushing against his pants. Only Justine could relieve his pressure—if he let her, if she was willing. All pipe dreams for the moment. He pushed the thought away as best he could and turned to the un-inventoried items. He wiped sweat from his forehead, saying, "I can't let her get to me like this. I just can't! I don't need another woman in my life right now." *Yeah, try convincing yourself of that.*

Justine replaced the receiver and relaxed, a satisfied smile on her lips, wanting to be with Darrius in any way she could—by taking photos or simply standing next to him. Whatever way he would let her be with him was okay with her. From the way he sounded moments ago, that was a distinct possibility.

The camera bag was still in the chair where she dropped it when she came in. She stared at it. "Another hour or so, huh?"

She took a spring-green tie-dyed sundress from the closet. She had never worn it but brought it along, hoping she would have a chance to while in New Mexico. She blow-dried her hair and curled it quickly after sprinkling powder everywhere. She added matching earrings, Darrius's bracelet and a little makeup and then slipped into the dress and headed westward.

The store lights were still on. Justine smiled, knowing Darrius hadn't taken her advice and gone home. But where was his truck? She parked her car and walked around the building. His white truck was right there, parked next to the back door. Camera bag in hand, she returned to the front and rang the doorbell.

In minutes, Darrius appeared. Smiling, he unlocked the door and held it open for her. "I knew you would arrive soon. Come in, take a load off."

Justine stepped inside and quickly faced him. "You knew I'd arrive soon? Let me guess, the stars told you this, too."

"Exactly right. That's the reason I've stayed another hour. I could have gone home, but something told me to stay." He pointed up at the starlit sky. "Look at the millions of stars out tonight. They couldn't help giving me a little advice." He saw the camera bag. "Tonight would be good for this, even better than tomorrow. There's no customers and the lighting is still good; we can talk, or do more."

"Talking is good. We'll see what comes later."

"Far be it from me to keep someone from doing her work."

"You let me worry about that." She placed her bag on the floor and turned to him. "You really are amazing, Darrius. You stayed here instead of going home and taking your own load off."

"A guy does what he has to, to spend time with the woman he likes. Come, let's get you set up."

He took her hand and led her to the showroom. "Will this do?"

Instead of answering, she asked, "What is that?"

"You like it?"

"It smells wonderful. Peyote?"

"Come on! It's just something I mixed up: a little juniper, sweet grass and badlands sage."

"I love it, and I was just kidding about the peyote."

"It's okay. Besides, who needs peyote when the likes of you are here?" He swung her in a half circle. "Look at you in this dress! If I hadn't promised to keep my hands to myself, you'd be in some real trouble here."

"I didn't hear you promise anything."

His eyes danced mischievously, but he chose to let his thoughts go unspoken and bask in the possibility of kissing her just one more time. "The showroom is completely stocked and dusted, the floors are mopped and the rugs in their places. Why don't we start? Where would you like me?"

"What?" *Don't tease me like this, Darrius. Where I truly want you is too obscene to mention.* "Oh." She looked around, saw the large showcase filled with jewelry, and lit by the traditional "End of the Trail" lamp. "Why don't we start where I first met you?"

"On your knees? When we first met, you were on your knees staring at the bracelets. You looked great in that position, if I may add. Hmm, maybe I should take the pictures. You on your knees before me would make for fantastic bedroom art."

"You're really something, Darrius." Being on her knees before him was an enticing thought, but she had to quickly suppress it or nothing would get done that night. "Pose by the lamp." She smoothed the fringes of his Western-style bandana print shirt, straightened his buffalo head belt buckle with nervous hands and then stepped back. It was sheer torture even touching his belt buckle because she could feel his heat, imagine the stiffness in his crotch, hear his shallow breathing. Everything about him was amazing, so amazing she could barely steady her hand to take the picture. "Smile . . . ah, yes, that's a good one." She took a few more of him posing by the cowboy boot display, but tried mainly focusing on the jewelry and other store items instead of the store's outrageously sexy owner.

"Why don't you pose by the cigar store Indian? Maybe put an arm around his waist." She then photographed him near the designer Native American T-shirts, at the basket displays and finally by the rack displaying the family's teas. The tea business was a story within itself, having started out as a small family business that grew by leaps and bounds over the years.

The atmosphere throughout the store was peaceful, serene. Even the CD playing in the background, entitled *Inside Desert Scenes* with its faint birdcalls and waterfalls in the background, added to the scene. Candles throughout the showroom and the dim lighting made the atmosphere that much more . . . soothing. Caught up in the fragrant and relaxing mood of the store itself, she lowered the camera, unable to take her eyes off the man who had made the evening possible.

She stood before him wordless, aimless, the camera on its leather strap dangling at her midsection.

He saw that she was unable to continue, and knew why. The feelings were mutual. He broke into the silence that had fallen over the room. "I've got a good picture for you."

Justine felt the perspiration on her forehead as she struggled to respond in an even voice. "Yeah? Of what?"

"Follow me."

Please don't take me to some forbidden little room in this place, because you'll find out exactly how weak I am when it comes to you. Her spirit made her follow him, but to where, her mind and body were not aware. All she knew was that wherever he walked, she would follow.

Darrius walked her into the kachina room. Expensive paintings of the Koshari covered turquoise walls. He remembered how much she loved seeing them when she first came in the other day. There in the background were the very portraits of Derrick dancing the clown dance as a Koshari. Darrius passed his hands before it. "Take one of me standing before the Koshari. I know he's your favorite kachina. I would still like to give you more details on him before you leave for San Francisco."

"Why not tonight?"

He struck a pose before the large Koshari painting. "If that's good for you." Strands of his hair fell against his shirt and he raised his hand to push them back.

"Don't! I like your hair like that, especially across the red hues of your shirt. I like the contrast. That's *so good,* Darrius; just stand right there. You won't believe how sensational you look against the gloss of the paint. Everything shines. This is the best picture yet." She lowered the camera, but her eyes were still fixed on him. Everything about the store was enchanting, the serene night atmosphere and the aroma coming from somewhere . . . and Darrius in his rugged jeans and fringed shirt. And *yes,* his hair! It was a black river of seduction, mouthwatering to her soul, feather-like to her touch. The memory of how it felt still made her fingers tingle. She wanted more, but wasn't sure how to ask. Instead, she asked about a new aroma in the air. "I smell something different now. What is it?"

"Ah, the tea is ready."

"Tea?"

"I started brewing some after talking to you. It's the Teepee Tales brew, good for relaxing. Served before bedtime. It's got passion flower in it. You will have some with me, won't you?"

"Passion flower? Who would say no to that?"

They were close enough to see the desire in each other's eyes. He agreed. "Yes, who would say no to that?"

"Good for bedtime, but it's no longer daytime, Darrius." *Where in the heck did that come from?*

"I know what you mean. Come with me. We'll have a cup or two and sit on the padded rug near your favorite place—the jewelry counter. There's plenty of room back there. Would you like that?"

Justine said nothing, taking his hand and letting him lead the way.

The steam from his piping-hot mug of tea filled his nostrils and made him relax against the wall behind the large jewelry display area. His gaze lingered on Justine. "I summoned you here from San Francisco. Did you know that? I remember the exact day, time and month it hit me: July 28, 5:06 in the afternoon. I knew you were coming, Justine."

His words got her attention. "July 28? You're kidding. Darrius, that was the exact day and hour my editor called me into his office. He had taken Wilfred Sands off the New Mexico story and was assigning it to me. He just suddenly took him off it, saying I had more insight and ability to capture the essence of the West. I was just glad for the opportunity."

"I did that. I know you probably think I'm nuts, but something roused me at that particular time, 5:06. I had fallen asleep at my computer desk for a brief afternoon nap. I had been tired, but I snapped awake and could feel you coming. I didn't tell you this before, didn't know how you would take it. I couldn't make out what you looked like—how tall, short, hair color, but I knew your spirit. It called to me." He sipped his tea, taking in the robust aroma as though it gave him courage to tell his tale of vibes, tribes and vision quests. "It must have been some kind of quest because days before, I went to the mountains behind my house for my prayers and something was so strong in my heart, but I couldn't capture it. Days later, I had the vision of your spirit. Please don't think I'm crazy. I'm not."

"I know you're not, Darrius, but tell me, you don't have Elvis sightings, do you? I mean, you don't see Elvis working at Burger Kings throughout Santa Fe, right?"

"I'm serious!"

She set her mug down and moved next to him, feeling the pressure of his leg against hers. "I'm sorry, and I know you're serious. This is just so much for me."

He brought her hand to his lips, kissed her delicate fingers and then looked deeply into her eyes. "I know exactly when you arrived in New Mexico. Your plane arrived in Albuquerque at 9:38 A.M. You stayed two days at the mission school and then departed. You had to wait hours for the bus but it never showed and you had to wait for the train. You stepped foot on Gallup ground at 3:12 Monday afternoon. You rented your car and then came here."

"I . . . did look at my watch. I remember it being almost 3:15, figuring I had lost time waiting for that damn bus."

He kissed her hand again, pulling her even closer to him. "It's karma, wisdom, callings."

Justine heard voices from the CD player—singers calling in a native chant. Everything was so mystic, strong, powerful—romantic. His hair brushed against her shoulders, tickling the skin above the neckline of her dress. With his hand still covering hers, she got on her knees, lifted the dress and sat between his outstretched legs.

He allowed her entrance, allowed her the opportunity to be that close to him. A gutsy move, and he loved that she did it. It meant she felt the closeness he felt—the same calling, perhaps. Turning and leaning back, her head rested against his chest as she continued to sip the tea. She smelled enticing, irresistible; hints of peach and avocado scent were in her hair, her skin, and the overwhelming desire to caress her tender skin haunted him. He restrained himself, but his hand still covered hers.

As for Justine, she had found her new safe place, her new haven, and he felt good. His hard stomach muscles teased her back, causing her to remember how they felt when her fingers had trickled across them in the dark-room. It was glorious, and she wanted more. She sipped her tea and then remembered something Derrick had mentioned. "Do you mind if I ask you a personal question?"

"Not at all."

"Why don't you dance anymore, Darrius?"

"Where did that come from?"

"Your brother said you don't dance anymore."

He rested his head against the wall again. Just thinking about how he used to dance made him uncom-fortable. Words seemed to stick in his throat as he tried to explain. "Derrick didn't tell you anything about it?"

"No. I guess he figured it was up to you to tell me. Does he even know?"

"Yes, he knows the entire story, and a sordid one it is."

Her hand smoothed the soft denim on his thigh. "You don't have to tell me, you know."

A soft brush of a kiss atop her head made him settle in. "I still dance sometimes, but not at the ceremonial anymore. Sometimes I'll dance at the lodges, sometimes for educational purposes at schools, but not often."

"I'm sure the kids get a kick out of it."

"Sure, but it's mostly for educational purposes—to carry on the oral tradition of our heritage. That's the main reason I don't do it anywhere else." He finished his tea and crossed his hands over her stomach. "There are a lot of visitors at the ceremonial each August. Some know the nature and tradition of the dances, but most don't. They come here for the shows, the crafts, the excitement, but they don't see the underlying meaning behind it. They just see tribes getting together to celebrate. And that's okay; I love to see tons of people trying their best to understand the plight and lives of a trampled people."

"I guess that would include me and my cameras."

"Yes and no. You take pictures to share with the world, bringing them into ours, and I'm sure your photos will be very enlightening."

"They will be, and I'm getting so much knowledge from you." Her face lifted to his. "I just want to do my best here, tell a great photographic story, do Native Americans justice."

"It's okay to say Indians, if you like."

"I'd rather just say Darrius."

A brush of a kiss landed on her cheek, so close to her lips that she could almost taste him.

His slight breath caressed her skin. "I hope I answered your question about the dancing. When I dance, I want people to know what it is for, to understand it. Sometimes it's not possible with large crowds. You understand?"

She saw the exact sharpness of his features not exposed by candlelight. "I understand because I feel the same way. I don't want people expecting me to cook great soul food because of the black in me. Hell, I can't even cook."

"You can cook, all right. Your kisses are steaming hot and delicious."

"Is that so?"

"Trust me."

And that she did. Leaning into him again, she still felt the after-burn of their kiss the other day. His warm chest gently heaved against her, his arms held her tighter, the wildness of his stiff erection probed her lower back. It felt like raw unadulterated sin, wicked, thick, hungry, savage and ready to make her savage as well. She shifted against him, wanting to feel more heat, passion, feel the length and mass of his erection move across her back.

Justine listened intently as he released a deep breath and spoke words only Darrius Red Sky could speak to her. "Stay right there. Ah, yes, that's a good spot."

He reclined deeper against the wall and slightly bent his knees. At that position, she could really feel him, feel his girth, his power, and her hands trembled under his. "Are you okay, Justine?"

Her dreamy voice floated into the air. "Never better. This is the perfect night."

"And the perfect company. Do you mind being this close to me?"

"Mind? No. Maybe I'm supposed to be here with you, this night, under these stars."

"Did the trees tell you this?" he asked, teasing her.

She shifted, moving deeper against him. "No, you told me. You've been calling me all day."

"Since San Francisco, remember?"

"How can I not? Each time I looked at the peaks of Red Rock yesterday I thought about you, Darrius."

"You didn't attempt to follow those peaks, did you? You don't have the right vehicle for that."

"I gazed up the path near the entrance, gazed long; wanting to know what was on the other side, what mysteries could be there."

"Plenty. On the other side of Red Rock are other cities like Zuni, Acoma and one of the Old Laguna Pueblo, as well as some of the reservations. It's getting past certain parts of the rock that's harmful."

"Can you take me there before I leave?"

"It *is* considered sacred by some people, mainly the Navajo. Many of our people celebrated, worshipped, were born and even died in those hills. It's an old place, dating back to the Mesozoic era, and it's not safe. The red rocks frame the park now." He kissed her hand, making her look him in the face. "Promise me you won't go up there. I wouldn't be able to handle it if you were hurt. Do you promise?"

She met his gaze. "I promise. I still wish I could go, though. I'm sure the sights and legends are remarkable."

"They are. I've been up there a few times, and that's why I know it's not the place for beautiful young photojournalists, no matter the breathtaking scenery."

"Breathtaking, is it?"

"But not as much as the sight sitting before me. Did you mind my kiss moments ago?"

"Mind it! I craved it, Darrius." Her face tilted to his again, spying a miniature medicine wheel in the background. Indeed, what they had *was* good medicine, and she replied, "I still crave it."

"Then let me ease your mind, take you out of discomfort."

The hem of her sundress fell below her knees, but was now rising. Her silken skin graced his palms and there was no stopping him from there on. As the fabric inched further up, dipping into the valley of silken delight, his cheek met hers and slowly brushed against it. "Are you comfortable with this, Justine?"

"I've been comfortable with you since day one. I just got a little uncomfortable in the darkroom, not knowing what you would think of me letting a virtual stranger kiss me."

"I can never have a bad thought about you. Just remember that."

Her hand covered his. "Don't stop. I like how you feel against me. I did the other day as well, but didn't know how to tell you."

"Tell me now." His lips grazed her jaw, and then her neck, tasting baby-soft skin, skin he knew felt like destiny . . . his destiny. "Tell me what you want, how you want it and for how long."

"You won't have that kind of time on your hands, Darrius, because I think I could live with you in this spot for an eternity."

"That long? So my vision was right?"

She pressed her back against his chest, making him feel just how much she wanted him. At the same time, she surely felt how much he wanted her. The thickness of his erection made her eyes dilate, wondered how he would feel inside her, how he would use what he had to make her dissolve into a mass of emotions. He was already doing that as both his hands and hers inched closer to her center. She was wet for him, was probably soaking from the minute she arrived almost an hour ago. It was unbelievable how much she wanted this man, and so soon. She had only met him two days ago, but if it's right, there are no time constraints.

Her hand still edged his as strong yet soft fingers dallied at the band of her bikini panties, the lace ones that barely hovered on her hips. The seat was definitely wet, and his fingers had finally found the moistness. His tender kisses moved to her collarbone, and with one hand he tugged her bra off. "You're sweet, like honey, and I can't stop tasting you."

"Then don't. I'm here, Darrius; all night if you wish."

"I *do* wish." He turned her face to his again and nibbled her bottom lip. His tongue stroked her lip line, circling, feathering gentle kisses before taking her mouth whole. It was a deep, tender kiss with tongues battling for ownership—and she caved.

Halfway facing him, she felt his hair blanketing her in soft dark whispers. Her body contracted just from the feel of his hair teasing her breasts, fingers, neck. As his kiss deepened, so did his assault on the rest of her. Where he had played with the rim of her panties was now an opening, gaping, exposing her sex as he cupped it. She gladly opened for him, letting him play his games of moving in and out, repeating the rhythm until she could feel her body tightening around him. Little moans escaped her as her inner muscles twined around his wet fingers. Cries of heated passion were muffled by his kiss, taking her in, pressing against her, massaging and opening her sex as he slid deeper and deeper inside. The thrusts barely lifted her from his lap, and he calmed her by holding her in place—movement against non-movement, making for deeper releases.

His hand reached between them, unleashing his belt buckle and zipper. A feverish erection sprawled out, and he lifted the back of her dress so it could pulsate against her. Yes, that was what he needed. To feel her sultriness against his own seething flesh! God, he wanted her. He would do what she said and only when she said it. He hoped it would be soon.

8

IN THE HEAT OF THE NIGHT

Justine felt Darrius's hulking rage against her back-side. It was glorious, wet, dark, hungry—everything she needed. She slid up and down against him, feeling his erection expand, the moisture of his droplets of eager cum, and the rigid, juicy tip massaging her moist skin. Her mind went crazy from want, and the very idea of his semen anywhere on her made her wild. She cupped the underside of her breasts—squeezing them together, matching each tight nipple, point to point. When her eyes were open, she could see the medicine wheel spin-ning, spinning potent vibes throughout the room, drawing her to the point where she had to face him, give him what they both needed. With that realization, she shifted in his lap. Their eyes locked, and in heated fury, Justine kissed him in openmouthed tugs, feeling his tongue as it swirled around hers. The movement of his fingers as they danced up her stomach and to her breasts, toying with and tugging at the hardened nipples as they kissed, drove her wild.

One touch of his lips against hers made her see dis-tant lands and times; he took her away, and to a place she never wanted to leave—total male inhabitation. Every part of her was awake now, from her hair follicles to the bottoms of her feet, and the deeper she kissed Darrius, the more her passion heightened. Her sex quivered, thrusting against him, wanting, needing him to explore it the way he would a hidden cave. She wanted him to hunt her, set a trail, dig in and claim his space within her body. God, how she ached for him, and her body jutting against his reinforced her need. She was insane now, and nothing could cure her but him pumping inch upon inch into her.

Needing it now, Justine relinquished her kiss, slowly pulling back and leaving him lunging for more. Without another word and without casting her gaze anywhere else but on him, she stood and slipped from the wet panties. Seeing his exposed length literally vibrating against his damp shirt made her drop to her knees again. Everything seemed like a dream, and that at any moment she would awaken in her room at the hotel. However, once her hands made contact with his penis, she, indeed, knew it *was* a dream—a waking dream that felt so good in her hands. Finally. His rich brown hue, the stiffness and heat of an incredible erection, consumed her. She had to have it, and without further delay, she had it.

His scent lingered long and hard against her palate. She let the tip of his sex play at her lips before tenderly embracing him with her mouth. His hands played in her hair, and he then slid the dress up her back; it made her take in more of him. He removed her dress, and within moments, swift, talented fingers dipped in and out of a juiced sex. He was now almost completely inside her mouth. If she had ever wondered what the best taste in life was, he had to be it. She was insatiable, taking in as much length as she could handle. Her soft tongue seduced the turgid veins of his phallus. Her gentle hand movements encircled his scrotum, letting the heft of his sac bounce in her palms. He was hot there as well, and her lips slowly moved from his phallus to the turgid sac, nipping at them, licking and lavishing. Her excitement heightened just from feeling his reaction to her. He bucked several times, but pushed deeper into her, letting her get all she craved and desired. The stroke of her lips soothed hot desire that was on the brink of explosion, yet he relaxed, letting her will him into submission. That was what Darrius Red Sky gave her, unconditional power over him, and she took it to the max.

Gently, he cupped her chin in his hands and made her withdraw from him. Their eyes locked briefly, and Darrius moved strands of dark-brown hair from her beautiful, flushed face. "Are you sure you want this of me?"

She could still taste him on her tongue and was weary from the lack of him filling her in any crevice. "I—I can't stay away from you, Darrius. Why? What is it about you that makes me crazy when I'm not around you? Hell, I'm nuts even around you."

"That's what I like, girl. You're supposed to be here, and I can't explain how or why." He delivered a quick kiss on her lips. "There's no going back now, Justine. We're here, together, and getting ready to do what must be done. There's no way around it."

"I'm too hot to go back. You have what I need, and in more than the physical sense. You feed my soul, and I think I'll die without you near me."

"I'll always be near. Have no worry."

She stood before him totally nude; her body was so toned, so succulent, so . . . in need of delivering to him that she trembled in his arms. He caressed the sides of her full breasts, traced a path to each taut nipple, and then down her belly. He played in the patch of soft hair above her sex while sucking lavishly on each hardened bud, taking one completely into his mouth, teasing it with rugged licks and suckling motions. While having his feast with one, the other nipple received its share of sensual caresses. He soon switched, giving the other as much delight as possible.

Justine's back arched, responding to the deep assault his tongue delivered to her torso. Now completely open to him, she wanted him open to her. "Completely naked, Darrius. You asked me what I wanted. Give me what I want."

He stood, taking her hand in his, smoothing it across his jutting phallus. "Take my clothes off; let me bury myself in what destiny has given me."

"No, you strip for me. Let me watch you unveil the rest of your secrets."

His unveiling started, and with each button undone, hints of deeply rich skin graced her. He loosened the cuffs and let his shirt slide to the floor. Air caught in her throat as she gasped at his marvelously chiseled chest, now totally exposed. Tight abs, strong, thick pecs and a trail of dark hair dipping into his underwear made her sex clench, wanting him so totally inside her she could barely stand it.

Her hand reached to him, wanting to help remove his jeans and underwear, but he stopped her. "This is my treat to you. Are you enjoying it, my mistress?"

Her throat was dry and the only word she could manage was, "Darrius."

"It's coming, baby. Watch me." And with seduction penetrating his mind and skin surface, he soothed his hand up and down his already exposed and engorged phallus. The purplish tip oozed for her while his eyes returned to hers. "Is this what you need?"

"Not just that. I want all of you. I want you on top of me, letting your hair and muscles taunt me. I want to revel in your feel, taste you, take you places you've never been before."

"And with you, that's everywhere." He released his smooth hold on the erection, let it wave in the air, stiff and hard—steamy and drizzling for her warmth. He tightened his abdomen for effect and slowly pushed his jeans down his hips. They landed with a thud at his bare feet, and he kicked them aside. To heighten the show, he massaged his scrotum, loving the look of dire need in her eyes. The look was sincere, and she was not the one-nighter type. Justine was there for the distance, and he wanted to give her the complete tour.

After teasing a warm, tight scrotum into a convulsive state, the Hanes dropped to his feet as well, exposing everything to her, in the night, in the dark, with the only light coming from a flickering candle—and their hearts. He kicked the underwear aside. Now nothing graced him but tight skin, skin so ready and able to fulfill, agitate and dominate her, if that's how she wanted it.

That *was* exactly what she wanted as she scanned the length of his perfect body. Shadows from the candle cast against his frame illuminated his hip-length hair and highlighted his phallus. Her legs automatically parted with anticipation. She was sticky sweet for the first time in her life from want of a man—this man! Again, she reached to him. "I can't believe how much I want you, Darrius. Slide inside and make me see things not of this world. Let me hear your flesh pounding against mine as you ride me into the wind."

"To the stars, Justine. I want a long, wild ride; slipping into a body that closes around me, traps me, pulls at me until I give . . . and I give hard."

"Then give hard, all night." She cupped her breasts as a type of offering to him, pinching heated buds that were ready to pop. "Take them into your mouth again and milk me. Milk me in every way imaginable, Darrius."

There were no words to match hers; none he would have said anyway. His was too intense to do anything but give what they both needed since the day their eyes locked. So, he surrendered, giving into the heat and pliability of her body.

He watched as Justine's hand wrapped around his shaft, jerking it in sultry thrusts, teasing him, running her tongue across it. But that wasn't enough for either of them, and Darrius knew it. The only way to be with

Justine was flat on his back since she was so determined to give him a sweet, aromatic taste.

Justine was now straddling him as he lay back. The shine of his hair splayed across the cream-colored rug, making the strands look like black silk. Everything tightened on her again, and nothing would suffice but having him in her every crevice.

Their lips met again, tasting, licking, nibbling, as his fingers played within her. She soaked him on contact, and she was his toy. Wet, sex-drenched skin slid across, upon, under for what seemed to be hours of play, but when Justine was ready for the ultimate in penetration, she regained her position on top. And he let her. Gladly. Together, they clad him with protection he had removed from his wallet only moments before.

Her hands moved over his face, loving the feel of his perfect features, tracing his large eyes, full lips, cleft chin, his neck. Desire moved her further south—soothing the pads of her fingers across his nipples and then feasting on them, making her tongue flick in circular motions around them. His back arched to the pleasure, landing her almost in midair. From there, her tongue traced a path to his navel, sucking, kissing, and lavishing hard on the sensitive spot. His erection stretched further to her, beckoning her, and she answered. Willingly.

Darrius felt words rush through his throat. It was time; his body spoke of the urgency of the matter. He stroked her bare bottom, feeling the curvature of her toned body against the hardness of his. "Now, Justine. Come closer to me; kiss me once more before we take flight."

She moved lengthwise across his body and tasted his hungry lips once more. At that angle, she could feel his tip poking at her folds, pressing his need for entrance. He was throbbing, pulsating . . . on the edge of release. He parted her thighs and slowly broke the kiss.

Now hovering just above his shaft, she lowered, sitting deeper upon inches of what she desired of him. Each thrust from both pelvic bones meshing together made her eyes roll in complete satisfaction. She knew he would fill her the way nothing ever had before. He was the only man who *could* take her beyond her own body and mind. And she lost control. He was so big, so large as he tried fitting completely in, and her body accommodated him by relaxing, opening wide, giving in to complete domination. Yes, he dominated, and with each thrust, she heard words, sounds. Was she talking, urging him on? That she didn't know, didn't quite understand, didn't quite care. He was fulfilling her needs, and that counted for more than breath itself.

Under her, he became a bucking bronco. The very contact of her flesh against his rigid, unrelenting member blocked any thought of all things but her. Sliding deep fulfilled a lifelong need, maybe because he was meant to be there with her—and he went beyond her depths. His body jerked, bucked, crammed devilishly inside her as he gained his momentum. The words and voices she heard were indeed his calls, primal calls, earth shattering.

Their tempos matched as they squirmed and tangled around one another. She reached behind and tickled his tight scrotum, massaging it as he pumped faster, deeper.

Her other hand wiped away tears of joy that trickled down her cheeks and onto his chest.

He wiped her face as well, knowing they were indeed the seeds of pure joy, pure sex. "Is this good? Am I taking you where you want to be?"

"Where I need to be, Darrius. Take it. Go deeper, wilder."

Their bodies meshed and their gyrations moved them from the carpeting and onto the middle of the floor. With him now behind her, his shaft grew larger, impaling her with deep, thick thrusts. Her body vibrated and hummed with each lavish bump and grind. He could feel her juices drizzling him, absorbing him like a wet sponge. His hips rocked her harder, making her cry out his name. But there was no mercy for Justine. She had what he needed, and he meant to get it all.

He craved release, but not until his Justine quivered around him. That's what he wanted, to be seized by her warmth. He went to a place where no one could hear his calls other than the woman orchestrating them. He gently eased her to her to the carpeting, kissing her once again. They hit the magic moment together and their voices echoed within the stillness of the closed, candlelit store. Their cries drowned out the distant music of the CD player.

In the semidarkness of the room, Justine could see his shadow stretching and reaching to the sky as he released. She could see his hair resting across his shoulders, his chest heaving, his head rearing back slowly. To her, he had a deliciousness that was hard to describe, impossible to pinpoint. Darrius needed to be bottled and sold; any woman would pay a premium for a man with his skill, his gift, his agility . . . his heart.

Moments later, he slumped to the floor, totally exhausted. She followed him, nestling in the curve of his body, staying quiet. His deep breathing lulled her, a mix of her hair and his served as a blanket that housed her.

Darrius's warm body against hers made her smile. "I can't believe how incredible tonight was. Never thought in a million years I'd be doing this with you, Darrius. I prayed, hoped, but never really thought I would have the chance."

"You knew you had a very definite chance with me, so don't deny it."

She looked at him halfway. "What?"

"It was as much on your mind as it was on mine. Taking pictures of me in here was a clever cover, a workable one. But, Justine, we both knew what we wanted the moment we laid eyes on each other. I told you this was karma, destiny. Admit it. I have."

"If I admit it, you won't think of me as being forward?"

"You belong to me, Justine. How can I think that? Don't you want to belong to me?"

"My mind is not mine to think with anymore. Does that answer you?"

The CD had started replaying, and distant chants again filled the air as he tried regaining his composure. "I got my answer, Justine, and I'm still hungering for you." His fingers entered her sex again, squeezing a clit that he had awakened, brought to life again; now it only hummed for him. Her slippery folds inspired him, wanting to taste it again.

Justine came again, and did a few more times that night before nestling against his smooth body. They rested on the bearskin rug, hugging, holding, kissing and taking in the scent of the lit incense.

Darrius switched the CD player off and nestled against the soft, heated body of his lover. Nothing had been more powerful in his life than the two of them together, and he smiled, knowing that he had found his niche in life. The gentle touch of his finger across the bend of her arm felt like heaven. She hadn't stirred, and he knew she'd fallen asleep in the comfort of his arms.

9

MORNING GLORY

Sunshine peeked through the closed window blinds, and Justine awakened with a smile. Darrius was still snoozing next to her, but instead of shaking him awake, she tried something else. Her first instinct was to re-ignite a sleeping giant with a great kiss. But that would be *too* typical. She found the small kitchen and began to brew a pot of herbal tea—one of his, the Galloping Stallion's brew, since that's just what he had been to her all night long.

Before it began to whistle, she removed the kettle from the stove, poured two steaming cupfuls and carried them and tea biscuits on a tray back to him. To her surprise, he was awake and awaiting her. He took the tray, allowing her to sit, and then handed her a mug. "Your brew woke me up." He sipped it. "Yes, the Stallion's Brew. It's sweet, like you." Watching her sip it, he smiled. "I see you like it. It lit your lips like—"

"Like you did last night?"

"Exactly. One thing, though. I didn't serve Teepee Tales tea last night. I fooled you."

"Yeah? What was it?"

"Indian Love Tea. Did you like it?"

"Couldn't you tell?" She caressed his cheek. "But it wasn't the tea that made me make love to you."

"What, then?"

"The stars, the moon—karma. It was . . . meant to be."

"I agree. Lean over here." He gave her a tiny tongue bath, one just big enough to hold her until he could do more.

A slow withdrawal from her lips was the best he could do without starting a sensual fire again. There were things that had to be done that day, and though he would have loved making love to her again, he couldn't. They sat in silence, holding hands and thinking back on what they had shared—midnight heat and morning glory.

Justine's body still tingled from him, still shivered from the mere thought of making love to him. She brought his hand to her lips, kissing it. "Was it really good for you last night?"

"I'd never done it like that before. I've never had that type of calling." His expression turned solemn. "What's most important is whether you are comfortable with things. We can never go back to being casual acquaintances. I can no longer be just the man who gave you a lovely bracelet. I only want what's good for you."

"What's good for me?"

"Yes. It's important to me."

"I wouldn't have visited you last night if you weren't important to me, Darrius."

A slow smile crept across his face. "Then you admit to coming here for more than just pictures, music and tea?"

"What can I say?" She took a few more sips of her tea. "It's your fault, anyway, for calling me here from my safe office in San Francisco."

"You willingly came."

"Touché, Mr. Red Sky." She smoothed his chest, feathering the small trail of hair down the middle of his stomach. "What's in store for us today?"

"I have to work. I won't have sales help today, and I open at eight-thirty."

"I have to go back to Red Rock for more photo shoots." She looked at the Kokopelli wall clock. "That gives us almost three hours."

His fingers traced her sensitive areola, making the nipple pucker against his finger. "Three hours to clean up, get you some clothes and eat." He took her hand. "Let's get today's tasks completed. And tonight, if you're not busy, maybe we can go back to Red Rock. I can give you more information on the Koshari, show you some caves—lower ones. Would you like that?"

"Is there enough room in those caves to make love? That would really be a good story, but only for us."

Darrius threaded his fingers through her tangled hair. "You live for danger."

For the first time in her life, Justine was glad to admit to falling for him, even if she had only met him a few days ago.

He pulled up to the Best Western and parked at the entrance. "Grab what you need. You can shower at my house while I make you breakfast."

"I'd like that. Maybe you can shower with me."

"Don't tempt me."

"I like tempting you. It's rewarding—know what I mean?"

"If you don't get outta here—"

"All right, give me a few minutes. Wanna come in and wait?"

"Too tempting. I'll stay out here."

The few minutes he had to wait, he tried everything to take his mind off her. Every song on the radio was some kind of love song; her scent lingered in his truck. There was no getting away from Justine; even if he cut off his own head, his body would still crave her. What to do? What to do?

Thoughts of her kept him quiet, still, even on the way to his house. She would occasionally ask why he was so quiet; he would only smile and run his hand over her thigh. Instead of going back to the store, he drove home where she could shower and then do some work on his laptop if she wanted to. He would make them a nice breakfast, getting their day started the right way.

As he prepared her breakfast, he knew she was in his shower splashing around nude, wet, warm, and he wanted to be with her, sharing her space.

Justine stepped into the spacious shower decorated in stucco desert tiles with primitive Native American historical figures embedded in the stone. This certainly made her dinky little bathroom in her loft look like a crack in the wall. Here, there was room to play, and she did. The large showerhead propelled jets of steamy warm water against her flesh, and naturally, it made her think of him. This time, imagining her body pressing against his wasn't what she wanted to do. It would take up way too much time, and there was so much still to do. She lathered up using a bar of glycerin petroglyph-styled soap. It smelled like spices and made her skin shimmer and feel soft.

While getting into the feel of the soap, the doors opened and Darrius stood there, naked. His voice cracked. "I need a shower, too. Mind if I share with you?" Without waiting for an answer, he slipped in and nestled behind her. His lips lowered to her ear. "I promise, just a shower. I'll bathe you and you bathe me. Deal?"

She handed him the soap without saying a word. His sudsy fingers traveled her neck and breasts, circling them, rubbing hard up and down on the nipple as he soaped them. He cupped her breasts in his hands, feeling the heft and slippery velvet of them while he nuzzled against her neck. From there, he moved down her belly and circled her navel, around her hips, to her buttocks, kneading each smooth cheek as he pressed against her. He parted her thighs, letting streaks of soap and water trail between them.

With a quick nibble on her earlobe, he moved them both into the stream of the jets, removed the detachable head and sprinkled her body from top to bottom. The jets lingered long and lavishly on her heated sex, playing on it, massaging with a slow, deliberate rhythm.

With quivering lips, she managed only one sentence. "I . . . thought this was just a shower?"

"It'll never be *just a shower* while with me. You should know that, since I can't keep my hands off you." He patted her behind. "All clean now, darling. It's my turn."

With the soap now in her hands, she lathered his strong shoulders, moving down his muscled arms and back up to his chest. The lathery bar traced his pecs, paying detailed attention to his hardened abs before slowly trickling down his stomach and sides. All along, their eyes matched, their stares lingered, lips dying to kiss, yet refrained. His erection pressed against her, wanting attention as well. No matter how long she saved the best for last, it was still there, and waiting for her soft, soapy clutch. Reluctance ended, and her hand slipped around his shaft, soaping it up and down. His back slightly arched from the pleasure of it.

Justine saw the magic working because, though his eyes were mostly open, her gentle touch made them close. Her hands wrapped around him, circling his tight behind, and then whispered against his chest, "All clean now." The cloth dropped to the bottom of the shower. Together they stood, staring lovingly at one another, wanting to do more than shower. In the end, however, they knew refraining would give them so much more— the coming night.

Dressed now in a bright yellow summer dress, she wore her hair in a high ponytail, and had a single strand necklace of turquoise around her neck. She was ready to get busy with her day at Red Rock.

Darrius walked in holding his laptop. "You can download the pictures on mine if you like."

Justine loved how he looked dressed in all native attire from the fringes on his sleeves to the feather in his hair. The clothing brought out his features. His dark hair glistened against the orange-red of his tunic. "You look great. I like the tunic, and the colors blend in well with your complexion." She then looked at the laptop he was carrying. "I remembered to bring mine along, but thanks. Is there anywhere quiet where I can download them for a little while?"

"Sure. Go to my den, and while you're in there I'll make us a light breakfast. You shouldn't have anything heavy today since it's going to be in the mid-nineties."

"That hot?"

"It's blazing around here in the summer."

"Yeah, also in Arizona. I like the heat, though."

He walked over and kissed her cheek. "You sure bring enough of it. But, yes, go to the den, and when breakfast is ready, I'll come for you and then whisk you off to Red Rock."

When he came back in forty minutes for breakfast, he casually looked at what she was scanning. There were pictures of buffalo dancers, the day parade dancers and the crafters from the craft show. He dryly asked, "You ready to eat?"

The lack of life in his voice got her attention and she turned, facing him. "Are you okay? You seem a little, well, drained of energy all of a sudden."

"It's nothing."

She looked down at the photos on the screen, realizing what he was looking at. "Do you miss dancing?"

"It's not important. Skip it."

"It is important to you, and that's why you miss it. I can see it in your eyes. You should dance again, if for no more than personal satisfaction."

"I dance for educational purposes when I feel like it, Justine, and that's it."

"But, you—"

"Can we not talk about this? It's a dead subject with me." To avoid any more questions, he left her alone and went back to the dining room.

Alone, but not wanting to be, she returned to her photographs, letting Darrius work out whatever he needed to. She'd apologize for pushing a touchy subject. She looked closer at two of the photos on the screen, not remembering taking either of them, especially the one featuring the outline of two teepees in the foreground. The other was of what looked to be small caves carved within the walls of Red Rock State Park itself. Her eyes squinted. A figure seemed to be huddled against a wall within one of the caves. *What is this?* She looked more closely but still couldn't make out what was going on inside the small cave. She figured she would see it later that day and get a better idea of what it was, photograph it better.

The other photo gained her attention. It was of the road that led to the dangerous side of the park, and for some reason it intrigued her. Justine wanted to see the apparent beauty of the place for her own personal reasons—it was the photographer inside of her, as well as her natural curiosity. Taking pictures of anything not related to the powwow was not part of her assignment, but she didn't care. She wanted to see it, see the majestic plains and never-ending landscapes, yet it was dangerous. Going up the road would definitely be a breach of Darrius's trust. He told her not to venture up the hill, and she wouldn't because she trusted his word. She quickly finished the pictures and went to join Darrius.

He stood in the middle of the dining room pouring juice into two glasses. Without calling to him, she walked over, took his hand and looked into his eyes. "I'm bad at keeping my mouth shut. Can you forgive me?"

"Nothing to forgive."

"Sure there is. You shouldn't have to explain to me about not wanting to dance anymore. I've heard your reasons, but you just looked so sad when you saw the pictures of the dancers."

"It involves more than my beliefs about dancing before crowds who don't know the story. That's all I can say about it right now, Justine. I really hope you understand."

She reached up and kissed his lips. His tense features then relaxed. "The only thing you have to tell me is whether or not I'm good for you. You sure are good for me."

"I think you can see that on my face—and on my body." He guided her hand across his beating heart. "You're always good for me." A devilish smile shadowed his face. "Can I be good to you again?"

"Oh, no, you don't; not until tonight. I have work, Darrius, and so do you." She tapped his butt. "Let's eat and then get a move on."

"Do I have time to check my horses?"

"Sure. I'd like to see the one you rode at the rodeo anyway. He was lovely."

"I have more than one. I want you to see my corral." They ate, talked of their lovemaking the night before and of the photographs she scanned. However, she failed to mention the one featuring the cave, and definitely did not bring up the one of the road leading to the other side of Red Rock. He would not like the picture and would assume she had her mind set on photographing more than just the powwow events. He would have been correct; her mind was on the plains and lands on the other side, but she was determined not to go against his word. At least, that's what she hoped she would do.

After breakfast, he took her hand, and led her through the back door and out into a large background. The mountains in back of his home simply amazed her. They looked as though they could part the sky with their gigantic peaks; with the sky so brilliant blue for their backdrop, the sight was breathtaking. "I wish I lived here. I could look at those mountains all day long."

"Could you?"

"In a heartbeat. My loft at home has a beautiful picturesque scene of the Pacific Ocean. Other window views are burdened with skyscrapers. I like the open space; so natural, crisp and clean. It's good living out here. No smog, like San Francisco sometimes has."

Darrius wrapped her arms around his hips. "It's not all roses out here, but I like it."

They came upon a large stable, and Darrius walked her over to three stalls with a horse in each one. The horses whinnied, sensing his presence. They loved him, and she could tell by their reaction that they didn't mind that a stranger was with him. A silver horse looked like the one at the rodeo, but it had no painted circles. But then, what might have been on him would have been washed off.

Justine stood aside as he poured grain into each of their troughs, stroked their manes and cooed at them, telling them how good they were. And then he turned to her.

"I have someone I'd like to introduce you to."

"Are you sure? I am a stranger to them."

"I'm sure. They won't hurt you."

Justine treaded lightly, not wanting to agitate them. She went to one side and watched him stroke the silver stallion. He was beautiful, with streaks of light brown mixed within brilliant strands of silver. "What's his name?"

"Gecko."

"Gecko? Why did you name him after a lizard?"

"Because he's fast. You should know; you saw him the other day."

Her forehead creased. "What do you mean?"

"I know you saw him, Justine. He was the one that impressed you at the rodeo. Only then he had painted circles of life all over him."

"I know you saw me. I saw you looking at me when the bull charged."

"I would have been there if you'd needed help. So would all the workers and ground keepers. Every reporter or photographer worth their grit goes to the rodeo. Red Rock has the most spectacular shows of any rodeo. So, am I right about you seeing me there?"

She couldn't deny it, and remembering how well he had ridden the frisky stallion made her hot again. The way he jerked, maneuvered and made the horse gallop to a smooth stride was a sight she wouldn't soon forget. "True, the pictures of the rodeo will be a great added feature for *The San Francisco Examiner*, but it was the rider that got my juices flowing." She briefly looked into the stallion's eyes. "Can I touch him?"

"He'd love to have a beautiful woman stroke his mane—like you stroke mine. You want to get on top?"

That caught her off guard. "Oh, you mean on top of *Gecko*."

Darrius kissed her cheek. "You can get on top of me anytime you like, but yes, I did mean my main man here," he said, patting the horse's rear end.

"Will you get on with me?"

"No, I'm gonna let him have his way with you and give you a rugged ride around the stable."

"Darrius! You know a city girl has no experience with horses. There's probably not one horse near where I live—"

"I'm joking, darling." He slid his foot into the stirrup and swung himself on, and then reached for her hand. "Just let me pull you up. You can sit in front of me."

Good deal! She could get first-hand experience and feel Darrius's hard body pressing against hers at the same time. Yeah, that would definitely be a good ride.

With that idea in mind, she willingly let Darrius pull her onto the horse and plant her directly in front of him. Once secure, she settled back, letting him enclose her, maneuvering her hips closer to his. As the horse trotted, she closed her eyes and relaxed, letting the slow, sensual gallop press her against him.

The feel of Justine's soft hair falling against his face and her fragrant skin made the ride harder to take. She smelled like the daintiest of flowers. He slowed the horse, making it tread on rough terrain simply for the pleasure of having her fall against him. Justine's hips moved with his, making him harder, ready to burst, and he moaned against her neck. "Are you sure you need to get to Red Rock today?"

She opened her eyes, realizing she wasn't in heaven, but with a man who made it seem so much more attainable. "Yep! Got a deadline."

"Too bad, because I'm loving this ride. Aren't you?"

She placed his hands over her taut nipples, letting him massage them. "Does this answer you?"

The pads of his fingers rubbed the fleshy nub. "I think it does."

She moved his hand under her dress and into her panties. "What's it like to make love on a horse?"

"I don't know. Never had the opportunity."

"You could now."

"What about your deadline? Forgot about it so soon?"

"It's just hard leaving you."

"We might have a little time to play, but aren't you scared our movements may make him move faster?"

"Not anymore. My knight in shining armor will save me, right?"

"You got it."

He kissed her neck and moved his hands to the front of her dress. Her hand slid against his as he massaged. He loved how this woman felt, her softness. He whispered into her ear. "Is this what you mean?"

"I'd like a little more, but I'll definitely take this."

Her body hummed for him as he continued his caress. The slow trot of the horse added to the tingling. What he was doing was a deliciously erotic second choice, and she rode with it, relaxed against him. Her mouth trembled as she felt herself going to that place—the very place that centers on total satisfaction and nothing more. Anticipation crowded her, making her body and mind so tight that all she wanted was release . . .

He gave it, and gladly.

Little moans of helplessness invaded his hearing, and he smiled, knowing she was so ready to be taken there— if only there was time.

Justine had always been scared of horses; was never taught how to ride growing up in the streets of San Francisco. Her uneasiness with horses seemed as though it had never existed now because she felt natural, mellowing to the slow trot while her lover gave her a sensual massage. Nothing had ever been hotter than them making love in open daylight. It was raw exhibitionism, thirsty, insane, uninhibited. She turned and faced him as he slowed the stallion almost to a dead stop.

There were no words that could explain what he felt for her at the moment. "What on earth have you done to me? I can't think straight anymore, and when I do think, it's about you, your smile, your ambition for life and love—your body thirsting for mine and mine for yours." He brought her face to his, his eyes narrowed, peering into hers, breathless. "Where the hell did you come from?"

"A long way, Darrius, and I've found what I've unknowingly been looking for."

"Me?"

"Only you." A smile touched her lips. "The wind told me to find you. Wind moved my plane straight into Albuquerque's airport and on into Gallup. Here I am today, hardly expecting to have a sensual massage while riding a horse."

"With me around, anything's possible."

They kissed again, and then the realization of Red Rock, more photo shoots and opening a store loomed heavy.

For once, Justine's mind was not on Darrius. Instead, those mysterious pictures she couldn't remember taking preoccupied her. She was determined, at least, to see the caves behind the teepees. Also, the winding road leading to forbidden places held her mind captive.

Darrius tapped the hood of her car. "Take good pictures."

"You're just going to work in the store today?"

"I have to finish my inventory. Besides, it's tourist season. I might sell another bracelet or two."

"You didn't sell me mine, if you remember. I would like to give you something in return for giving me such a fabulous piece of jewelry."

"Yeah, like you haven't already."

"Darrius . . ."

"Okay, okay, since you're so determined to give me something, why not treat me to dinner, and then we can check out one of those little caves in your picture. I already know what they're all—"

"Wait a minute! You know about the pictures? How?"

"I just do. I also know about the picture of the road leading to the other side of Red Rock." His eyes were penetrating. "Don't go there, Justine. I'm very serious. There's power up there, and you're not equipped to handle it."

Simply by his tone of voice, she knew there had to be something to that road. Now it really scared her, yet intrigued her. Yet for his benefit, she conceded. "I promise I won't go up there. I'm scared to, anyway."

"Not scared enough. I know this about you." He released her hand and locked her door. "I'm serious."

There was worry in his eyes, something that she wouldn't have guessed could appear on such a handsome face. His somber expression made her nervous, so she tried to break the tension. She poked his belly. "How can I ignore the warnings of such a powerful man?"

"Stop kidding around. I just want you safe. There are more than legends up there."

"All right already! I said I wouldn't go!"

"Good, then how about eight tonight for dinner at Red Rock?"

"Cool with me."

"Meet me at the main arena near the entrance, and we'll explore the *safe* places."

As she reached for her camera bag on the front seat, he took her arm. "I know you can't explain how you got the pictures, but the one of the road is a warning. You took it for a purpose, and you may never be able to explain how you got it."

She still couldn't decipher the look in his eyes, but knew his words were dead on. "I'd better go before I miss the real reason I'm here."

"You're staring at the *real* reason, but remember, eight o'clock at the entrance."

"Got it." Words hung in the air, words she had no idea she would ever say to a man. "I really like you, Darrius, despite the fact that you won't let me roam free."

"You're right, I won't, and if it makes you feel any better—I like you, too. A whole lot!"

"It does."

She waved goodbye and drove away. She had been in such a rush to get away from Darrius to what was up that hill, despite his warnings and her own promises to him. Then again, in the past, she had never lived up to too many promises. What made her think she could suddenly start now?

10

TEMPTATION SINGS

The mountains of Red Rock seemed even higher even and more majestic to Justine than they had the first time she'd seen them. She figured that maybe the peaks looked more tempting *because* he had told her to stay away from them. Then again, she had always been one to look danger in the face and laugh at it. But before, there had been no sexually and emotionally stimulating man to warn her. Now there was, and her feelings were mixed. She trusted and respected Darrius too much to ignore his warning, but it was unsettling to not be able to do what she wanted. Ultimately, she knew not violating Darrius's trust was more important than shots of outstanding scenery. *Is it? Sure it is—just keep saying that to yourself.*

Never had she experienced a man who knew her thoughts and possible actions before she did. Yet he did. It would take some getting used to, considering the men in her past barely knew *she* was in the bed with them. All they had wanted was a hot, wet body that came with plenty of moans—fake or real. She had done both and was tired of the bullshit. It was high time to have a man in her life who actually knew her mind instead of what to do to make her come. Thinking of her past lovers made her aware of just how bereft of emotion her romantic life had been. Darrius had already proven that a man could be more than an erection. Finally. And that was the *only* reason she took the longer route to Red Rock and avoided the cliffs. However, temptation was hard to clear from the recesses of a wandering mind.

Fooling around with Darrius on that damn horse made her late for the youth Buffalo Dance, but being late was a small price to pay for pleasure: Her body still quivered from his touch, and she desperately wanted to return to him. The way her mind was going, she could have easily sat on a rock and daydreamed about him and not gotten any work done. Nothing doing. *The Examiner* would fire her, and all over a wickedly decadent remembrance.

Justine followed the sound of drums from the smaller arena where she was in time to see the boys in buffalo costumes performing. She had not seen many of the dances, but she did know they encompassed legends, creation stories, tales of the hunt and the thanksgiving rituals. She did not know precisely what this particular dance represented, but she did have some idea. Of course, the dance movements themselves would provide clues. And she was able to gather pieces of information from different tribesmen.

Given permission to photograph the dancers, she proceeded to take scores of photos of the boys doing their Buffalo routines—enough, actually, to do a separate spread on dance. In their buffalo-inspired getups and their faces painted black, red and white, the boys—no doubt masters-in-training—danced around the makeshift teepee conjuring up images of buffaloes on the prairie. Each dancer carried a rattle in one hand and a large rod in the other. The green and yellow boughs on their heads symbolized the time of year the buffalo would be expected to return. Each bough represented willows in full leaf.

The smell of fry bread and the rhythmic beating of drums drew her to another arena. She trekked over to a small fry bread stand and purchased a piece of the bread with a side of chili sauce. She then headed in the directions of the drums, tapping her hand against her thigh, already feeling the beat and rhythm in her soul. Inside the arena, Justine saw tribesmen dressed in colors of the elements, like browns and greens for the earth, white for the wind and red and yellow for fire. She took a brochure and then asked permission to photograph the ceremony. With permission denied, her only option was to settle back and be a spectator.

As the activities got underway, Justine scanned the brochure, reading that the mound of dirt in the middle of the arena was called the buffalo mound. A plate containing maple sugar was atop the mound. She had no idea what it signified, thus read on. An emissary seeking volunteers to participate in the ritual drew her attention. At first, she was reluctant to step up and participate, but then her other side—the side that was bold enough to do anything for a good story—stood up. She was in the Land of Enchantment—what better way to get up close and view the festivities than to actually participate? When the emissary arrived, she waved her hands frantically, and with a smile, the young man chose her and several others.

The next step involved selecting someone from the Buffalo Clan to lead the dance. The appointed dancer donned a buffalo head and other ornamentation. Justine and the others were directed to follow him to the plate of maple sugar on the mound. First he, and then each of the volunteers, lapped up small portions as a buffalo would. Each participant then got the chance to beat the drum. When it was Justine's turn, she was hesitant about licking the mound of sugar that had touched many other tongues. Not wanting to break tradition, however, she tasted the sweet mixture. She thought it was the sweetest of sugars imaginable, but really couldn't say if she was responding to the sugar itself, or if the festivities had gotten to her.

Then came her turn at the drum. Beating on the deerskin took her to a place in her mind that was new to her. The sound of her own taps on the hide took her mind to a serene, magical place—a place where calm was the norm, life was easy and the chanting voices of distant tribesmen enfolded her as she drifted into daydream mode: Before her stood a man, her husband—Red Sky. His arms folded across his bare chest, he smiled down on his wife, who had fit in so perfectly with his clan . . .

Someone nudged her and Justine quickly returned to reality—her reality. A vision. If so, it was her first. In a way, it scared her, making her wonder if perhaps she was being drawn to this life a little too much. That didn't explain Darrius's image. He was as clear as day, from his shining black hair to his only article of clothing, a breech-cloth. Yes, only a breechcloth! Justine had a sudden yearning to return to that vision, make it reality, be in the loving embrace of her husband and the old ones, living a simpler life . . . loving in a simpler way. She wouldn't have to travel to distant lands to find her lover as she had in reality. He would already be there. That was also her reality.

Justine checked the time, two hours before reality met her for dinner at eight. *Her lover would be there.* She handed over the portable drum and felt a thin layer of perspiration on her forehead. Indeed it had been some type of vision; so short, so sweet, but it had ended, and the rest of the ceremony awaited . . .

The focus then shifted to a plate of wild rice in a cen-tral spot. It was meant for the leader and was to be shared with whomever he asked. Justine hoped she wouldn't be asked since she was still a little unsteady from her vision. It was something she couldn't shake. She stayed for the rest of the ceremony—observing. She wanted to do but one thing: return to the vision; see Darrius . . . be one with him again.

With more than an hour left before meeting Darrius, Justine stood against a cottonwood tree, still trying to make heads or tales of her short vision. There were no conclusions, just truth—the truth that Darrius was embedded inside her. Her mind saw nothing now but the only man she had ever wanted to kiss her. He was so alive and vibrant, so vivid.

Distant drums beat again taking her from her reverie. She followed the path to the larger bandstand where another dance was underway. In the center were four men representing the points from where the buffalo would be expected to appear. Two other dancers were dressed as bears poised to attack. Justine, again, found herself in the middle of the action.

She became engaged in the ceremony as an onlooker. In the middle of it, an actor in the disguise of Famine scared her with his wild antics, chasing cast members around and getting so close to her that she could see his features, see his anger, even though he was supposedly an actor. His acting was that real, that believable, and it made her take flight. Before she could flee, Famine took her arm and tried his best to pull her into his lair of doom, but she escaped, running to the back of the sidelines. He was the only aspect of Native American mythology she truly feared. She decided to go back to her word and keep her distance at ceremonies from then on. All she wanted now was to see her lover and have a nice quiet dinner—alone with him.

With everything that had gone on at the ceremonies, she had to clear her head, to get ready for Darrius, so he wouldn't see the mixed emotions on her face. He would inquire, but what would she say to him? Would she tell him of her vision, or even the Famine character who scared her? Though the Famine character was not always a fearful being, this one was, and she didn't want Darrius knowing that a mere character like that had scared the bold and vivacious Justine-Roberts Paretti.

Earlier in the day, Justine remembered that she had left her 35mm camera on her bed at the Best Western. She had wanted to use the camera for shots of some of the dancers, and then she and Darrius could develop them together. It had been fun developing his few pictures together and besides, she still liked the old way of developing pictures. She looked at the time and saw that she still had over an hour before meeting Darrius. Though she had not really wanted to leave the park, she did so anyway since the hotel was only ten minutes away.

On her way back, she knew she had to pass the road that led to where she ultimately wanted to be—the other side of Red Rock, the dangerous place that promised both beauty and danger. It was where she would find spectacular shots. She looked at the 35mm camera on the car seat and decided that she and Darrius would not develop pictures together after all. She would take the photos, leave the film inside the camera and develop them at home. Those would not be pictures for *The Examiner* anyway. They would be hers. Taking a trip up there, even in a car not right for the journey, would present images she would never forget. But to get them, she would have to overcome two obstacles: betraying Darrius's word, and risking her life!

After re-entering Red Rock State Park, she veered due east up the hill towards danger and enchantment. If she was lucky, no telltale trace of what she was about to do would show on her face, nor, she hoped, would he pick up any vibes.

She looked through the windshield and saw hills so high and breathtaking, so rich in desert colors that she stopped the car to look at them for a moment. She started driving again, and the hills and valleys looked that much more outstanding against a pinkish-red setting sun. She would be alone up there—and in the dark if she chose to venture forward. Yet the small car kept moving, slanting backwards at an arc the higher she went.

Her heart practically beat through her chest, but the job of a photojournalist was sometimes a risky one, so she kept on. Her only regret, other than the car being on a complete upward axis, was betraying Darrius's trust. What the heck! She knew she would be back way before she was to meet him. She only wanted a peek at the other side, see what all the fuss was about, and then return as if nothing had happened. Sure, it was a flawless plan, but the higher she ventured, the more edgy her nerves became. *He warned me for a reason, so why am I doing this? Because of curiosity.* Her hands shook, her mouth was dry and panic was steadily creeping though her nervous system.

Now more than halfway up the winding road, all she could see, other than the rapidly approaching darkness and brick-hued behemoths, was blurred vision due to fright. And Justine knew when she had been beaten. The mountain had won. Now her problem was how to back down without losing control of the car. Behind her was the road that had assisted her in the climb, which was of no help now. Before her was the goliath that piqued her curiosity, but also forced piercing fear into her heart. Again, she asked herself: *Why the hell did I do this? Darrius was right. I could die up here.* Her mind was racing, her breath fogging the windshield, her hands almost too nervous to steer. *My God!*

She had no choice but to go in the direction of the mountains and pray that there was a side road that would lead her back down. With eyes almost shut, she pressed the accelerator and the car shimmied and rattled, and could hardly make it with its limited power. It definitely wasn't an off-road vehicle, and she knew that going up. But hey, the car started out great, crunching small rocks, digging into the rough terrain.

Tears dripped onto her dress, her lips trembled. There was no way out! The car was tilting and beginning to slide, yet she had to continue because there was nowhere else to go. She finally came to a small fork in the road and took a deep breath, seeing this as maybe a way to turn around. She inched into the middle of the fork and backed the car to the right, finally heading in the right direction back down. Suddenly there was life in her fingers, her head, her heart, and she could breathe. It was a steep climb back down, but she was no longer on the slope backwards. She cautiously drove down and came to a stop where the road merged with the entrance to the park.

After parking, she looked into the rearview mirror and saw a person she barely recognized. Her hair was a mess, her cheeks a darker red against brown skin, eyes swollen, the front of her dress wet from tears. *What a stupid-ass move!* The car clock read seven-thirty. She had exactly a half hour to look like the human Darrius remembered making love to on a horse. What would she do? What would she say to him? The day had been a mix of fun and fear, all at her own hands; and most certainly the uneasiness would show on her face. Darrius would see it right off if he hadn't already picked up her bad vibes.

11

THE HIDDEN TRUTH

By seven fifty, Justine was perfect: no traces of puffy eyes, no shaking hands, no wet dress. In the small restroom near the main arena, she checked herself in the mirror, fixed her hair, refreshed her makeup and was good to go. Her secret was safe and would never turn into a lie unless spoken and then denied. Darrius was good at reading her; hopefully, not that good.

Justine could see the stick-frame teepees in the distance near the main entrance as the setting sun cast its last glow upon the earth. Behind the teepees stood her photographed caves that looked to be carved in the center of a large mountain. For the life of her, she couldn't remember photographing caves. Then where did the pictures come from? She had to have taken them. As if in slow motion, she walked toward the caves, wanting to see the images on their walls; remembering seeing sketchy figures on the photos. Would they be petroglyphs? She hoped so. There were risks, though, either emotional or physical. Did she still want to go? Yes, but for her own knowledge.

Justine saw the rope and sign barring everyone from getting closer to the teepees and caves; nonetheless, she was about to slide under it when she heard her name.

"Justine!"

She spun around and saw Darrius holding his hand out to her and looking from her to the teepees. "Darrius?" It was exactly eight. "Right on time, aren't you?"

"Apparently. What are you doing over here? This is forbidden. Don't you see the ropes and signs?"

"I . . . yes, but—"

"Come on. I'll take you to another set of caves later, ones we can go inside."

She looked at the cave before her. "Why is this one so different?"

"Unsafe, mainly."

She accepted his answer. Yet, her questioning persisted. "But since you were supposed to meet me at the entrance by eight, what are *you* doing here?"

"Since I'm on the board of directors for the park, I scout around at times, making sure everything is in order—like the caves you were about to violate."

"I'm really sorry. Forgive me?"

"No sweat. They're a mystery to every outsider."

Outsider! By now, she hoped she was more than that to him. She let it pass, knowing how he truly felt about her. "So, what's up for tonight?"

"Buffalo stew, for one thing. I'm hungry. Have you eaten—?"

Her eyes winced. "Buffalo stew! That sounds so . . . well, not appetizing."

He pulled her toward a food stand. "No different from the buffalo burger you had the other night."

"I suppose that's safe to say."

"Don't knock it until you try it. It's just as good as anything made with cow meat. They're both animals. We honor the buffalo by partaking. Come on, you've gotta try it. Besides, I've been waiting to have dinner with you all day."

Darrius led her to a secluded little picnic table and went to get their food. He returned with two heaping bowls of stew, sodas and corn muffins. Savoring the stew's rich aroma, he told her it had been made with Indian ingredients he had grown up on. "My mother makes it all the time." He handed her a spoon. "Eat up."

He watched as she tasted her first spoonful of stew, expecting to see signs of distaste on her face. To his surprise, a pleasant smile appeared instead.

"You like?"

"Surprisingly. I thought it would taste—"

"Bland and gamey?"

"Yeah!"

"It can, if it's not made correctly, as would be the case for any food, right?"

"Right, and it goes well with the bread."

They ate in silence for a while. And then Darrius's eyes met hers, locked in position as if reading them. "What did you see out here today? I know you've taken great pictures for us to develop in the morning."

A coy little smile appeared on her face. "Would that mean I would have to get up early and drive to your house to develop them or—"

"I think you know the answer. You will stay the night, won't you?"

She rolled her eyes playfully. "I don't know. Any man who makes out on a horse might not be trustworthy."

A slight hint of tongue moistened his lower lip. "Umm, I've been thinking about that all day, too. It was a blast."

"I'm not afraid of horses anymore, if that's any consolation."

"It is."

"Good, so you know I'll stay the night, Darrius. To answer your question, I did a few things. I went to a few buffalo dances and—"

"The spirit of Famine scared you, didn't he?"

His abruptness took her aback. "Yeah, he did. I've never seen a famine character look so—

"Scary?"

"Yes. I've seen people play that character at the Arizona powwows, but this guy was something else."

"That actor is Anderson Healy, a very well-known actor in this area. He's actually had bit roles in native movies like *Dances with Wolves* and *Geronimo*."

"Really?"

"Yes. He's very good, because I can see uncertainty in your eyes."

Is it fear from Famine or the damn mountain that she was so curious about? Whatever the case, she definitely had been scared of something. Keeping quiet about going up the other side of Red Rock was her only choice. To avoid any more talk of the terrifying character, she took another sip of her drink.

"Anything else?" he asked.

"I took more stills of dancers, walked around, ate a little, watched more shows."

"What else?"

His eyes were penetrating hers as though he were reading her soul. "Nothing else."

"You did something else, Justine."

"I haven't had time to do anything else, Darrius. After being scared by the famine dude, I just settled back and took it easy."

"He is a hard act to swallow; beautiful young women are usually frightened by him. You could have called me. I'd have come sooner to comfort you."

"Who would have watched your store?"

"Derrick. He hung out with me today. He was taking it easy because he'll be doing a lot of dancing for the main powwow over the weekend." He studied her a little closer. "You sure you didn't do anything else?"

"Darrius! Cool it. I had fun today."

He settled back and finished his drink. "I'm sorry. I just want to protect you."

"From what?"

He knew he was scaring her, causing her more grief by being so persistent. "Nothing. Forgive me for being protective. I get weird like this sometimes, although I haven't been this way since my last girlfriend. She was also a hard one to protect, always wanting to do her own thing. You know the kind, right?" His brow arched playfully.

"Perhaps. What was she like?"

"Fun-loving, kind. Most of the time."

Justine saw a hint of something on his face, leading her to ask, "Did you love her?"

"Yes." He then did his best imitation of Dracula to break the tension of having to talk of a past lover. "But I love you more. She may have had all the qualities I just mentioned, but so do you. In the end, she was way too aggressive, never listened to advice and eventually got into some trouble with the law."

"What did she do?"

"Something I never would have suspected. She held up a liquor store. I knew she liked to drink, but that was carrying it a little too far. Funny thing, I never got vibes from her about that."

"I'm sorry, Darrius. You won't have that to worry about with me. I hardly ever drink liquor—and I'm scared of guns."

"Good girl. Guns and liquor will kill ya."

However, something he said did concern her: the willfulness of his last girlfriend. She was willful as well, having gone up Red Rock after he had asked her not to. She decided she would try to rein in her willfulness.

He kissed her hand. "What are you thinking about?"

"Oh, uh . . . just you, as usual." *That's right, play it off well and he'll suspect nothing!*

Darrius helped her up from the table. "Let's see more dancing. Once the sun completely sets, we can go back to the smaller caves at the back of the park—the *safe* places—and talk, show you what's inside. Your picture showed up a few things."

"Yeah, like what?"

"You'll see. You can take more pictures."

"I almost have enough. Some things should remain sacred, right?"

"Yes, some things."

Justine was glad that he hadn't pressed the subject of Red Rock's other side, hadn't confronted her with what she knew she shouldn't have done.

By sundown, the arenas filled with jingle, grass and buffalo dancers, among others. Tantalizing aromas, from incense to a variety of native foods, wafted through the air. With her hand in his and their hearts attuned to one another, Justine was happy. During open dances in the main arena, she danced in line with the other participants. Holding her cameras, Darrius waited on the sideline. She still wondered what his real reason was for not dancing. It had to be more than what he had told her earlier.

She kept step with the others, dancing, listening to the dancers chanting, being one with a nation. Yes, the children in her neighborhood were Native American and that is where she learned things about the culture. They taught her a little about the kachina dolls, told her about the powwows they went to, the things they did while there and also about the dances. As she grew older, her quest for knowledge about the Indian culture grew and the children who had remained in the area were able to explain more aspects of the culture to her. So, her experience with native people went far beyond the games they played as children. She became one with them as she learned more about the culture. Even her best friend,

Fara, had told her a great many things about Native Americans since her mother was Pawnee, but now she was learning even more about their culture by being at one of the biggest powwows in the west.

By moonlight, Darrius led Justine to the restricted cave area in the back of the park where hardly anyone went, and lifted the rope. He saw the confused look on Justine's face and explained, "I'm on the board of trustees of Red Rock, remember? That gives me certain privileges. I know these caves like the back of my own hand. We're safe."

"Then why is the rope around it?"

"To keep spectators out. Many don't know the story of Red Rock or the lesser-known stories of the fascinating things found here—like the caves. Open access would invite exploitation."

"I was about to a few minutes ago."

"True. You're naturally investigative."

Holding a flashlight in one hand and her hand in the other, he lifted the rope and led her into the cave.

Justine entered the semi-darkness and looked around. Without Darrius guiding her, she touched the walls, ran her fingers over the petroglyph drawings, feeling their depth. As she explored the cave, her mouth went dry from excitement. Awestruck, she turned to him. He looked calm, serene, as he watched her.

She said, "This is a different cave than the one in your pictures."

"Right. We can't go into that one because it's not as safe as this one is—though, we really shouldn't be here, too, because of the cracks here—and then over here." He pointed to a few gaps on both walls. "We can stay for a little while, though."

"I—I can't believe this. It's so interesting here."

"I take it you're happy with your find."

"I'm happy with everything here."

He came up behind her and kissed her neck, pressing her body against his. "I have more delights for you, my love."

"Really? What? Making out on the horse again?"

"I think he's safe in his stable." Darrius moved his hand down her dress, stopping at the juncture of her thighs. She was already moist for him, and he wanted to play, plunder, spread her across continents and delve inside. "What we did on my painted glory was fun, but this will be as well." He turned the flashlight on, uncovering a large blanket, a bottle of white wine and a few throw pillows. He whispered in her ear, "Does that look inviting?"

Were her eyes deceiving her, or had Darrius been there earlier than planned? Had he been witness to her stupid trek up the other end of Red Rock? If so, why hadn't he chastised her? So many questions flooded her mind as she turned and faced him. "How long can we be here tonight?"

"Maybe long enough to make out, talk."

"Or do a little more," she said with a twinkle in her eye.

"I don't know about that. The park closes at a certain time, you know. But we'll see."

"How long have you been here tonight?"

"Ten minutes early. I promise I wasn't watching you, because I knew you had work to do. I just wanted to make our night together special, talk to you about the caves, the kachinas, the—"

"The Koshari? I would still like to hear his side of the story from you instead from out of some book or remembering what the kids in the neighborhood told me."

"Sure. If you want to hear the story."

"You're a hell of a man, Red Sky."

His nose nuzzled hers. "I've been told that, my love. Come, let's sit on the blanket so I can answer all the pondering questions."

Justine wiggled between his spread thighs, feeling the heat of his swollen erection already willing and anticipating contact with her. She liked that, loved the idea of a man so ready for her that he could barely think of anything else. For her, that was living.

His breathing lulled her, making her a slave to any and all things he could possibly do to her. His voice drew her in as he told her exactly what animals were on the walls, what the stick-like people were doing and how hunts were so great back in the day of the roaming, plentiful buffalo. He told her the story as though he had actually been there. Maybe he had been. Reincarnation was more than just a word, and with Darrius's sixth sense, who knew what to believe—or disbelieve. But she believed because he was a master in every sense of the word.

His voice took her out of her pleasant reverie and made her pay attention. He poured her a glass of chardonnay. "Do these walls live up to your expectations?"

"That and more."

He nibbled on her earlobes, making her ready to completely relax with him to let him take her right then and there, but he was reluctant to. The place wasn't right enough to make it real to her. She deserved more than a blanket, a musty cave and only a flashlight as ambiance. Justine was the luxury suite type of woman as far as he was concerned. But for the time being, he was glad to tell her stories, do a little making out and just spend some quality time together.

He massaged her nipple through the thin cotton dress and ached to kiss her in so many places, but again, she deserved more and he planned on giving her only his best. To not concentrate on how much he wanted to make love, he lowered to her ear. "Want to hear a story?"

"The Koshari one? I know a lot about him, but not enough."

"Not him—not this time. I have another one; one that's so grand in scale it makes Koshari pale in comparison."

"Yeah? What story could surpass Koshari?"

"The one about Red Sky."

"Hmm. I'm beginning to like the sound of that. Where did your last name come from, anyway?"

He nuzzled against her ear. "What will you give me in return for delivering my sordid story?"

"My soul?"

"That's a start." His hand moved down to the V of her thighs, tracing the thin panty line, rubbing the pad of a finger across the center and against the swelled nub of opulence. She shuddered at what one stroke could do to her.

"I know you love what I'm doing to you. Don't deny it."

"I can't deny it, Darrius. You make me insane."

"What about the rest of you? When do I get this?" He cupped her slick passage.

"After I get my story. Deal?"

"Deal." He settled against the dirt cave wall and unfolded the generations-old tale of a family. "Legend has it that on the night of my great-great-grandfather's birth, a storm raged; it raged like never before, with streaks of gray and yellow lightning illuminating the sky. Alone in her village, except for her grandmother, a young woman gave birth to a son, and at the exact moment of his arrival the heavens opened up, seemingly wanting to swallow the Earth. In its wrath, the sky turned bright red, hailed, boomed. The birth was a difficult one, rendering her almost dead, yet she held on to give life to a nameless baby who she knew would be great in his days on this planet."

Justine was spellbound. "Did she die soon after naming him?"

"She survived and named him after something more powerful than himself—the elements; thus came the name Red Sky. He was the first of three sons and a daughter born to the young woman, and all turned out to be powerful in his or her own way. My great-great-grand-father, along with his brother, went on to become a legendary hunter of the Bear Tribe. The other son became a powerful medicine man. As for my great-great-aunt Nereid, she became known as a notable sea-maiden."

"Are you serious, Darrius?"

"Very. Thus my great-great-grandfather's name stuck, using his name as our last name. I don't know who decided that, but it stuck. Throughout my family history, there have been powerful men and women."

"Like you."

"Hardly. I'm just a man."

"You're more than a man, Darrius; you're someone I could get lost in forever."

The tip of his tongue played at her ear, savoring her feel and aroma, getting hungrier for her with every move she made, every word she spoke. He captured her lobe, pulled on it, tugged softly, feeling his nature aching to be set free to overpower her, and in such luscious ways. "I guess I have been on the hunt for you since looking into your eyes."

"A hunter, are you?"

"When I want to be."

"Really, though. Do you hunt?"

"I can but I don't. It's not my calling. I believe most of what I have came from my shaman ancestors. I love getting to the truth of things, seeing and talking of greater things than us humans, trying to understand forces that I know are way beyond our scope. I'm the religious one of the clan."

"What about Derrick? Is he religious, too?"

"He's the one we call the fool, but we mean no harm by it. He's the one who amuses, takes away plight, brings levity to sad situations. He's the dancer."

That was the very word that could bring Darrius to his knees. *Dancing.* Justine sensed there was more to his story than the dances being exploited by visitors to the various powwows. He could never make a living as an actor. He was too down to earth, too anxious to get to the heart of things; he could never successfully hide what he was thinking. But what *was* he thinking? What was the reason behind his lack of dancing?

Her demeanor became solemn, she knew he was touchy about the subject and could quite possibly turn away or evade it by any means necessary. Yet, she had to know. She stroked his cheek, feeling his cascading hair brushing her skin. Was it her way of buttering him up? Who knew? But it was worth a shot.

"Don't kill me over this, but it's something I really need to know. I want the total truth—all of it. Okay?"

The "okay" was shaky, and he heard the quiver in her voice. His arms encircled her small frame. "Why so serious all of a sudden? Just ask me. I told you I'd answer anything you want me to."

"Truthfully?"

"There's no other way, is there?"

"I hope not." She hesitated a bit and then plunged ahead: "Well—tell me the real reason why you don't dance anymore, Darrius."

His body shifted and he released a husky breath. A husky breath from deep within his soul. "Ah, sounds like another one of those questions."

"What questions?"

"The kind of question that requires me getting something for my efforts. What will you give me for the answer?"

"I'm serious!"

"So am I. That's a touchy subject. I gave you an answer."

"Yes, but not *the* answer, not the answer that gets to the root of the question."

"You really are some woman, Justine. Okay, but if I tell you, you have to promise not to get scared."

That alerted her. "Scared? Why would a story about you no longer dancing scare me?"

"Because my dances have been known to kill!"

12

DANGEROUS LIAISONS

They were face to face, and Justine stared into deadly serious eyes. Not expecting his explosive revelation, her voice cracked with surprise—confusion. "Excuse me?"

"You heard right, Justine."

"Why would a dance be dangerous, Darrius?"

"It wasn't just a dance, darling. It's *the* dance, the same dance you'll see Derrick perform tomorrow night. It's the Koshari dance, one I thought I'd perfected until that ill-fated evening—in a large arena, in front of hundreds of people."

He lowered his eyes, his voice fell silent and Justine saw him fishing for words. Nervous hands now played with strands of her dark locks, and she could feel his tension. She laced her fingers through his, pulling him back to the matter at hand. "Just tell me what happened at the dance. You won't frighten me. Had I been scared of anything, it would have been traveling up the . . . never mind." Letting on about her trip up danger mountain would intensify the moment, not lighten it. Besides, she wanted Darrius's story and nothing more—for the moment.

"Traveling up what, Justine? Finish what you were about to say."

"Not a chance. No way are you getting out of telling me about the dance."

"Why do you need to know?"

"Because I want to know everything about you—even the bad, if that's what the dance was."

"It was, and I'm ashamed of the outcome, but if you need to know—"

"I do."

"Then hang on, because it's not pretty." He took a deep breath and settled back, not wanting to relive an excruciating night years ago. Knowing Justine, he knew she'd stop at nothing to dig the truth out of him. If she had a flaw, her need to know everything was it. He did know it was an expected part of her trade, but it was also part of her personality.

There were so many emotions surrounding the dance and he didn't really know where to start, but the beginning was probably the best place. Starting out easy, buying time to soften the expected blow, was the only way to ease into it.

"Justine, I no longer perform at powwows because a death did occur as I danced the ludicrous dance eight years ago. It was a powwow much like this one—a more traditional powwow with many of the legendary kachinas performing. They don't dance in the powwows every year, just on occasions—years apart. This year the Koshari dances in public again. The last time he did was eight years ago—I was the dancer then. As you know, the Koshari is a clown, a trickster who does everything he can do to disrupt the kachina ceremonies. He makes a mockery of everyone there, dancers and spectators. He's silly, slovenly and cares for nothing but his own entertainment, whatever it may be. I was exceptional at that. I had a way of getting the crowd so riled up and into the ceremonies that I became the main dancer at one point."

"I'm sure you were phenomenal."

"I was the best, until one night when I became too much like the character and got careless."

"What happened?"

"You see, the audience is encouraged to participate in the rousting, get the Koshari agitated to the point where he selects someone to take his frustrations out on. Their primary function is to amuse the audience during gaps in the major ceremonies. They teach a lesson on how not to behave. They serve other functions, as you well know, but my dance was for amusement."

"I know a lot about the Koshari, how he entertains, what his other roles are. Now that I know you danced as the character, he really is my favorite."

"Don't be so high on them because of me. Hear the rest of the story first. There was a young woman doing her best to get me into action, enticing me, so I acted accordingly. She was beautiful, smiling, enjoying the performances . . . and I was attracted to her. I was only twenty-one years old, and if any situation arose where I could show off my prowess, I seized it. I pulled her into the main arena, grabbing her each time she tried to make her escape. I tossed my fruit, water and anything at her that wouldn't injure her. I could see she was becoming embarrassed by the crowd laughing at her. She was sticky from the watermelon and her clothes were wet, but I hadn't had my fill. I was proud of the fact that I was the best Hano clown in the area, even better than my brother, and I wanted to show off."

Darrius rubbed his temples to relieve the pressure, but with each word, imaginary screws drilled into his skull. "I got my claps, calls, hoots and chants from the crowd and that fueled me, got into my blood, making everything inside me race. Before I knew anything, I picked her up, hoisted her small frame above my head and kept in step with the drums and other music. I lost my footing."

His hands draped to his sides, his voice becoming listless and his tongue heavy with grief. Justine's impulse was to calm him, tell him he didn't have to go on, but since he had started, she thought it better to get it out of his system. Maybe he had never talked to anyone other than family about what happened.

What *had* happened?

Darrius listened to her even breathing, not wanting to interrupt it with the story of a dead girl, a girl who will haunt him for the rest of his life. Somehow, talking of it relieved the tension in his soul. Spitting it out was the only remedy.

"Her body flew into the air and landed with a thud. I was powerless to break her fall, since I was already on the ground. The arena fell silent and there was only the stillness in the night until her sister screamed out and ran into the arena to hold the body of a girl who lost her life at my hands. My hands!"

The story hit Justine so hard she could feel his suffering in her own beating heart. Her hands cradled his, kissing them. "It was a mistake, Darrius."

"I was careless."

"You didn't want it to happen."

"Yet it did, and I still see her when I see my own face in the mirror—well, at least until you stepped into my life. All I see is you now. The very idea of losing someone, anyone, curdles my blood. I can't lose anyone else to a tragedy."

"You didn't know her."

"I didn't have to. All I could do was watch her as they took her away on a stretcher. Her sister attacked me, pounding my arms, my chest, and all I could do was let her. I deserved it, and I felt if that was the only way for her to give me a little payback, then so be it. The police and security took the sister away. Moments later, a squad car came for me. My world spun around as fast as a spinning globe on some history channel."

"They took you away? It was an accident, Darrius."

"A girl died, Justine. It was a death, and I caused it. It . . . was murder."

Justine faced him, trailed her hand across his cheeks, feeling the sweat caused by telling such a heart-wrenching tale. It didn't seem real; seemed more like something on the Lifetime network—not the real life of a man, her lover.

Feeling his pain, she herself trembled as he continued. "There I was in some cell wearing black and white paint, a breechcloth, moccasins and handcuffs. My hat fell off at the arena, leaving its mark on the same spot where she lost her life. Her name was Asia, and she was nineteen years old."

"How long were you there?"

"My father's lawyers got me out two days later, but I'm still in prison, Justine, at least until I look at you." His hands grazed the sides of her face, wiping tears away. "Why are you crying?"

"Because I hurt for you."

Perplexed, he narrowed his eyes. "Why? This didn't happen to you."

"Don't you dare say that! Somehow or other you bull-dozed your way into my heart, and I can't shake you. I feel what you feel, hurt along with you. I hear the pain in your voice, and it stabs at me, too."

He kissed her lips. "I'm sorry, Justine. You're the last person I want to hurt. That's why I didn't want to tell the story."

"You had to, and you'll feel better. Have you spoken of this to anyone since it happened?"

"Not really. Once the lawyers got me out of it, I kept it to myself. My family walked around on eggshells for a while when I was near. They didn't know how to talk about it with me; I didn't know how to with them. I sent her family cards, money, anything I could find that would make their heart lighter, but they returned every-thing to me—unopened. I couldn't blame them. Asia was dead and I couldn't resurrect her no matter how many visions I had. I'm just a man."

"You're more than a man."

His arms tightened around her. "I'm glad you think so. Will you stay with me? Not run away?"

"I couldn't leave you if I wanted to, but you have to forgive yourself, Darrius. That was eight years ago. I know the pain and memories will never go away, but you didn't mean for it to happen. You were doing your job, entertaining a crowd. I know Asia forgives you."

"So now you know why I don't dance."

He lifted the bottle and poured more wine. "Stay with me, right here, right now in the sanctity of this cave. Feeling your body next to mine takes me away, Justine. No woman has ever done this to me." He finished his wine and lay back on the blanket.

She lay next to him and watched his reflection flickering against the candle-lit walls. Her body craved him, wanted him to fill her, overwhelm her with his strength and power, part her valley and climb steeper hills with her. His story only made her want him more, want to protect him, want to make him feel more like the man she knew he was.

They rested together, saying nothing, watching the images on the wall that were illuminated by his flashlight. Her hands smoothed up and down his shirt, relaxing brick-hard muscles covered by velvet skin. Not fighting the urge to taste him, she lifted the hem of his T-shirt, stretching it to his pecs. The will to lick his smooth skin awakened every fiber of her being—and she partook in loving, swirling licks, starting in the middle of his chest. Her tongue moistened his flesh, making a trail from his heart to the pucker of his navel, making his stomach rise and fall. Her trail continued to the band of his Jockeys, flicking her feverish tip around the perimeter.

His body tightened to her moves and alluring enticements. The rise in his pants quickly became more than arousal. He wanted her in every possible way. The more her tongue moved towards his hot, seething phallus, and finally conquering it with wet licks and caresses against the roughness of his jeans, the more he knew she was the woman to make his dreams come true, to make him finally trust himself, to finally allow himself to feel free to love another woman. He cupped her face, feeling her lips attacking the material, begging access.

He knew it was neither the time nor the place to truly make love to her. Guards were still in the general area, though he had access day and night—all night, if need be. What he really wanted was to lie with her, cuddle, feel good again without benefit of intercourse—if it was possible with a woman like Justine. Was it?

He tilted her face to his, whispering, "We can't make love here. It's not private enough."

"I know it isn't, but we can kiss, right?"

"We can kiss all night."

"We can kiss everywhere, whatever we want, right?"

His thumbs massaged hardened nipples pressing against the sundress. "Let's start with this." His lips pressed against hers, opening wide to her, chasing her tongue, capturing it and mating—hard.

Justine felt the boiling point of his erection, and nothing could satisfy her more than satisfying *him* more. She slowly withdrew from him, lowering her hands past his shirt and belt and onto his zipper. Without words, she followed her need and unzipped the mountainous hurdle . . . taking what she wanted.

He sprang to life the minute she unleashed him. A hard, glistening shaft shown in the stillness of the cave, and Justine wrapped her hands around pleasure. Soft veins of virility throbbed against her palms, making her passage constrict with need, yet it was about him, only him, and she was there to please him that night. He'd done so much work moments ago, spilling his guts about a painful episode in his life. She was simply there to take away all thoughts of the terrible incident.

His salty tip pumped harder, swelling against her inner cheeks the deeper she took him. The smooth, easy strokes of her hungry mouth relieved him, made him wonder what he could have done to deserve her. Everything. He was the perfect man for her and in every sense of the word. Justine knew how to satisfy him, from the mere sound of her voice to pumping his shaft with hard, rugged strokes. Yes, she was the only woman who could take him from sad to happy all in one night.

The more deeply she went down on him, the tighter he got, feeling like pumping his seed nonstop. His sac tightened as her nails grazed it. And at the same time that very talented tongue stroked the underside of his erection, moving back to the tip, circling it. Double action, and he could barely stand not being in her, pumping in long, stiff strokes over again, feeling her hidden treasures as she covered him. He imagined being inside her, sliding against walls so wet and famished for him, spreading her thighs wide apart, gyrating in circular motions. His hips would vigorously rock against hers, and almost pull completely out before pushing right back in. He could feel his lips around her nipples, licking, flicking, sucking. God! He needed the release so badly, and with her—only her. Imagining rubbing his fingers across her labia, and then moving straight to the magic little button that set her body ablaze was what he lived for. She'd constrict around him, hold him tight and milk him into the hardest orgasm a man could have.

That was enough, and he pulled away from her.

Justine watched him, amazed by how he had reacted to her. After he calmed, she kissed his moist lips and rested against his pounding chest. Her words softly filled the night air. "Was it good for you, Darrius?"

"Beyond reality. Was it good for you?"

"Anything with you is good for me."

"It was awesome. Lie against me. Let's just stay here, still, quiet, listening to our hearts, our minds, souls." His lips met with the softness of her cheek. "We really are one, aren't we?"

"Something I hadn't planned on was being with a man this soon. But then came you and I couldn't help myself."

"I'm glad." He sighed and relaxed against the smooth cave wall. "It's been a long day, but a good one."

"Indeed it has been." The back of her mind was still cluttered with things that had gone wrong that day; being scared by the Famine dancer, not being able to take as many pictures as she had wanted to, going against the wishes of a man she adored. All of what she had accomplished with her photos and falling for Darrius could have been lost by one stupid move she simply couldn't forget. Her little day excursion up Suicide Mountain would remain forever a secret, yet something about the mountain still wouldn't let her rest.

13

SHOPPERS PARADISE

Friday Morning

Justine awakened the next morning still wrapped in Darrius's arms. They had fallen asleep kissing and holding one another. Their new love was so amazing, so earth shattering, that nothing else mattered more than being together. That is what carried her through the night, and that is what awakened her to a new day surrounded by the love of a man.

In the glints of an early sun coming in from the cave opening, she smiled a smile of total contentment. Normally the idea of wearing the same dress and panties and having unbrushed teeth would have made her cringe. This time it meant the culmination of the best night ever. She stirred in his arms, willing to stay right where she was, seeing the hot New Mexico sun set the sky ablaze. Yes, now she knew what living and loving was really about.

Her barely audible sigh caused him to stir; he soon awakened with the same syrupy, heaven-filled smile. Her hair was tangled around his fingers. He slowly caressed the silky strands of a woman who had again made her own magic with him. "I can't believe we slept here all night. I don't even remember falling asleep."

Her voice cracked with the newness of the day. "That's a good thing. It means you, too, were into what we were doing."

"Well, as much as I would love to stay here and continue doing just that, we'd better get a move on before security comes around."

"I thought you had access here."

"I do, but they don't expect me to ever stay the night." He helped her to her feet and kissed the tip of her warm nose. "Actually, this scene would be better finished off in your lovely hotel room on a nice big bed, don't you think?"

"We could go back to sleep."

"Or do *other* things."

"You're intent on wearing me out, aren't you?"

His arms wrapped tighter around her, their lips briefly met. "Indeed, I am."

It was high noon and Justine again awoke next to her lover, but this time their warm, sexually stimulated bodies huddled under a damp sheet—slick from lovemaking. Instead of awakening him, she stared from the top of his jet hair, moved to his fantastically toned torso, to knees partly spread exposing a shaft that filled her effortlessly and endlessly.

How lucky she felt to be a part of this man's life after living a life filled with Mr. Nobodies. A lot of Mr. Nobodies, and that was the sad part. There had been men in her life, yet her job was the only thing that made her feel her existence mattered. Being defined by her job hadn't been what she wanted, but it was all she had other than her family and the few true friends she'd managed to hang on to.

She looked over at his closed eyes again and smiled. This stranger, this total stranger, drifted into her life and gave her air again. He was a deep breath of incredibly fresh air, and she couldn't breathe in enough. Touching his golden, damp skin electrified her to the point of needing him inside her again. But she didn't awaken him. He was exhausted, exhausted from his work and their sex life—but what a good sleep it made for.

She left him on the bed and headed straight for the shower. Funny, showering was the last thing they thought about upon entering her room. Snatching off every scrap of clothing and diving heart first into bed was the only thing on their minds. They partook for hours.

When she returned to the bedroom wrapped in a thick bath towel, he was sitting up on the bed, wrapped in the sheet. "Why didn't you join me? We had such fun showering together before."

"We all need our privacy, and I assumed you needed yours, you know, to clear your head. I sure needed to clear mine."

Her eyes softened. "Dredging up those old memories of the dance didn't help, did it?"

"You needed to know, and I'm actually glad it's in the open. It's like a weight off my chest, though it still happened no matter how much I wish it hadn't."

She sat next to him, her towel brushing against his skin. "Then let's do something else fun today to take your mind off all those bad memories."

"I can't. I have to meet a buyer at the Zuni location by two."

"Can you reschedule?"

"Not really. Besides, Friday is the best day to see what's been collected over the week. He's known to locate rare finds, things I know the store could make a mint on. He's the one who found your bracelet. It was actually at an estate sale. One of New Mexico's most famous Pueblo women, an artist, owned the bracelet, having purchased it somewhere in Mesoamerica only months before her death."

Justine studied the bracelet hanging from her wrist; she had not taken it off since he had put it on her wrist. "I didn't know it had such a history. Is it Toltec, Mayan—"

"Looks more Aztec, actually."

"Really? What kind of art did the woman make?"

"Sculptures. She was famous for her work with underworld pieces."

"Underworld?"

"You know, demons, Satan, other dark forces." Her expression suddenly changed. "But don't worry. She was very important to our people. She was the one people also called a spirit guide, telling us what forces were around—which ones to pay attention to, which ones to avoid. It has partly to do with kachinas. I'll explain more about them over the weekend or on Monday." He brought her face to his. "You'll still be around on Monday, won't you?"

"I did tell my boss I would be back on Monday. Maybe I can stretch it into another day or so. After all, you haven't told me your version of the kachina story."

"Tomorrow will be a good day for that. I'll have the entire day free. I have a friend watching the store for me tomorrow."

"That's good." She smiled dreamily. "We may never leave your bedroom, since you won't have to work tomorrow."

"But I do have work today, unfortunately."

"Yeah, maybe you'd better meet that guy at two. Who knows, he may have some type of upside-down cross or something to sell to you."

"Not a chance." He pulled her wet body against his. "How about we meet for dinner and then go over to the ceremony. They're doing some of the minor dancing tonight, and Derrick may be dancing there, too. I'll explain all the mystical things you'll see tonight—well, those you don't already know about: the dances, outfits, what they're for."

"What about taking pictures tonight?"

"Probably not, but ask Derrick. Cameras are prohibited at most dances over the weekend, though some photographers have gotten away with it."

He peeked into the V of her gaping towel, teasing her flesh with light strokes. "You got anything else to do in the meantime?"

"Lots. I'd like to go into town and take pictures of the locals, business owners, give our readers more than a superficial view of what Gallup is all about. I want them to be able to truly see the place, envision themselves in the middle of the action. "

"Spoken like a true photojournalist, and from the work I've seen from your very expert lens, you'll achieve it. I'll give you keys before we leave my house. Maybe you can stop by the Zuni store. You haven't seen it."

"Maybe, but what time are we having dinner tonight?"

"Seven! After that, we can get ready to watch the dances."

"Seven it is!"

With Darrius now taking his shower, Justine sat down to upload more pictures. Another picture caught her eyes. It looked to be a landscape. It was the road less traveled—literally. Suicide Mountain! *How on earth did I shoot this?* It was a clear shot of one of the highest peaks on her insane trip up the dangerous mountain. Then she remembered. It had been taken before panic struck, before she got too high on the mountain to calmly move back down.

She was glad Darrius was not in there to see it. Trust was a big issue with him, and this photograph would make him seriously doubt her character. He already had an ex-girlfriend who was also a liquor store burglar. Being part of a duo of painful women was the last thing she wanted to be for Darrius. A liar and a thief—what a winning hand!

Unfortunately, in this case, the shot was a spectacular one, despite what a wreck she was—a bundle of nerves, sweating like a wild boar and with teeth chattering. Yeah, wouldn't that make a great, lasting impression on him?

Every picture turned out great with Red Rock as its backdrop. There were pictures of teepees, dancers who stopped and posed for shots, jingle dress and fancy dance dancers. Yes, *The Examiner* would be proud of the job she was doing there with her photographs.

She put the last picture up to dry just as Darrius opened the bathroom door. Within seconds, he was in her arms, smelling like fresh rain. His hair was still damp and felt like silk. Their lips parted, and her nose quickly nuzzled the crisp strands of his mane. "Umm, I could play in your hair all day."

"If only we had time."

"We do have time for one thing, don't we?"

"Like?" Darrius questioned.

"Going to your house and showing me your bedroom. I wanted to see it this morning, but you wanted to come here. That's the only room in the house I haven't seen. It's like you're avoiding something in there."

"Maybe I am. Then again, maybe I have something in there that I'm waiting to show you tomorrow tonight. Something special that's taken me a while to get up the nerve to even want to show to you."

Her eyes lazily studied his. "Come on, show me today."

"No way. Now that I've gotten the guts to show you later, showing you now would spoil the surprise. I don't allow just anyone in my room—especially after my last girlfriend, who I thought was the love of my life. Instead, she had a love affair with a gun, several bottles of Jack Daniel's and Mr. Smirnoff." He smiled ruefully as he thought of his gun-packing ex. "You know, she's probably having the time of her life playing hard to get with several guards at some prison in Santa Fe."

"Forget about her, Darrius," she said, her finger trailing down the front of his T-shirt. "I'm not just anyone, am I? So surely you'll be safe showing me the bedroom."

"No, you're not just anyone, you're everyone; everyone I want you to be, friend, lover, confidant—hopefully, girlfriend, now that I want to chance it again."

"Aren't I already?"

A smile lit his face like a rising rainbow. "Just the answer I was hoping for."

"And I hardly drink. Pistols and I don't mix, either."

"Good attributes. Let's go. Today will be remarkable. Tonight will be astonishing, and tomorrow night will be mesmerizing."

Her hand joined his. "I'm ready."

Darrius was the only thing that could have taken her mind off food. They'd been together all morning, making love, talking, and both had totally forgotten about breakfast. There was still so much to see of the town, and although Justine was getting hungry, she didn't want to stop. She was in her mode, visiting storeowners and taking pictures of their shops up and down Coal Avenue. The streets were crowded with people who were either natives or visitors who had come from wherever to take part in the ceremonial.

On occasion, she would see people walking around in traditional native outfits who were either part of the ceremonies or just showing off their rich native legacy. Either way, they made for astonishing shots. Traditionally, it was always best to ask for permission, but she snapped a few on the side—a few more pictures to add to her pictorial record of beautiful New Mexico. Yes, her spread would be awesome, maybe even award-winning. Shots of the upper hills of Red Rock would improve her prospects of winning. She was still aching to see what was beyond the foothills, but one thing stopped her: she had given her word to Darrius that she would not tamper with that area. She loved Darrius too much to go against him, no matter what marvels awaited her camera.

Justine entered the last store on her list, Peko's on Coal, and asked the owner for permission to photograph his store. And what a beautiful place it was, with huge dream catchers on all four walls, along with a variety of cow and other types of animal hides in decorative designs. The scent of sage incense filled the air, reminding her of the outstanding love she and Darrius made that famous night in his store. It was the start of something that had taken over her body, mind, soul.

She gravitated to a large jewelry display looking for something she could afford to take home as a memento.

What else at a decent price could she buy and take home as a remembrance of the wondrous trip to another land?

Inside the display case was a stunning squash blossom necklace, something she'd had set her mind on buying since seeing her first one in *New Mexico Magazine* two years ago. And it matched the bracelet that had become so precious to her.

She crouched in front of the showcase and studied the necklace, marveling at the intricate design of the horse-shoe-shaped silver backings with a mix of Arizona and Chinese turquoise. Above each cluster was a two-millimeter spot of red coral. Justine knew her gems, having grown up visiting her parents' small jewelry shop every day after school to marvel at the new gems that had come in. Back then, she couldn't linger. As the oldest girl, she had to rush home and mind the other siblings until one of her parents came home. On very special occasions, her mother would bring her small, leftover pieces of gems that were too awkward in size to fit into the cabochon. She had always wanted to put the pieces together and make her own jewelry. It never happened; her mind strayed to other interests because one day she got a camera for her birthday and she had been hooked on photography ever since.

"Ma'am, is there something I can show you?"

Justine rose and slowly turned to face a short, older man with a long beard. He wore a white shirt with bolo tie and a pair of sharply creased jeans. "I love your squash-blossom necklace. How much is it?"

"I have several, all varying in price."

He walked over to the display, unlocked it and took out rows of necklaces. "My most expensive one is this one." He held it up to the light. "You'll not see anything like this one in any store in New Mexico—it's from an estate sale."

"Was the owner an old woman who made sculptures?"

"No, but I know who you're talking about. That would be Lilly Brook, passed away several years ago. Her pieces are in museums here and in Taos." He took out one necklace and said to Justine. "This one's a beauty and would look wonderful on you."

True enough, she hadn't seen anything like that in Darrius's store. Then again, after seeing Darrius, she hadn't looked too closely at anything else in the store.

Her fingertips traced the inlay patterns, feeling the smooth turquoise grace her fingers. "It's gorgeous. How much?"

"For a good price this week. I always lower my pieces during the ceremonial for visitors—$1,250. For you, I'll take another twenty dollars off," he said, offering her the necklace.

"Really?" She didn't want to pay that much and asked to see the others. "What else do you have that's similar? I can't quite spend that much."

"I have one that's $900." He took that one out, too, but still, it was too much.

"Do you have anything less than that?" Justine asked.

"This one is $480 but it's not all pure silver; still, it's very pretty." He held it out to her.

"May I try it on?"

"Sure. It'll match your bracelet. Red Sky Jewelers, is it?"

She looked up in surprise. "That's right."

"Yeah. Darrius is good. He has wonderful pieces."

More wonderful pieces than you think! Yes, her mind had gone off on a tangent again, and always would when Darrius was concerned. She couldn't wait to see him later, and thought she might stop by his Zuni location and surprise him.

She smiled down at it. "I love the weight—heavy enough, yet light."

"Made right here in town by one of our best silversmiths, Harry Takai. How it got to Wilber Silver Arrow's home in the hills, I'll never know. The old man died about six months ago, and this necklace was brought in with some of his other possessions."

Her eyes skeptically moved from side to side as if in deep thought. "Four eighty, huh?"

"That's right." After examining each piece, she decided she liked the cheaper one. "I'll take it."

"Excellent choice. May I wrap it for you?"

"No, I'll wear it." Then she remembered her mission. "Oh, would it be okay with you if I take some shots of your store? I work for *The San Francisco Examiner.* I'm doing a spread on the Intertribal Ceremonial."

"Help yourself. I'll just ring this up for you. Cash or credit?"

"Cash! I hate credit card bills. I do have travelers' checks if you take those."

"Anything you wish."

Justine wandered around looking for good prospects to photograph. She saw all kinds of staffs, walking sticks and war masks carved of the best mahogany, cottonwood and oak. She stopped and lightly touched a Mississippian cedar mask with shell eyes and mouth. She had remembered seeing one similar to it in one of her reference books on native cultures. Then she entered a room that contained native pots from the Pawnee and Algonquin. She took a few good shots of the room and went on to one decorated with animal heads. It had a surreal quality, giving her a sense of being in a hunt, in the middle of a prairie, having to fend for herself with nothing but a 35mm camera as a weapon.

Standing in the middle of the floor, the eyes of bears, caribou, elk and buffalo all seemed to follow her, tracking her every move. She quickly snapped what she wanted and got out. It was an eerie room, but might be very interesting to the readers.

Taking one more shot of the showrooms, she noticed some items on the sale rack. Could they actually be what she hoped they were? Were they rare finds in the form of T-shirts—the T-shirt of all shirts? She removed two shirts from the rack and, indeed, they were rare finds. In her hands were two kachina shirts—one was of the Crow Mother Darrius had spoken of; the name was painted onto the bottom of the shirt in red-flecked puffy paint. She would wear that one today. The other shirt was simply amazing to her and she was barely able to take her eyes off it—a white Hanes T-shirt with an airbrushed version of the Koshari across the chest. He was outlined in black against the white, but the black coordinating pattern stuck out in what seemed to be the darkest of ink. His striped, tasseled hat drooped over a face painted in stripes and circles. Large eyes were rimmed in dark ink; his chiseled body seemed to be moving in a rhythmic dance, giving him a 3-D effect. Justine held the shirt up, stared at it and flatly said, "Darrius! This is you."

The man came up from behind her. "You like?"

"Yes."

"Another local artist painted this about eight years ago during a tragic incident that happened at one of our powwows."

She knew about it, all right, but wasn't in the mood to bring up what Darrius had told her. The story had scared her, especially coming from his own lips. On the other hand, the shirt was too good to pass up despite the fact it was painted during an accidental death! "I'll take both shirts."

"Is there anything else I can help you with, Ms . . .?"

"Roberts-Paretti." She handed him a business card. "I'll pay cash for these, too. Thanks for letting me take the shots. We'll send you a copy of the paper."

As the man began to bag the shirt, Justine stopped him. "I'll wear the Crow Mother shirt. Can I change somewhere?"

"I have a dressing room."

Minutes later, Justine stepped out wearing the shirt with her faded jeans and sandals. She looked down at her bagged Koshari shirt and smiled, knowing Darrius would be on her chest tomorrow and would hopefully be in her body later that night.

14

PRE-FESTIVITIES

Driving down Route 66 wearing her squash necklace and Crow Mother shirt made her really feel like a part of all the festivities. She smiled knowing Darrius would be more than happy to make her a part of his life and his culture, and she would let him.

The Ranch Kitchen was just ahead, and she could hear her stomach growling for its famous Southwest barbecue. Her stomach had begun churning while she was in the basket room at Peko's on Coal. She hadn't had anything to eat since the buffalo stew at Red Rock the night before.

Food. That was her immediate goal. By two, she was sitting in front of a plate of pork, barbecued to perfection, with side orders of coleslaw and corn on the cob. Her server was the uncanny image of the 1920s actor Tom Mix—or so he seemed to think he was. He was dressed in the typical Western attire, including a ten-gallon hat and cowboy boots pointier than the tip of a Ginsu knife.

As she ate the tender ribs, her mind drifted to Darrius and his question—being his girlfriend. The thought warmed her, making her smile at the possibility of being in a man's life after being alone for so long. Past lovers had been duds, so instead of getting hooked up with yet another one of those, she had thrown herself into her photography. Destiny, and her ability to capture the perfect shot landed her straight into the arms of a new lover.

Sipping from the tall glass of iced tea, she wondered how a long-distance relationship would work for them. California wasn't too far from New Mexico, but far enough to be lonely for a lover in the middle of the night. Even if she left California to live in Gallup, what about her job? She loved her position, had the freedom to select almost any assignment she wanted. Would she have that freedom at a major magazine or newspaper in Gallup? She'd probably have to start on ground level and work her way up. She already had a track record at *The Examiner*. What about leaving her family and friends? Could she really leave them? She had a life in California and wasn't sure whether she wanted to risk it for the sake of an incredible love affair that could possibly last until . . . infinity! Choices!

She could find excuses for not staying in Gallup, though the possibility of remaining pressed on her mind persistently. Darrius was a priceless find. He treated her like a queen, catering to her, giving her everything he knew she wanted even before she knew she wanted it. His tender touch was so unlike anything she had ever experienced. She didn't know if she'd be able to give that up. Justine always found herself between a rock and a hard place, always letting her imagination take her to far-fetched places. This was a new relationship with

Darrius—if that was what it truly was. For Christ's sake, she had just met the man and knew she had to slow down.

First things first was the only way to handle that kind of situation. Number one: Call her editor, Sid, and tell him she needed at least another day and would fly out Tuesday. Number two: Take more pictures and try to shoot for photojournalist of the year in the Southwest region with her photos on native people. Third: Get away from the table before she ordered another plate of ribs.

Ordinarily, the scenery along Route 66 was awe-inspiring and would take her mind off everything, but her suddenly acute awareness of circumstances predominated her thoughts. It seemed the only way to clear her mind was to visit Darrius and talk about it. Not an option. He had things to do. Instead, she pulled to the side of the road and took pictures of the mountain ranges against a clear blue sky. The peaks of the ranges seemed to pierce the sky with their upward stretching points. Shadows of desert red, chocolate brown and tan never ceased to amaze her.

Having to pass Red Rock State Park on her way back to the hotel presented a dilemma. There was that ever-present desire to return to the road that had led her toward danger; the same place that had made her teeth rattle, her skin sweat, her eyes swell shut—yet she was driven to see if she could make it to the top. There was something she had to prove to herself; was she actually afraid of the mountain itself, or afraid of disappointing Darrius?

She didn't want to be afraid of anything because it would eventually get in the way of her career. There were always more peaks to discover for the sake of that once-in-a-lifetime shot. Did she love her job that much? So much that she was willing to try to prove herself invincible? She would never know unless she tried it again.

The entrance to Red Rock seemed to call her, and upon passing through the park entrance, she faced that forbidding winding road that had made her hair stand on end. She stopped at the foot of the road and peered up. Eyes barely open, she stared into the great unknown—the road to stories, petroglyphs. What a story awaited her and her camera.

Justine pressed the ignition and heard the car's engine rev, rocking back and forth. The rounded cliffs and jagged edges seemed to be holding their arms out to embrace her. Her throat tightened and her skin was becoming moist under the Crow Mother shirt. Her sweaty hands pressed against the shirt while her eyes fixed on the sight before her. The muscles in her driving foot wanted to press the accelerator; her right hand ached to put the gear in drive. She didn't. There was something not right about where she was, and she truly hadn't any idea if it was physiological or out of respect for Darrius. There were no answers to any of her questions that day.

She saw a way out. Then and only then did she put the gear in drive. Once she felt the car easing away from the road to doom, her throat loosened, her skin dried and her mind relaxed. No, she didn't have to do it. She could just get back on the road and go to the safety and comfort of the Red Rock Best Western—the safest place in town.

Just one look up the forbidden road of Red Rock had made her so thirsty she had to pull into a service station for a bottle of water. By the time she made it to her room, the large bottle of water was gone. What was it about that place that intrigued her? Maybe it was both monsters agitating her at the same time: Darrius, and the smallness of the car. Right, as if a larger vehicle could make everything else go away. Whatever the case, Justine removed her clothes and jewelry and plopped naked onto the bed. She fell into a deep and restless sleep.

Justine awakened and stared through a window now playing host to a fading sun. *God, what time is it?* Six o'clock; she had slept a good two hours, but still had time to take care of business before meeting Darrius at the powwow.

She flipped on her phone and called her editor's cell. "Sid, Justine. You got a minute?"

The booming voice of the fifty-ish, go-for-the-gusto editor answered loud and clear, "Sure, what's up?"

"I need another day or two here."

"Problems?"

"None to speak of, but I would like to take shots of them dismantling the powwow grounds on Sunday. I think seeing the remnants of the ceremonial grounds after the powwow will make a great ending to the story.

Think of it; I start with photos of the opening of the day parade, have all the extras in the middle, including the night parade and end with the exciting dismantling of the grounds. Sound good?"

"You can make anything sound good, Justine. You've shown me with your other assignments. I got the other pictures you sent over and they're terrific. See, I knew you would do the powwow justice—just like you did for the one in Arizona."

"I was glad for the opportunity. It'll take me another day to pack everything up and tie loose ends. Can I have until Wednesday, maybe?"

"We'll need to get those pictures in if it's a go for the first paper in September."

"It goes out mid-August anyway, and Wednesday will only be the ninth of the month, so there's time. You'll be really ecstatic with what I have. Come on, two more days, Sid."

"Fine, but your ass better be back here Wednesday morning."

"You really are a sweetheart, aren't you?"

"I try."

"First thing Wednesday. My ass and everything else will be on the plane. Promise."

She hardly wanted him to know that she needed more time with Darrius, so she had made it a business-only request. Darrius was her little secret, for as long as she could keep him a secret. The way things were developing between them, he would soon take over her life. And she would let him. Gladly.

She next called the airport and changed her ticket. She then took a long shower, sudsing up with the frankincense soap Darrius had bought her. She wanted to smell like heaven to him that night and dress to show she had an appreciation of his people's customs. Though she would wear the Crow Mother T-shirt, she would change into clean jeans and wear her new jewelry. And simply for his benefit, she would wear her hair tied back in a long braid, wrapped in a silver braid clasp—she wanted to look as traditional as possible. The squash blossom hairstyle wouldn't work for her; it stuck out way too far on the sides and made her ears look bigger than they already were. Besides, she knew the style was only for women with an impending marriage. She thought about the statement again. "Marriage, huh? Maybe the squash-blossom style is just what I'm looking for. If I'm married, wouldn't I have to stay with my husband no matter where he lived? I wouldn't have to worry too much about my career." She smiled, knowing she would never give up her career and would insist on having both it and Darrius. The idea of marrying so soon after meeting a man was a far-fetched one, but it amused her nonetheless. The long braid it was.

Justine entered Red Rock State Park by seven that evening, but deliberately did not look at the forbidden road that seemed to plague her each passing day. Instead, she checked her makeup in the rearview mirror and put on more Pink Passion lip gloss.

Once parked and inside the main arena, she looked down at her camera bag, hoping she'd be able to take more photos that night. That would be a fantastic added feature for the photo spread. What she really hoped for was to get more pictures Saturday night at the main event where Derrick would be dancing. His dancing would be part of the Palolokong performance; it was a traditional dance usually done on the mesas, but there would be a special performance for this year's powwow. Lucky for her she picked the right powwow and the right year. Also lucky for her she had the right spirit guide to tell her of such things—Darrius.

Minutes later, Darrius came up behind her holding a tray with two corn enchiladas, two bowls of buffalo stew and something hot in Styrofoam cups. "Right on time, as usual. How was your day?" he asked.

Justine spun around. She hated to think she was reacting like Pavlov's dog, but the sound of Darrius's voice could easily make her salivate. Her eyes widened at the sight of him. He gleamed, looking super healthy and sexy, with remnants of the fading sun shining against his dark hair. His turquoise necklace resting within the V of his half-opened shirt gleamed brilliantly against his honey-tinted skin. "Well, look at you. I love the feather in your hair and the fringes on your jeans. If I didn't know any better, I'd think you were here to dance."

"Hardly. You know my views on that subject." He saw the camera bag on her shoulder. "You know, you may not be able to use your camera tonight. The traditionals are very skeptical of cameras."

"I know, but maybe you can convince a few of them to give a poor working girl a shot."

"It's not a matter of convincing; more a matter of tradition. We'll see. Derrick may let you take some of him since he's the overseer of the performances this year."

"Really?"

"Maybe. Here, I brought food. I knew you'd be hungry, and you should have something in your stomach."

"I had a great lunch at The Ranch Kitchen."

"That's a great place to eat."

"Would have been better had you been able to join me."

"Lots of inventory at the Zuni store. Weren't you going to try to join me there?"

"Yes, but I got so busy with taking pictures of other stores. By the time I finished, I was so hungry that all I could think of was eating and then taking a nap. I wanted to look good and feel good tonight. I know it's not the main event, but I didn't want to be tired while watching other dances."

"The dances tonight are minor, though very spectacular. You'll have to get some rest before the ceremonies tomorrow night. They're long and you may be too taken with the dances to even think of anything else."

"You're a hell of a man to think of me like this." She took her bowl and enchilada and sat down with him.

Her smile persisted and Darrius stared at her. "What's on your mind other than food, girl?"

"There's something else I want." Her brows rose suggestively.

Darrius quickly caught the message. "Justine, we don't have time for the cave. Besides, it's too light out for that."

"A kiss, Darrius!"

"Oh, how could I forget? I've thought about kissing you all day. I get here and totally lose track. You look so beautiful."

Without responding to the compliment, she leaned into him, brushing her lips feverishly against his. Lips opened, and tongues wanted to play tag, but knowing they would draw a crowd, they quickly separated.

"Umm. Any more of that and I may just lead you into one of those caves."

"I'd let Darrius Red Sky do anything he wanted to, and whenever he wanted it. However, the buffalo stew is smelling mighty good."

"Let's eat." He then noticed the necklace. "Where'd you get the squash?"

"Peko's. You like?"

"He's a good guy. He has a marvelous store."

She teased. "Almost as good as yours?"

"Nothing is as great as my store—other than the woman who walked into it and made me fall in love. I think for the first time."

"What? Weren't you in love with Annie Oakley before she was hauled off to some prison in, where, Santa Fe?"

"A born kidder, aren't you?"

Justine smiled and shifted in her seat, feeling her heart warm a few degrees to his words. "Falling in love can be a wonderful feeling."

After taking a sip from his cola, he stared into her eyes. "Then I take it I have the same effect on you."

"I don't know. Love is an awfully strong word to use, but if the look in my eyes and this constant smile on my face is any indication, then—"

"There aren't any formations at this table, Justine. So, I guess I have my answer."

He kissed her hand, inhaling the scent of her frankincense soap. "I can't believe how quickly I've fallen for you. But I knew I would the minute I saw you."

"The air told you of my beauty?"

"This time you're right. I think this is destiny."

"I sure hope so, Darrius, because you're all I think about. Today at Peko's I saw a Koshari shirt and the face on it looked just like you, or so I thought. I see you in everything."

"Did you buy it?"

"Sure did, but I decided to wear the Crow Mother tonight and save Koshari for the big powwow tomorrow night."

"That's fitting. Was it hand-painted?"

"Yes. Do you know the artist?"

"Not sure." He remembered a man sitting in the audience painting shirts the night of the fatal dance accident. *Why would she have to buy that particular shirt?*

"I think the Koshari on the shirt is you."

"Could be anyone who portrays the Koshari; might even be Derrick."

"It looks like you."

"Whatever you say."

"I have something else to say to you, something you'll like, I hope."

"Yeah? What?"

"I convinced my boss to let me stay an extra day or two. I won't have to be back until Wednesday."

"That's great, darling. That'll give me more time to, you know, take advantage of you a whole lot more. You can go golfing with me on Monday."

"Great. I would love to. Maybe you can teach me a few things about golf."

Darrius looked at his watch. "We have twenty minutes before the first minor dance starts. After that, I need to take you home—alone. You're going to have a busy day tomorrow and again in the evening with the main powwow dances."

She pouted. "Will you come home with me? I know you won't show me your bedroom yet, but I can show you mine, even if it's only mine until Wednesday."

"That's an offer too tempting to pass on. You've got a deal, Ms. Justine Roberts-Paretti."

15

LORD OF THE DANCE

Saturday Night

Excitement was in the air as spectators hurried toward the main arena. Dancers were lined up at the entrance to the park awaiting the start of the Grand Entry, which consisted of the formal opening of the powwow.

Among the spectators were Justine and Darrius, holding hands and anticipating the start of the first of many performances that night. She held Darrius's hand and smiled at him. She didn't see the expression on his face that she had hoped to. As he looked at the dancers ready to walk into the arena, his expression had changed to that of being sullen. She thought maybe he was remembering what had happened to him years ago as he danced the famous trickster dance. Her objective that evening was to take his mind as much away from that as she possibly could. To help accomplish that, she wore more native attire, including the squash-blossom hair-style that she thought looked silly on her. She wore it anyway, along with fringed jeans and the Koshari T-shirt. She looked down at the shirt, thinking maybe wearing another shirt might have been better, but he said he liked it.

She clutched his hand tighter. "I'm so excited about tonight. This is the real deal, one of the main things I came here for." She reconsidered her words. "Actually, now that I've met you, the dance is the second-most important thing to me."

"Glad a mere mortal like me can have that kind of an effect on a goddess. I'm glad you're here. Grand Entry starts soon, and I want us to have a great spot. We should get as close to the front as possible. There are a lot of people here tonight."

"Why so close, though?" Justine asked, curious.

"So you can see everything. Also, having you at the front will make it easy for me to find you."

She quickly turned to him. "Aren't you going to be next to me?"

"Yes, but I have to help Derrick put on his paint for the dance. It won't take too long, and then I'll return to your side again. You're safe here."

"Well . . . if you say so."

"I do. You'll see some very interesting things tonight, and you'll be so close to them that you'll see them in your dreams. The traditional first song will start soon."

"Good. Can't wait to hear it."

"Every dancer and contributor enters the arena by this song."

"Even the Koshari?"

"Derrick will walk out, too, but not in the Koshari costume. Believe me, you will see plenty of that outfit soon."

Justine stood in amazement as the dancers walked into the middle of the arena. However, as the dancers walked in, Darrius's face seemed to express that he missed the dance, that it was something he was raised to do and understand in all of its intricate details. She felt sorry for him, wanted to find a way to help him, lighten his mood, but there was nothing she could do. If Darrius wanted to get over this, he would have to find a way, but she would always be willing to give him support.

She smiled and leaned into him. "Who will be the honoree this year?"

"You know about that?"

"Sure, I have studied the culture a bit before coming here. That's why I was so anxious to get the assignment, to learn more. I'm sure I will get a wealth of information tonight—to add to what I already know."

Darrius kissed her cheek. "There's plenty to see and learn here this evening. If there's anything you have questions about, just let me know. There are a lot of intricate moves and steps you may not be aware of; some are not mentioned in many of the reference books unless written by dancers. Basically, the powwow has turned into a competition to see who is best, who is the most creative, the most outstanding. Let's watch the Grand Entry. Each group of dancers enter the arena to the song. First the flag bearers enter and then the head dancers, veterans. But I'll explain it all when we see them. There's also contest and honor songs, like what you asked about a minute ago. Every year someone from around here has something to celebrate. This year Demario and Caitlyn are celebrating their marriage this October."

"Marriage, huh. Ever thought about marriage yourself?"

"Lately." He smiled and then turned to the dancers marching into the arena.

Justine smiled a secret smile herself, and then returned to the onslaught of dancers marching to distant drums.

Before the ceremonial dancing started, Darrius bought two more corn tamales with deer meat, sodas and bottled water.

He bit into his tortilla and wrapped his arm back around Justine's shoulder. "I know you're getting used to the taste of buffalo meat, but I figured you could use something different."

"I actually like it now. The taste was a little gamey at first, but it's good. Deer is good, too."

"Buffalo used to be our main meat."

"I know, from years ago."

"*Our* meat is all of us from the Paleo-Indians to the present. We are all one family."

Justine pointed into the crowd. "Look, the Northern Traditional Men Dancers. I was hoping they'd be here."

"And they are, of course."

Both watched as more dancers entered. They wore native outfits from beaded moccasins to beaded belts. What impressed Justine most were their headdresses, breechcloths and eagle-feathered fans.

After the Northern Traditional dancers came the Southern Straight, representing warriors on the lookout for enemies. They made Justine a little wary, causing her to shy away when a dancer came too close.

Darrius held her hand. "Don't be scared. They won't hurt you; I won't let them."

"I know I'm a little skittish, but their movements are so garish and rough, like the Famine dancer. He really scared me, but it was his purpose and I understand that."

"And like his was, this is only for show, darling. The dance lets people know what a real war party was like for Paleo-Indians."

Justine watched in a mix of wariness and amazement. Dancers wore mock animal skins, trailers, turbans and other traditional garb.

After the Southern Traditional dancers joined the others at the edge of the arena, the Grass Dancers began their march into the arena. Darrius introduced them. "What's coming out now is, I think, the oldest of the powwow dances—the Men Grass Dancers."

"What's their story? I do know it is one of the oldest dances, and I think that is what Derrick was doing the other day—it looks familiar."

"He does do the grass dance. It's essentially religious, and there are several accounts of its beginnings long ago. One account describes warriors in search of a place to practice their thanksgiving rituals and worship. The dancers move in the formation, swaying back and forth. Just watch, it actually describes itself—if one looks hard enough. We worship nature and are thankful for our home—the Earth."

Justine watched the graceful movements of the dancers as they offered their thanks to Mother Earth. A sense of calmness came over her as she listened to the sacred music accompanying the dance.

After the last women's Fancy Shawl dance ended an hour later, Darrius kissed her cheek. "Derrick is due up soon for the kachina dances. I shouldn't be too long."

"Can't I go with you?"

"Not this time. I'll be in the men's dressing tent. You wouldn't want to be in there with a bunch of sweaty men, would you?"

"I've seen the time when I would have said yes. Now the only man I want to see nude is you."

"And so you shall, but not now. I promise you'll be okay, and I'll be right back at your side." He stroked her chin, and then he walked off in the direction of the teepees.

Justine watched him walk off until he totally disappeared. She missed him already. And then she returned to the dancers, watching the women's Jingle Dress dance.

The night was hot and humid, and for the life of her, she couldn't understand how all the dancers made it through the night wearing such heavy costumes. The Jingle Dress dancers were no exception, coming out in full regalia with bells and thimbles. She had read about the tradition of the Jingle Dance and knew it originated as a kind of medicine for curing a variety of ailments in the old days. The dancers twisted their feet in unison to the right and left while moving sideways.

Darrius hadn't returned after nearly half an hour, but she stayed where she was. She could see the heat in the air, could smell smoke from food stands and watched the differing dances with acrobatics. It gave the appearance of a large, outdoor cookout. She rubbed her eyes to get a clear view of the arena, and was ready to see the antics of the kachina dances. The 'traditional' kachina dances didn't normally take place at powwows, more so inside kivas and on mesas, but as Darrius said earlier, the kachina dances were involved this time for added enjoyment and also to teach lessons not normally learned at traditional powwows. It had been Derrick and a few others' decision to include the kachinas this time; it made for a more spectacular event, and Justine felt honored to be able to experience it. During her brief stay, she had gotten a few good shots. All in all, everything she had experienced had been worth the trip.

She stood on the sidelines of the arena watching the nominations for the contest songs. Once the nominations, which were based on creativity, beat and timing, were announced, the traditional dancing was soon over. Everyone returned to the arena before the start of the famous kachina dance. From what she had read and learned from Darrius, it was a serious ceremony, but had its share of levity—at the hands of the Koshari.

Darrius returned with cups of tea for the both of them. "Glad you stayed put. The dance is about to start."

"I told you I would go nowhere without you, but why hot tea on a hot night like this?"

He stared at her blankly for a moment, and then remembered what he was supposed to say to her. "This is the real Teepee Dreams tea that I didn't give you the other night. It's to get you in the mood for after the dance."

"Why? What's going on after the dance?"

"Us, as soon as we leave the park."

"Care to show me a little bit before the ceremony?"

"Can't. We should concentrate on the dance or we'll miss something."

"I think snuggling against you is worth missing a few things."

"Not tonight. Not yet, anyway."

She sensed his apprehension, but kissed his cheek anyway. "Umm, you taste great. I'm always in the mood for you!"

He pulled back, confusing her more. "Are you okay, Darrius?"

"Sure. Why?"

"Just seem a little distant all of a sudden."

"I'm fine, just excited about the dancing. Want food, bathroom, or anything before it starts?"

"No, I'm fine. I sneaked off to the bathroom during the Shawl Dance."

"Good girl."

Justine watched him for a few seconds longer as he stared into the large crowd. She wondered if he was fearful that his brother's dance would end in tragedy, as his did. Then she thought for a moment. *Derrick has*

*danced many times before. What would make Darrius
nervous about this all of a sudden?* Discarding the idea as a
figment of her imagination, she, too, stared out at the
crowd.

The lights flickered off and on and Darrius took her
hand. "Ready to see my brother do what he does best?"

"More than ready."

The announcer stood in the middle of the arena
dressed as the Crow Mother kachina. Justine listened
carefully as he explained the ceremony, what would be
happening and who would be represented. In the background, she saw some of the arena.

Darrius whispered in her ear. "What you see now is
considered the Guard Kachinas."

"I know. Remember, I told you I've done some
reading about kachinas?"

"Oh?

"Darrius, I know you remember me telling you that."

"Just kidding. Wanted to test your knowledge. Then
since you're so smart, tell me who you see."

"I see the Broad-Faced kachina—"

"What does he do?"

Why was he questioning her? To test her?

She took a deep breath. "Well, if you insist on my
telling you. He has something to do with being on all
mesas during the bean dance, and he's a guard. He keeps
a close eye on the Palolokong dances."

"That's some of it."

"Any more questions?"

"Yeah, who are the others in the center now?"

Barely able to take her eyes from him due to his rapid-fire questions, she stared into the circle and pointed. "Well, I think I see Warrior Woman."

"Right. H'e-e'-e, is the native name. Who else?"

"Can't I just watch the ceremony?"

"Sure, but name two more for me and I'll leave you alone."

"I don't want to be left alone, Darrius. I just want to enjoy the ceremony, maybe have *you* tell me a few things I don't know. I see Toho, Ahote and Ewiro. Hey, doesn't Ewiro guard the clowns?"

"You're right. You *do* know a lot about my customs and beliefs."

"Comes from growing up with native children. I've seen their kachina dolls before, but when I was a child, I never could fully understand the lessons the doll represented, no matter how much the native children explained them to me. Can I watch the ceremony now? They're really getting into it."

"I suppose."

"Good. Wrap your arms around me and tell me everything."

He did as asked, but he held her loosely, as if he had left his feelings for her inside Derrick's teepee. No matter how she tried getting closer to him, he kept his distance. It almost brought her to tears. This from a man who talked of marriage only an hour or two before. This from a man she made love to on a horse, of all things.

During a break in the kachina dances, she caught a glimpse of frantic antics from another kachina. Darrius whispered in her ear, "Here's your boy."

Her eyes lit as the Koshari pranced into the arena, immediately followed by Ewiro. "Wow, it really is him!"

Koshari danced his way into the arena sporting the rhythmic style and agility of an African tribal dancer and the ease and depth of a ribbon dancer. Justine stood there in Darrius's arms, amazed that she was actually seeing her favorite kachina perform. She had no idea Derrick had so much soul in his movements. He was fascinating to watch as he chased several of the guard kachinas around the area. "I . . . I had no idea he could move like that. He's awesome."

"He's incredible at what he does; the best dancer I've ever seen."

Only the Koshari could rid her mind of Darrius and his sudden distance. Koshari was a feast to the eyes, something she had always wanted to see since seeing her first Koshari clown as a child. Now she was witness to him, seeing him in the flesh, dancing like a wild man— an erotic wild man. His moves were so smooth, almost sexual, that she nearly felt ashamed to watch him in the company of Darrius—almost. He was lyrical in movement. The man painted in white and black stripes with tassel hat mesmerized her beyond reason.

Koshari was on the other side of the arena in front of a group of fans who were egging him on. Apparently, they knew his antics and wanted him to display the actions of a very un-Hopi-like individual. He brought a lesson, that of being the last person to be like, and thus avoid being shunned from the group. He was a glutton, an antagonist, a . . . clown who exemplified all rude behavior; the lesson was exaggerated in dance. He did it so well.

Justine watched him as he doused the guards and onlookers with buckets of water. His fruit tossing made a slimy mess of many people, and Justine was amused enough to actually want to be part of the action. He was the most amazing character she'd ever seen.

The way his body moved heightened his physical strength, and from as far away as the opposite side of the arena she could see his muscles. His bulging thigh muscles under the breechcloth excited her. His nude, striped torso rippled with each heavy bucket of water he tossed. The way he ran, stretching his long, lean, well-toned legs almost made her own legs weak. If only she could see Darrius like that. Being a twin to this fabulous dancer and witness to his sexual strength, she knew he could dance just as provocative and be just as stimulating.

Darrius was clearly enthralled by his brother's dance. His expression said he was itching to do the same. She held his hand tighter, kissing it. The kiss made him antsy for some reason, and he continued to avoid her.

Justine returned her attention to the amazing dancer. Koshari had proceeded to paw at the audience, traipsing around the left side of the arena in a frantic search for a victim. He stopped in front of a young woman, pulled her into the crowd and dowsed her with the remaining bucket of water. The poor young woman just stood there, not knowing what to do with her wet clothing as Koshari danced around her, tossing more fruit, making a mess of his unwilling participant. Suddenly, Koshari decided to show his true prowess by lifting the young woman above his head, stunning the audience. The crowd oohed and aahed, and at the same time Darrius's hand gripped hers tighter, nervous. Apparently, once Derrick hoisted the woman it brought on visions of what had happened that night eight years back. Justine looked up at Darrius; his eyes were fixed on the action.

"Are you thinking about what happened when you did that?" Apparently, the accident was very much on his mind, and she wanted to make him feel at ease. It didn't work. His jaw tightened, his muscles clenched and his eyes stayed fixed on the field.

"Darrius? Are you okay?"

"I'm . . . yeah. He hasn't done that in years."

"I thought it was part of his act."

"Not usually."

"Don't worry. He's doing a great job."

That produced a smile. "He sure is, isn't he?"

They watched Derrick totally embarrassing the young woman as he slowly lowered her to the ground. As he did, Justine noticed the rippling muscles in his back accentuated by the black and white paint and how his muscled arms constricted, showing off pure power! His bare feet stood sturdy on the lumpy dirt, his legs straining even though he tossed her body around as though she were a rag doll.

In the midst of the frolicking, his tasseled hat fell to the ground; again, Darrius's grip on her tightened. She knew why. The night the girl died, his hat had fallen, too.

He quickly retrieved the hat, replaced it, returned the girl safely to the audience and continued his prancing.

Derrick moved closer to her side, teasing the audience, egging them on as they dared him. There was nothing the guard kachinas could do to stop him because he was, at that point, sheer energy. Justine could feel the heat in her shirt and panties just watching him. Why would he have to be Derrick?

Justine cringed when Koshari moved closer to her side of the arena. She did not want to be pulled into the action, no matter what she may have thought just minutes ago.

Her back was pressed against Darrius's chest, inching away, yet he failed to hide her. He pushed her forward. "What's wrong? I thought you liked Koshari?"

"I—do, but he's coming closer. He's a little too up close and personal."

"So what?"

Not a typical response from her lover. "What? What are you saying?"

"He's not going to hurt you, Justine. Get up close; take a good look at the legend you have wanted to see since childhood. You did say that, didn't you?"

"Yeah, but—"

Koshari was now before her, smelling of watermelon, sticky from heat and a combination of sticky-sweet delights. His eyes focused on her, his chest heaving.

Ahote, a hunter kachina, came to her rescue, but Koshari pushed him aside as if tossing a bag of feathers away. That's how strong and how determined Koshari was to obtain his ultimate kill. His ultimate thrill.

Justine pushed her shivering body against Darrius's for whatever protection she could get. Just as she thought she saw a way out around Darrius, Koshari grabbed her arm, pulling her mercilessly into the crowd and into his muscled, fruit-tainted lair.

She reached back for Darrius to save her, but all he did was stand there smiling, his hands thrust deeply into his pockets. It was as if he wanted her to be tossed into the air and humiliated. Though the dancer was Derrick and not Darrius, couldn't the same thing happen to his brother—to any dancer? She was in the clutches of a purposeful maniac. It was his job to be insane, crazy, intimidating, silly. Then why did she like the Koshari so much? *Because, despite his aggressive and unscrupulous behavior, he excited her.*

Something about a wild and aggressive man had always tempted her, and this time he was hidden behind a façade, something she would like to look at hard to see his distinct features. She did not plan to get close enough to Derrick to see anything. Wouldn't that make Darrius jealous? Sure. The way he was acting, standing there on the sidelines laughing as his apparent girlfriend getting humiliated; he needed to be jealous. *Jerk!*

But was it *really* important enough to have her body twisted and conforming to the body of another just to make Darrius jealous? Again, sure! The only thing, she'd have to get rid of her nervousness and let this man, this brother of her lover, touch and caress her body much the same way a lover would, only on an exhibitionism-type scale. Would her nerves allow it? She was soon to find out, because Derrick's strong arms were lifting her to the stars as others laughed.

Before she realized anything, she was face to face with the stars, up so high in the man's arms that the ground was a world away. Fear was her first reaction, but then she remembered what she wanted to do—make Darrius jealous, and prove to him that she could relax in the arms of another man. The trick was how to do it. Her heart rate soared and she could hear the laughter of the audience; she assumed Darrius's laugh was mixed in somewhere. The silver bracelet resting partially against her and partially dangling felt like it weighed a ton, as did her precious squash necklace. She couldn't do it, she was too scared and had decided to give in to Darrius—let him win, in a way.

Her body seemed to relax, suddenly just as limp as a rag doll. Her mind had relaxed due to over stimulation. There was too much going on and shutdown was the only recourse.

With her eyes now staring at the sky, her body felt relaxed, and the ground seemed so far away. Koshari slowly lowered her to his midsection, and she felt the power of his erection practically bursting through the covered jockstrap. At that moment, not a thought was given to the scores of people watching them.

There was utter attraction between them heightened by Derrick squeezing and manipulating her to his pleasure. She could hear the audience cheering for this barbarian, this utter heathen, and her loins were now ablaze.

With his knee now between her thighs, she could feel him pressing hard, felt that tremendously muscular thigh edging itself closer to her sex. His body rocked hers back and forth, causing sensations to rush through her that she didn't want to have with Derrick. What on earth was he doing to her? Was he even conscious of what he was doing to her in front of so many people? Surely, his mind had been stolen by the dance. By that moment in time, however, her mind's eye saw him as Darrius.

Nothing mattered now, she was in this hooligan's arms and there was nothing she could do about it. She continued to relax against him, knowing he would never hurt her.

The very shirt made in his image was now soaked with sweat, both his and hers, and traces of watermelon were pressed firmly against them both. The outline of her erect nipples poked through the fabric for any and all to see. Only one set of eyes truly saw—the Koshari's! It was both embarrassing and exhilarating.

Not caring who saw what at this point, the Koshari's hands touched and rubbed her breasts, making the hardened buds reach to him. Fingers of one hand moved towards her heated core. His thigh inched closer as well, feeling her fire, thirsting for it—wanting to mate with the thick, liquid center and have it drip all over him. He didn't care who she was, or who she belonged to now. Darrius was but a mere obstacle in the way of attaining pure sexual relief.

Their eyes met again, and only then did she have the common sense to look squarely into the face of the giver. Eyes circled with black paint looked, for some reason, lighter in hue than Derrick's darker eye color. Was it her imagination, or was she seeing who she *really* wanted manipulating her? Mind tricks. She glanced to the audience and saw Darrius looking amused.

Casting her attention back to Koshari, she saw tiny laugh lines most unnoticed on Derrick. His full mouth encircled with heavy black paint, but with rosy, full lips aching for the touch of other human skin—hers. His jet hair flowed down his back and across his shoulders in tangled, wet masses, yet illuminated by the arena spotlights. In the thick of dust, heat, wetness and paint, this Koshari managed to look like the epitome of sexual exertion. Justine loved it; she was no longer afraid of being so close to the action.

Those perfect rosy male lips brushed against her cheek as he bent over her, moving in a frenzied dance of copulation, and her limp body followed his rugged, full-body strokes up and down.

He was truly *her* Darrius. At first, she thought her mind had gone—seeing a man in her arms who was supposed to be in the audience. That explained why he had acted so strange next to her, not wanting to kiss her. Now, the right man definitely wanted to; his jig was up.

The heat of his lips against her cheek and lips fumed her. His sweat-tainted fragrance fueled her, making her thighs part wider for his access. They both wanted it, and in front of everyone. That was the very sad part. She wasn't into exhibitionism, but with this particular clown, she would do anything to please him—even be made a fool of.

Koshari stood erect, looked at the crowd and saw their flushed faces. They were all waiting for the next act, the live sex show. But it wasn't that kind of party, and he was overcome with embarrassment. He lowered Justine to her feet and stared at her. Their bodies were still touching, still emitting a combination of heat, seduction and everything associated with sexuality. His thick manhood tented the garment. His well-contoured chest heaved up and down, expanding muscles and the painted black flowers around his nipples. He asked in a hushed voice, "Are you still afraid, Justine?"

"No," she replied, her voice low.

"Tell me why?"

"Because I know you."

"Then who am I?"

"Only one man has lips like yours. Only one man has a speck of blue in one of his light brown eyes. Yes, I noticed that just a minute ago, but you had me fooled for a while. How would I have explained enjoying your brother's exotic caresses so much? Surely, you saw how my body responded to his; how I relaxed and let him do pretty much anything he wanted to me, and in front of this crowd. I couldn't have delivered a believable explanation to you, but thankfully I no longer have to."

"When did you really find out it was me?"

"When I relaxed and went with the flow. Darrius, only one man has a touch like yours. You can seduce me anywhere, any time, day or night."

"And I plan to, my love. Every chance I get."

The crowd began to clap and cheer, trying their best to bring Darrius and Justine out of their reverie. It didn't work. Darrius continued to hold her close, almost whispering. "I didn't embarrass you too much in the beginning, did I?"

"Sure you did, and I was scared. All I could think of was that poor woman who died during your dance. Did you think of her, too?"

"Only for a few minutes, but when I took you into my arms, nothing else mattered but doing this the right way, and with the right woman."

"Am I the right woman, Darrius?"

"You know better than to ask me that."

A smile crept across her paint-smeared face. "What an idiot you are to fool me like this, Darrius. But the worst part was that I kissed your brother thinking he was you."

"So long as he didn't like it."

"He did."

"Figures. He's always been a sly fox. Come, let's join everyone before the natives get even more restless. Oh, but one thing first! I have to complete my mission or I will never be considered a true Koshari dancer."

"What would that be?" she asked.

He picked up a large bucket of water. "This, but I'll be glad to dry you off when we get home."

"Darrius, you better not dare." She tried to run but he caught her by the shirttail and dowsed her. For good measure, he tossed bits of melon at her. "Now you're a real victim of the Koshari."

Darrius returned her to the sideline, back to his brother/partner in crime, and then ran after the squirrel kachina to complete the ceremony.

16

FAMILY TIES

Relief mixed with anger, Justine playfully punched Derrick in the stomach. "You and that damn Darrius planned the whole thing, didn't you?"

"Yeah, and it worked. You should have seen your face when he pulled you into the arena."

"Didn't I look like a perfect version of a ripe tomato, ready to burst?"

"You did, but try not to hate me too much. Darrius told me the story of your not wanting to get too close to the dancers, despite being a fantastic photographer. What's the deal with that?"

She straightened the front of her now wet Koshari shirt and brushed strands of hair from her face. "The Famine dancer scared me the other day, and with Darrius pulling me into the arena, it made me think about him. Besides, when photographing landscapes, you don't have to fear being made a fool of."

"But you snap more than landscapes."

"True, but until coming here I had no fear of being pulled into the action. I was always left alone to do my thing."

One look at Derrick told her that he only half believed her do-my-thing story.

"What else are you scared of?"

"How do you know I'm scared of anything else?"

"Just a guess. Crowds can be hard if you're not used to them."

"The crowds are fine. Naturally, they would be since I also take pictures of things other than landscapes. That can be scary at times, too. I don't let that stop me, though. I can't."

"Whatever the case, I think you may have helped Darrius get over his reluctance to dance."

"I sure hope so. He's so good at it."

"I take it he told you the story of the girl who died at the powwow."

"Yeah. How sad."

"Because of that, he'd never considered dancing again, though he loves it so much. He's the most graceful and poetic dancer I've ever seen. I think he should do more kachina dances."

She looked at Derrick skeptically. "What about not exploiting sacred dances for outsiders?"

"True. He thinks dances should be educational as well as enjoyable. Powwows can be educational for those ready to learn about another culture. That's why he comes to them. Now he may be dancing in more of them, thanks to you."

"I'm glad."

"Some dances are kept from outsiders and will never be seen at open powwows. They were originally done in kivas, an underground gathering place back in the old times. So, yes, there are dances none of us will do in public. But he was using that excuse mostly to hide behind his self-doubt."

"Possible. When is Darrius coming back? I'd like to get out of these wet clothes."

"Soon. The dances are mostly over, but there is the—" Sounds of the host drum ensemble, Southern Splendor, who were located behind the large arena, took his attention. "The drummers are starting up again. This means they're going to do either an honor song or a giveaway."

Derrick was pointing at a large group of drummers standing in a circle. Several drums had paintings of sacred animals. "A giveaway? What are they giving away?"

"A particular person is selected for one reason or another—maybe someone who helped with setup; a needy family or someone who is to be honored for some other reason. They are presented with things from money, housing or whatever." Squinting, he stared into the audience, his voice now a whisper. "I—I just don't know who the honoree is this year. I know of no family in need other than the multitudes who are always in need in the area. There is a wedding, but the couple is honored with a song."

Justine looked around but did not know exactly what to look for. "Can I at least take a few pictures?"

"It would be okay now to do that."

Quickly, she grabbed her camera bag from the ground and hung her camera around her neck. She stooped and took pictures of the dancers still in costume.

When she heard the beating of drums, she looked up from the camera in time to see Darrius walking into the arena. There was something in his arms covered by a muted color shawl. *What? What is he doing now?*

The host drum ensemble, Southern Splendor, maintained the drums in a melodic, sensual tempo that matched every barefoot step Darrius took. Being a true photographer, she snapped a few photos of him as he approached a man in the audience holding a cane.

She watched as Darrius handed the man a metal sculpture of a war hero bearing a flag. Then the coordinator returned to the microphone, saying, "This year, our honoree is Justin Fleming, who returned home in one piece after risking his life in Iraq for the sake of America." Everyone clapped and cheered and Justine continued with her photographing, knowing this would be a great picture to add to the others of this very special powwow. She saw Justin's mother, Rita, the woman who had served them at the Eagle Café. Then she remembered the story of her son returning home alive. She smiled and knew that if anyone would be the honoree, it *should* be him.

After the cheers subsided, Justine saw Darrius walking in her direction with something else in his arms still covered. She looked at Derrick. "What is he doing now?"

"He also has something for you."

"Me? But why? I'm certainly no hero." She looked around the arena as people began to congratulate Justin. Then she looked straight into Darrius's eyes. He was still in the Koshari costume, wet, sticky and looking a total mess. Then again, to her, he was perfect.

She stood to greet him, smiling. "What do you have covered in that beautiful shawl?"

"Please, accept my gift to you.," he said, placing the item into her trembling hands. "Unveil it."

Justine removed shawl and revealed the most exquisitely carved Koshari clown she had ever seen. He was a miniature of a real man. The delicate cottonwood figure had the musculature, proportioned paint, tasseled hat and face paintings of the one on her shirt. Justine looked up at Darrius, speechless.

"I haven't done anything to deserve—"

"Don't say a word, darling. I originally had him carved for myself by my main man Frederic K, the most talented carver I know. But now he's yours. I want you to have him. Cherish him."

Justine's voice was choked with emotion. "But . . . why?"

"Because I'm in love, Justine. This is a first for me."

He moved into her, taking her jaw into his warm hand. "I love you. I've never really wanted to love again since my last relationship, but it has happened, and I'm glad. You complete me. I felt it as you rode the plane into my land—into my heart. I beckoned you."

"You beckoned me. I know. I felt it the day I looked into your face, Darrius."

He gently kissed her lips, holding her slightly around the hips. When the kiss broke, their eyes locked for an eternity.

Finally, Justine's voice creaked, penetrating the muggy warm air around them. "What's next for us tonight?"

"Meeting my family."

"They're here?"

"Always here for Derrick and me. Only this time, I'm the main attraction—next to you. Now, answer one important thing for me. Are you still scared because of the famine dancer?"

"No, I'm no longer scared. He was only a dancer. Sometimes I can get spooked by unusual things."

"Understandable. So, will you meet my family?"

"It'll be my honor."

"Do you like the kachina?"

"I love him."

"And me?"

She kissed his lips once more. "I think I do."

"Good enough—for now. Come, meet the rest of me."

Hand in hand, the couple, along with Derrick, walked across the arena. Justine felt as though she was meeting the first family of New Mexico. Maybe she was.

In a little huddle stood two women and two men. Justine knew they had to be his family because they were the only ones waiting aside from all the action. She felt uncertainty rising again—not the fear of utter terror, but the fear of not fitting in. Although Darrius was a man who meant everything to her and made her feel like a queen, there was that little matter of withstanding a family's scrutiny. After all, she wasn't Native American. But what should it matter? She wanted to fit in, live her life with him. As far as she was concerned, nothing would get in her way. Yet, there they stood, four pairs of eyes watching their approach.

Her nerves seemingly tightening into knots, she let Darrius lead her into the middle of their group. She waited for Darrius to speak first, looking from member to member. His mother, a delicately framed woman, was as beautiful as she was dainty. Her hair was pulled into a bun at the nape of her neck and secured with a hummingbird clasp. Her clothing was airy and simple, consisting of a silk-flower blouse and denim skirt. The twins looked like her.

His father was a tall, thin man who wore the traditional Western attire—bandana shirt, battered cowboy hat, jeans and boots so pointy they could have been considered 'roach-killers' in certain circles. His complexion was dark—dark caramel, like his twin sons, and his silver feather chains hung down the front of his shirt. He was very, very handsome.

Their brother, Jemez, was a younger version of Darrius and Derrick, but he also looked like their mom. He, too, was a tall, slender man with a flow of dark hair down his back. From the looks of him, he would never be seen in traditional Indian attire. No, he was decidedly contemporary in his jeans and white T-shirt with a Discman hanging from his belt. His eyes were darker, more mysterious looking than his brothers'. Now she knew why he was considered the trickster of the bunch, even more so than Derrick. His eyes gave him away, told of the levity within him. He, too, was very handsome.

Standing next to her father was the favorite of the family, the delicate rosebud, the pride—Asinka. She was as lovely as Darrius had said she was. Her long dark hair rested against her back in a loose knot. Within the mix of soft wave and endless dark layers were several kachina-shaped hairpieces, including one Justine recognized as Crow Mother. She was the one who epitomized a blend of tradition and the Western world. Though she wore jeans, her top was poncho-style in desert colors of rust, sand, turquoise and green. All the colors spiraled in unison, making a 3-D pattern. Around her neck was a double-strand necklace of coral and jet nuggets, draping down her neck and into the delicate V of her breast. Asinka was, by far, the most beautiful female Justine had ever seen. Her eyes were big and dark, her cheekbones were prominent, her lips full.

This was his family, and all were part of one another.

"Well, everyone, here she is."

Justine saw the sheepish smile on Darrius's face and was reminded of a teenager introducing his first girl to the folks; much like the smile her brother Justin had the night of his prom. Darrius's words even sounded school-boyish, but she loved them.

"What do you think of her?"

His mother stepped forward and held her hand out. "I am very pleased to meet you, Justine. My son speaks so well of you. We had to come and see for ourselves. Well, we did have ulterior motives. Darrius is quite the dancer, isn't he?"

Almost speechless, Justine spoke up. "He really did fool me. I'd heard he was a wonderful dancer, but feared I would never see for myself."

At that, Darrius brought her closer. "Dad, Justine."

Drake Red Sky had penetrating eyes that looked at her as if sizing up what kind of a woman she really was. After the intense once-over he wrapped his arms around her and gave her a big hug. She then relaxed. "I'm so glad to meet you, Mr. Red Sky." If the parents were pleased, so was she.

"We were anxious to see Darrius carry out his plan to perform his Koshari dance. I'm so proud of both sons and how they dance." He glanced sideways at Jemez. "If only we could get this one to follow suit."

Donning a nonchalant expression, Jemez spoke up. "Come on, Dad, you know I won't dance, but I am proud to meet the one woman who has made my brother dance again. You must be a heck of a woman. Pleased to meet you."

Realizing she had hardly spoken, she stepped back, smiling. "This has been the best night of my life. I've wondered about all of you, and wanted to meet the family who produced the man who has taken my breath away." She shook every hand, but when she came to Asinka, the girl stood motionless for seconds, silent. She spoke only after Darrius gave her the okay to. To Justine it seemed as though her brother had to give her permission, but sensed that wasn't the case.

Darrius touched Justine's shoulder. "My sister is very shy."

"Darrius has been the love of her life since she was three," her mother explained. "Now seeing him with another woman is rather—well, hard, for lack of a better word."

"That's not it, Mom." Finally, her little wings spread, and Asinka took Justine's hand. "I *am* pleased to meet you." She brought out a covered item from inside her poncho. "I made this for you. It's not as grand as what Darrius gave, but . . . I hope you like it."

Justine graciously accepted it, touched by the unexpected kindness of the teenaged girl. "I . . . like it already. What is it?"

Asinka lifted the covering and handed her a small totem of a turtle—the Picasso marble totem lay flat in her hand. Her voice soft and clear, she said, "He's a very special totem, and I think he represents you well."

A confused Justine asked, "Represents me? What do you mean?"

"Don't you like him?"

Justine ran her fingers over the glassy surface of the turtle. "I love it. Picasso marble is one of my favorite stones."

"He's more than marble. The turtle teaches us to be careful in new situations, to be patient while we await our goals."

Darrius cut in to explain what his sister was trying to convey. "The turtle teaches us to take things slow, something both you and I aren't very good at, right?"

"But I like what we have, Darrius."

"So do I, but this totem says we should go slowly, for it gives us time to figure out if we need to protect ourselves or go forward. That's for any situation, not just what we share, Justine. It applies to both of us—our endeavors, journeys, our trek through life."

She moved closer to his ear, whispering, "Don't you still love me like you said a few minutes ago?"

"Never question that, my love. I'm simply saying we should take it slower, work things out before we fall in heart first all the way."

"I'm willing to try." She took a closer look at the turtle and then asked, "Does it mean all that?"

"Afraid so."

Asinka rejoined the conversation. "This is a strange land to you, Justine. You don't know the area legends, the mystique. Yes, New Mexico is very beautiful, but there are ways of the land that must be followed. Think about where you go, what you discover. That's what's most important. The turtle will be your guide."

Asinka looked at Darrius and smiled. "As for you, I have a gift for you as well. You conquered a giant dilemma, and we're proud of you." She watched her father and brothers exchange manly ribbing and punches. It was always a happy moment for her when she saw Darrius smile. Asinka had seen the despair caused by his failed relationships and his reluctance to do what he had loved so much—dancing.

Amidst the laughter, Darrius stepped over to his sister, who held out another covered item. "What do you have for me? The turtle is not exactly my totem."

"Indeed it isn't," she said, handed him the object.

Darrius stared at a magnificently carved dragonfly. "Wow! This is great."

"I thought it was appropriate because I know you, what you think, who and what you think about." Her eyes cut quickly to Justine and then back to Darrius. "I think you will need this one day."

Darrius and Justine examined the totem. "Did you carve this as well?"

"No. I cheated with yours and bought it at Elliot's Trading Post."

At last, the beautiful girl smiled and it lit up her face. Indeed, beauty ran in their family—for both men and women. But one thing was as clear as glass: She had to be part of Darrius's life, hook or crook! Justine looked at her turtle totem again, and then placed Darrius's next to it in her hand. "They're a complete team, land, sea and air."

"Yes, complete, like us."

Feeling the family's eyes on him as he stared into the face of his lover, he quickly moved back. "I'm in sticky paint, sweaty and standing next to a woman in wet clothing. I think it's time to depart and look human again. You agree, Justine?"

"Wholeheartedly. It's been very nice meeting you all and, I hope to see you again before I leave in a few days."

She and Darrius then joined hands and headed for his truck. Before they got in, Justine looked at him rather anxiously. "Are you not sure about your relationship with me? We *have* only known one another for almost a week."

"Justine, don't let the totems and time frames fool you. I love you and nothing will ever change that. What I mean by taking things slow is just that—getting to know one another more completely. I hope you understand that."

"I do. I just wanted to be sure of your feelings."

"They're intact."

Once inside the truck, she asked, "Aren't you going to get your clothes from Derrick?"

"Why would I? I certainly won't need them tonight." He wriggled his brows at her and smiled. "Know what I mean?"

"I do. Start the truck. Now! Baby has a mighty big appetite tonight."

17

PLEASURE PRINCIPLE

"Did I fail to tell you that you were fantastic tonight?" Justine asked.

With his eyes still fixed on the road, he answered lightheartedly. "You can always tell me again."

"I will. You were—"

"Better yet, show me."

"Right now?"

"Yeah. I saw how you looked at my breechcloth even though, at the time, you thought I was Derrick."

"You're right. I'm sure family traits go beyond hair color and perfect teeth, but you're the only Red Sky I truly want to experience—again."

"Then give me something that can satisfy me until we get home."

"While you drive? What if you crash the truck?"

"Then we'll die in seventh heaven, right?"

"What about my totem that says to take things slowly?"

"Baby, that doesn't apply to everything; we've already done the deed. Besides, I'm only asking for a kiss."

Trying her best to avoid taking him on in the dead of night on a lonely stretch of highway, she looked through her window. In the distance were mountains that looked like crouching giants; their dark, deeply rooted forestry looked as though they had eyes, eyes that could see her kissing her lover, getting her fill of him—delighting in his pleasures. Yes, she had been taken by his breechcloth, knew the power beyond it and wanted more of it, then as well as now.

Her eyes returned to his profile, observing the keenness of his features, the beauty of his blue-black hair as it blew in the wind. She wanted him more and more. "Just a kiss, right?"

He looked as though he were about to say something grand, but only said, "I promise nothing more—at least until we're in the shower."

"There is no such thing as having *just* a kiss when it comes to you, but I'm going to trust your word this time. Pull over; can't have you killing us over one kiss."

"One of my kisses will kill you—but it's a lovely death, my sweet Justine."

"I like the sound of that."

Darrius pulled over and indulged her in a kiss that was so dangerous that he knew he would lose control of the situation if he wasn't careful. However, he wanted to do more, could feel his breechcloth tenting the deeper he kissed her. They were alone, it was dark and no one was around for miles, yet this wasn't the place. Justine was a special person and she deserved having more than a quickie in the middle of nowhere, New Mexico.

But then he realized that in her arms, there was no such place as "nowhere." He was everywhere with one single touch of her precious hands. Her breasts felt like heaven in his hands; the feel of her still damp hair against his neck and shoulders almost made him weak from want. He slowly drew back and stared into her eyes. "I can't believe how amazing you are. Are you a dream?"

"A dream is the last thing I am, Darrius."

"Whatever you are, I need you in my life, and nothing less will ever do."

"Then let's not stop. Let's enjoy the moment a little longer, explore. We're completely alone and there is no one around to tell on us," she said. "We can have each other now—and later."

"But it will be so much better in my bed."

"You mean I finally get to see the bed that envelops this precious body?"

"I told you we were going home."

"I know, but I somehow assumed we were going back to my hotel room. You've been so secretive about this bedroom of yours."

"Best of all, we will have the entire night to do exactly what we want to do. No interruptions, no ringing phones or doorbells." He cradled her face in his hands. "I have gifts for you tonight, my love. Not just any gifts but physical ones, sexual ones—ones you will never forget. It all starts with a bubble bath, candlelight, me and you."

"And after that?"

"Hot, wet sex! The wettest and hottest that you've probably ever experienced."

"Then start the truck and let's get a move on."

He gave her a short, sweet kiss. "I knew you would see things my way."

One disheveled clown holding hands with a wet girl wearing a clown shirt finally made it to his garage. A perfect match—a hot, perfect match, and they were crazy for one another. They went to the stalls to check on Darrius's horses one more time before going into the house. The beautiful show horses were sound asleep in the middle of large hay beds. Darrius tenderly brushed the mane of the silver horse with the back of his hand.

Watching Darrius tenderly stroke the animal made Justine think of how he touched her, how he made her feel special. He had been the first man to actually show her the kind of tenderness a man is supposed to show a woman. Love was the key word—loved. Yes, he'd admitted it. Love didn't have to take years or months to develop; and Darrius had proved this in a matter of days.

Her arm rested around his hip. "You really love those horses, don't you?"

"Sure do. All of them. From the moment I saw Gecko three years ago. I already had the other two. I feel the same about you."

"I don't know where I rank in that answer. You've just equated me with horses."

"Well, think about it this way, you are wild, like them."

"Only at heart."

"I beg to differ. Girl, you ride me like you've lost your mind. And I love it."

"So do I."

"I love all things, Justine, from the smallest of animals to very smart, beautiful women. I have an affection for love, I guess." He walked over to another horse, James, and patted his mane. "James, here, actually had a brother. I bought them both at the same time. Billy died in a riding accident. He broke a leg in several places, where I only bruised my side."

Her arm wrapped tighter around him. "Glad you made it out alive."

"It killed me having to shoot Billy. That's why I take such good care of these. Now I want to take care of you. What I said tonight was true, Justine. I'm in love with you. I think I always have been. It's like I conjured you here, worked some kind of magic, because before I knew it, there you were. I didn't want to accept the fact that I was immediately attracted to you, but after seeing you . . . I couldn't help myself."

"Do you really think you used powers to get me here? Because all of a sudden I got the assignment, though I had lobbied for it."

"I prayed. I went out alone to the mountain because my heart was heavy for some reason. There wasn't anything wrong, but I just knew something was missing. Fasting on that mountaintop and talking to my ancestors helped me discover what was really wrong with me." He moved Justine closer into his warm embrace. "Now, as far as the magic, I don't know. I think I have some powers, and maybe the vibes I cast out were strong enough to send you here. Could have just been fate. I hope that answers your question."

"Maybe. I've seen situations like that on television— people summonsing others by power of the mind, but wasn't sure of the validity."

"Maybe it works, maybe it doesn't. I'm no authority on that subject. One thing I do know is that my feelings for you are real." His fingers traced the neckline of the damp Koshari clown shirt. "Let's go inside where we can talk."

"We can talk in the morning. I'm anxious to get to bed."

"Sleepy?" he asked.

"Nope. Just want to relax with you."

"I would like that." He sweetly kissed her on the forehead. "I have good relaxation methods inside just waiting for you."

Justine dutifully followed him. Hand in hand, they walked from the stable and across the open land to his home. Ahead of her, she could see the shadow of his house, the ranch style of it aglow against the backdrop of distant mountains. A single light shone from the kitchen; a welcome light of sorts that gave off a homey feeling.

There was a constant mingling of aromas in his house, spices of the Southwest, teas, essential oils and man—all man. It reminded her of the night they made love in his store. She felt at home, though she had only been there twice. She felt natural there and never wanted to leave. As she looked around the living room, a startling remembrance crossed her mind that she would have to leave in a few days. Thinking of that was hard, so she chose to put the thought away—at least for the evening—and enjoy Darrius whether they talked all night or made love. It didn't matter to Justine what they did, so long as they were together.

They sat by a small fire in his living room and had a small glass of wine to toast their relationship. As they sipped, Justine couldn't help but wonder what she would be like after leaving him. She looked at his profile as shadows of flames flickered across his skin. "Darrius?"

"Yes?"

"I tried not bringing this up, but something is bothering me."

He kissed her hand. "What could be wrong? The mood is right, the evening was perfect and we're together."

"That's just the problem. Soon I won't be here. What will we do then? A long-distance relationship is a hard one to keep."

"Not if the people involved are insistent on making it last. I know I am. Are you?"

"Sure, but we'll be apart for long periods of time. I won't be able to fly out here as often as I would like."

"I know, but haven't you heard the expression absence makes the heart grow fonder?"

"Many times, but since knowing you, I won't want the absence."

"You won't have to be without me for too long. I can come to you, too, you know."

"You have your work. I have mine."

He slid her into his lap, kissing the tip of her nose. "We can make this work, Justine. I'm not about to give up on seeing you, talking to you—even emailing you." He finished the last of his wine. "Let's not talk about this right now. We have tomorrow for that, but I don't want you worrying. We *will* be together—all the time. In fact, we'll be together so much that you may get tired of me."

"Yeah, like that could happen."

"It could."

"Never, and you're right. Let's save this conversation for another day." She touched his chest. "I need to get you out of that paint."

"And how would you like to do it?"

"The old fashioned way—a shower. But not just your regular shower. I want a warm, bubbling one with sensual candles all around. You know, romantic."

"I know just what you're talking about, love." He lifted her from his lap. "Let's walk in naked, step into a warm shower and make it warmer. Would that be a good start?"

She answered by pulling her shirt off and unsnapping the back of her bra. Darrius slid it off her shoulders and let it drop to the carpeting in a heap. In one quick motion, he unzipped her jeans and slid them, and her panties, to her feet. She kicked off her sandals and stepped out of the heap of clothing.

Before him stood a naked seductress. His eyes never left her slender frame. The heft of her breasts made him moisten his lips; the dark patch of hair covering her sex made his fingers tingle, wanting her like never before. His erection parted the buckskin breechcloth, reminding him that it was now his turn to disrobe.

Easy.

The jockstrap and a single knotted strap behind him pulled free, along with the breechcloth, releasing him. Both items dropped to the ground, covering her bare feet. She stepped back to admire him. From the single light coming from another room, she could see his frame; a tall, slender black-and-white-painted man with flows of hair gracing his back and sides. The only unpainted area of his body was a stiff erection. The sight both excited and amused her. She smiled.

"What is it?" Darrius asked.

"You're a little mismatched."

He looked down and saw his phallus was a shade lighter than the rest of his painted body. "There was no way in hell Derrick was going to help me paint this." He turned and showed an equally bare derriere. "He wouldn't paint that, either."

"That's for me to paint." She took his hand. "The bathroom awaits, doesn't it?"

"Ready and waiting."

Inside the bathroom, he lit two frankincense candles on each side of the large shower. Jets soon sprayed into the stall, steaming the walls and enhancing the fragrance of the candles.

Now face to face and skin to skin, he kissed her, swirling his tongue around hers, battling for dominance as he held her tighter. His erection pulsed against her upper stomach. His natural liquid mixed with water beaded against his tip and he stroked it, making it harder.

He let Justine take over the task, wrapping her hand around the thick phallus, feeling its rigid veins, his smooth tip, the soft, wet skin of it—skin more sensitive there than the rest of it. She slightly jerked it, caressed the underside, raking gentle nails across it. A man had never been as hard as he was to her that night.

Darrius was the only man who could take her to a world she had never experienced. Images would explode in her mind as his body filled hers. She wanted to be crazy from him that night; wanted to be crazy because of him, and she was more than halfway there just by looking into his eyes.

Darrius took the bar soap from the dish, wet it and held wet fingers under her nose. "Lavender; your favorite."

"Did I tell you lavender was my favorite?"

"No. I just knew. I *am* right, aren't I?"

"Right as rain. Drench me, rain on me, fill me with every pleasure of the night." She stroked his erection harder.

"Is that what you want, total and explicit carnal pleasures?"

"It's what every woman wants; especially me, but only with you."

He responded with mouth-watering kisses that trailed from her lips down. He paused at her breasts, taking one full, beaded nipple into his mouth, tugging lightly. The other received equal attention as water poured, covering them both as if in torrential rains.

For Justine, no other sexual experience had matched what they were doing, not even their previous lovemaking. She couldn't believe his lovemaking got better with time, like aged wine, only sweeter—much sweeter. With each tender stroke, with every sensual caress across her naked, wet flesh, the tighter the strings within her sex pulled, wanting release, that unbalancing of everything within her.

Darrius kissed down to her belly and let his fingers play at her juncture, soon kissing her there as well, with teasing tongue strokes. She was too hot and delicious to part from, and already, he missed her kiss so much. Again facing his lover, they kissed in a hard, wild battle that made her wrap her arms around his shoulders. He pressed his body closer into her, gyrating hip to hip, sex to sex. The more Justine squirmed against him, the more he felt an intolerable fever swell within him.

Amid the rage of caresses and steam, Justine opened her eyes and saw a mixture of black and white paint glide down his body and pool with the water at their feet, which was now a creamy white color. His hair, now in sheets of darkness, was molded to his back and her hands. The heavy strands lay between her fingers as they kissed beyond control of their emotions.

Minutes later, Justine pulled away, stared into his flushed, paintless face and said, "Now."

"No!"

She blinked in disbelief. "What? We're so ready, Darrius."

"We are, but I have more planned. I don't want anything quick. I want this to last all night, all morning, all of tomorrow—if that pleases you."

Her hand traveled the length of his torso, stopping at his engorged erection. "It does, but I want *this*. I want you on top of me, beside me, under me . . . in back of me."

"In back of you. I can fix that now, draw out the fantasy, make you so ready for me you'll explode upon contact once we move to the bed. I love looking at you when you come. You look like a goddess."

"Then make me look like one now."

Darrius placed her under the jets and turned her back to him. He watched the water sheet across her dark hair and African/Italian-rich skin and knew he had no choice but to move with her—or go crazy from his own desire to take it slower. There still would be no penetration—not yet, but something so damn pleasurable he would be weary from the act.

He moved the hair from the back of her neck, kissed it, and had her bend ever so slightly. With one hand leaning against the wall above her head for balance, his other held tight to his length, moving it in a steady pace up and down. He felt her body tighten, aching, wanting more. Still, he teased. His length slid effortlessly across her labia from behind, yet without entrance. Now both of his hands rested on the wall above her head while his hips rocked against her.

The water splashed between her back and his chest. Her calls echoed throughout the petroglyph-etched walls of the candlelit bathroom. His body tensed, his lips trembled, and his throat constricted as a wave of silky white erupted from him.

His chest heaved for seconds only, to gain momentum. Then he kissed her once more and shut off the water. Helping her from the stall, he wrapped a plush towel around her and blew out the candle. And then they walked dripping wet to his bedroom.

Staring at the heavy oak bedroom door, Justine knew paradise was on the other side. His bedroom was a place she had seen only in her mind. She waited in anticipation as he turned the knob.

What lay beyond was darkness, and he chose not to turn on a light. Instead, he opened the door wider and ushered her in. "Walk with me and lie face down on the bed."

"Shouldn't we towel dry first?"

"No, I still want you wet in every thinkable way."

He was fiddling with something on a counter. "What are you doing?"

"You'll see."

"Will it hurt?"

"Of course not, silly."

"What about the lights?"

"They'll be off soon. Now, tell me what you think this smell is."

He uncorked the bottle and let the aroma fill the room.

Justine sniffed the air. "Sage?"

"Good. It's desert sage, one of the essential oils of my . . . our people. I'm giving you a massage, but first I have to show something else to you."

He turned on a little lamp by the bed that cast a lazy low glow around the room.

She looked up and saw on the back wall a large oil painting of a Koshari clown in a rhythmic dance, his long dark hair swirling around him. The rugged black paint clumped in parts, indicating musculature of the insatiable dancer. Justine sat up and pointed. "My God! This is the best one I've seen. Is this . . . you?"

"Look at the face and tell me."

The picture painted every aspect of Darrius's person from his keen features to his feet. The jet background cast an effect of motion—still motion.

"This is amazing. When was it painted?"

"The day after I was released from jail. The same artist asked me to pose in the studio. I have the original, but there are many prints. The artist can't keep them on hand."

"No doubt. Look at the muscles, the movement, the excitement on your face. You must have really been excited while he painted you."

"But I wasn't, what with the girl's death still so fresh on my mind. The artist, Eva Germaine, even played Native American soundtracks while I posed to help get me back in the mood."

"Did it help?"

"Some."

"A woman painted this?"

"Sure. Why not? Aren't women just as talented?"

"That's not what I mean." Justine continued to gaze at the painting. "Look at the breechcloth painted in white with a buffalo skull. She really hit you where you live, didn't she?"

"Then, yes. I still love dancing, as you saw from my performance tonight, but where I really *live* is in my store . . . and here with you; especially here with you, tonight."

She continued to stare. "She made it a point to capture the bulge in the breechcloth. Was she beautiful?"

"For a sixty-year-old woman, yes. Jealous?"

"Not a chance. I have the real thing in bed with me."

He moved closer. "And as every one knows, the real one is always better."

"Sure is." Her hand smoothed against the turgid erection that was ready to part her.

His hand gently brought her face to his. "Lie back and let me do what I need to do with you."

As if in a trance, she did as told. "Do I get my massage?"

"Lie on your back. I'm waiting to deliver one."

"On wet skin?"

"To me, oil and water mix very well."

"Then mix with me, Mr. Poetry in Motion."

Darrius took the cork off the glass flask, dribbled the aromatic potion into his palms and rubbed them together. The scent hit the air in waves and Justine became more relaxed, anticipating the magic to come.

He planted his thighs on either side of hers and began massaging the tender, moist skin under her ears. Then he moved down to her neck and shoulders. His hands then circled her breasts.

Her back arched, bringing her breasts almost level with his chest. The hardened nipples pressed against his palms, tickling the oiled flesh—making his erection almost unbearable. But this part of the act was for her . . . solely for her. He continued, raking his rounded nails down her torso, circling her ribcage, navel, stopping just before the gentle tuft of hair that covered a marvelous sex—a sex he craved, mixed well with, wanted to partake of . . . immediately. But it wasn't about him—not yet.

The scent of desert sage heightened her senses as Darrius cast spells on her body, making the winding spring well within her sex tighten. The closer he moved to her core, the less she could control her words, actions, thoughts. He played at the sides of her mound, oiling her hips, her upper thighs, but returning to the very place where all life seemed to begin. He teased her there, fingers hovering at the opening, but never entering, only a suggestion of the act. Hoping her moans and stretches would entice him more, she put on her act as well as any actress in Hollywood. Her body stretched, splaying curvature, sprawling like a satisfied feline, stretching muscles that had been dormant for months now. Her knees captured him, gently squeezing his sides, playing at his pelvic bone while his hands continued swirling and playing her body.

Now slick from neck to toes she demanded he sample her natural slickness, wet his whistle and delve into desire. This time it would be better, more; no time restraints, no store hours to be careful of, no rocking, clumsy horse swaying two bodies in the middle of the desert sun. They were in paradise, and at that moment, Darrius slid two fingers into her blazing cove, her eyes rolled, looked beyond her to the back wall. For the life of her, she saw his painting come to life—as if he'd stepped from the canvas. Was there peyote in the room or was she really seeing this? The deeper his fingers moved into her, the more she could see shadows of his portrait sprawling across her.

Black and white blurs filled her mind as his rigid fingers entered her. Her hips heaved from the mattress, keeping pace with his gyrations. She reached for the flask, poured the mixture into her own hands and saturated her dancer's neck and shoulders. What had he slipped her? This was the best foreplay ever created? Genital penetration hadn't even become a thought yet, but there her body was wet from water, sweat, desire, mind-altering something . . . but what? Nothing, just uninhibited foreplay.

Darrius was now way beyond the ability to control anything. Once the oil met his heated flesh, he was on his way to nirvana. Seeing Justine in a new light now took him all the way there. She was wild that night, uninhibited, primal—everything he needed her to be. Sure, sex with her had been nothing less than a harrowing experience, one that constantly took him over the edge, but this was different. Sweat-lodge material. He, too, was seeing things, feeling things that were so foreign, yet so right for his body. His erection spun into knots, pulsating, dewy from need.

His eyes bore into hers, and her words were all he needed to make foreplay a thing of the past. Now sex to sex, his body trembled, his arms above her head were shaking from raw power, he lowered and kissed her, gently pulled and tugged on her bottom lip before moving down to each succulent nipple. There, too, he tugged, licked, and with one motion he moved his hard, stiff phallus into her thirsty sex, drawing back briefly before thrusting inside again. He was home, comfortable, snug . . . very, very energized.

Messy, sticky silk sheets barely covered each body. Soon the sheets were kicked to the carpeting. Justine, now in the mood for tasting him another way, pulled from him. Her now hollow core that had drunk so lavishly from him felt as distant as a dwindling lightning storm. Yet she suffered it to be so in order to get more of what she wanted.

Darrius, now flat on his back with an erection parting the air, was an enticing sight. She bent over him, letting her hair dance across his chest. Her mouth lowered to his seedy tip, tasting him slowly, and then taking him in even strokes. He filled her mouth so well, like he was a natural fit for only her, and she for him. She barely raked his scrotum, feeling it tighten to her advances. Soon his fists pounded the mattress, his throat tightened and she knew he was ready.

The condom on the table rested in a wolf ashtray, and she released it from its foil home. Together they slid it onto his shaft, and she lowered onto him. Justine looked to the painting, seeing it move once again in her mind, moving to his rhythm. Within seconds, an explosion shattered her, leaving her breathless. Her sex continued to drink of his with each convulsion—draining him. Tired, satisfied. Justine slumped onto him, and there they rested for what was left of the night.

18

SWEET DREAMS ARE MADE OF THESE

Sunday

Justine awakened to a bright New Mexico sunrise and delectable aromas coming from the kitchen. But how? Darrius was still lying next to her. She looked around the disordered room—covers everywhere, the scent of desert sage lingering in the air, pillows on the floor.

She swiped hair away from her face and said, "What a night!" Her body was still stiff and hurting from the workout Darrius had given her.

Darrius stirred on his side of the bed and then opened his eyes. "Something sure smells good."

"What is it? Do you have a maid or something?"

"I got up early and put a few things together. I also packed us a picnic basket."

"A picnic—"

"Yeah! Today is ours, baby. I've got plans for us."

"Can I take my camera?"

"Leave it in the car, but you'll be so excited when we get to where I'm taking you."

Justine sat up completely. "Where are we going?"

"We eat first and shower, and then I'll surprise you."

"You're already the best surprise of my life. Until I met you, I was just plain ol' Justine from the streets of San Francisco. Now look at me. I'm in bed with a prince!"

He tossed back the sheets and slowly stood. "Don't send any Hail Marys my way yet. I'm just a man, Justine."

"Not from my side of the bed."

He saw the contented smile on her lovely face. With her hair tossed in a frazzle of curls about her face and neck and the sheet barely covering her breasts, he had the urge to take her again. But there would be time for that later. He knew if he touched her again that morning their picnic would not happen. "You lie there and relax. Let me finish getting breakfast ready, then you can come in and partake. Okay?"

She said, "Okay." She was drifting off, dreaming of their lovemaking when she heard him call her.

"Not asleep, are you?" he called from the kitchen.

"I soon will be if you don't hurry and give me a reason to get up."

"Just you wait. These aromas will lure you so wickedly you'll float in here to me."

More tantalizing aromas soon filled the air, and Justine wrapped Darrius's robe around her and walked unannounced into the kitchen.

A mixture of sage, meat, baked bread and berries filled the air. Darrius was at the stove mixing a concoction of batter and mixed berries, not seeing her, but feeling her presence the moment she walked in. "Come on, you cheated. I wanted to have the kitchen prepared with a set table and full plates before you came in."

"The aromas beckoned and I had to come." She peered into the mixed bowl. "What are you making? More of your fancy bread?"

"Corn batter flapjacks with mixed berries."

"And the aroma coming from the oven?"

"Jackrabbit links."

Her smile suddenly turned upside down. "You *are* kidding, aren't you?"

"Why? Doesn't jackrabbit sound appetizing?"

"Frankly, no!"

"Good, then I'll turn it into wild turkey. That sounds better?"

She stood behind him and wrapped her arms around his hips. "Much better. Wild turkey, huh?"

"Ever had it before?"

"No, but I have had a wild stallion." The palm of her hand rubbed against a half-saluting erection.

"Well, if you keep hanging around here, no telling how wild I'll get." At that, he ladled batter into the pan and watched it sizzle around the edges. "Just perfect. Umm, smells better than usual. I love how you inspire the best in me, Justine. Everything seems better when you're around."

Plugging in the coffee maker, he said, "A little caffeine to get us jumping while on the road. Tell you what, since you're here, set the table for me, will ya?"

As if pretending to be the dutiful wife, she opened the spacious cupboards and took out a couple of reddish-brown plates with vibrant yellow and red hummingbirds in the middle. She ran her fingers along the rolled edges of the plates, admiring them. "These are almost too lovely to eat on."

He turned and sweetly kissed her cheek. "But we have a lot to accomplish today. But before that, I have something that belongs to you."

"Let me guess; my heart?"

"Cute, but I think I already have that, don't I?"

"Indeed. What do you have?"

"Something I thought you liked enough to keep with you." He ducked around a corner and returned with her basket. "Look familiar?"

"My basket! I completely forgot it, being so wrapped up in you these last few days." She took it from him and examined the etched details, the delicate carvings. "Thanks so much for keeping it for me."

"Just don't forget about it again."

"No way. It goes in the truck with us, right next to my suitcase. I'll send it ahead tomorrow along with my Koshari clowns and the rest of my trinkets."

"Good idea." He took the sausage out of the oven, flipped the flapjacks into a platter and filled the pan with more batter. He filled both plates and added fresh blueberries, watermelon slices, kiwi and strawberries on the side.

Justine was awed by the feast he had whipped up. Not only was he a great lover, but he could cook, too. Yes, he was definitely a keeper. Her old thoughts were returning—the marriage game. Her thoughts were running ahead of her because he hadn't mentioned a thing about marriage or engagement. That was another problem she saw in herself—jumping the gun.

She asked brightly, trying to redirect her thoughts, "So, where are you taking me today?"

"El Morro National Monument."

"Near the Zuni mountains?"

"One and the same."

"I've studied parts of New Mexico and other states. At first it was in school, then I realized I liked geography and studied maps while in college. Maybe I was mapping my way to areas I wanted to visit."

"Could be. Now you'll have a chance to see some of the things you may have studied. El Morro is a fabulous place, rich in history. You also know that where we're going is close to sacred Anasazi ruins, right?"

"I wasn't sure of that. Can we see them?"

"It's sacred and very hilly, just like the land beyond Red Rock. It would be disrespectful, not to mention dangerous, to go there, but I can show you some other sights."

"I want to see as much as I can see."

His hand stretched across the table to caress her cheek. "I don't think there's anything I dislike about you."

"Even the bullheadedness?"

"That is part of who you are."

"And you know this because . . .? Oh, let me guess, the eagle told you."

"I know you're kidding, but a totem did tell me—my dragonfly totem. I don't take kindly to just any woman; namely, those with guns and liquor bottles."

"I'm glad you're able to joke about that. I know she hurt you."

"She did, but that part of my life is over. You're with me now. How we do this after you leave tomorrow is the trick."

"Well, as my totem says, take things slow and let things work out on their own. And they will, Darrius. Trust it."

"You're right." He looked at the wall clock, noting the time. "We must eat quickly. You still need to shower, without me—"

"What a drag!"

"Indeed, but if we're to explore, we must do it during the best of light. Besides, you need to get more clothing. Your clown shirt is wrinkled, your sandals are wet and your jeans are stained, though you would look beautiful in a sack."

"Sweet talk. Words like that could make me move in here with you if I wasn't leaving in a day or two. Would you let me?"

"In a heartbeat!"

Past the visitor center and in the near distance stood rows of tall pointed sandstone rocks called Inscription

Rock, a.k.a. El Morro National Monument. Justine was speechless at the breathtaking sight.

"The bluff is a hell of a place, is it not?" Darrius asked, reacting to the awe he saw on her face.

"Wh—What?"

"That's what it's called, the bluff, and aren't you glad I insisted you wear ground-grippers instead of those pretty sandals?"

"Oh, yes. I was just so taken by—"

"The beauty of El Morro?"

"It's incredible."

"You have yet to see how incredible it truly is. Let's walk another half mile so you can see the inscriptions. They date back to the fifteenth century. You'll have to hold my hand, though. The terrain is hilly. Can't have you falling off a cliff."

"Could that happen up there?"

"Only near the ruins, which we *won't* be going to, though I know you want to."

"Can't we?"

"Justine," he said sternly.

"Okay, okay. Show me the inscriptions, then let's tour. Surely, there are *other* places you can take me to."

"There are, and just so you could have something tangible to remember this day, *I* have one of your cameras. I slid it into the picnic basket."

"Quite the man, aren't you?"

"Quite! Let's roll. I think you'll like Inscription Loop. There are over two thousand signatures and petroglyphs to look at."

"Really? Who are some of the signers?"

"Mostly the Spanish on their trek to conquer many a Native American lifestyle. I can't remember some of the names, but you'll see them. They're very old, and preservationists are constantly finding ways to keep them safe."

Inscription Rock was a wealth of sights that Justine was eager to capture. She was thankful Darrius brought one of her cameras. *The Examiner* would be indebted to her for years to come for these pictures. She only wished she could shoot the ruins, the old Anasazi villages at the top of the mesa and whatever it was behind Red Rock, but values and traditions were not something she dared tamper with. It would be like someone coming into her parents' home, uninvited, and rifling through their most prized possessions. Besides, her lover would send her flying back to her own ancestors, and she was not ready to go yet. She took his hand and followed him to the wall, which was covered with inscriptions and petroglyphs.

Darrius led her to something he thought she would love: the first English inscription made by Lieutenant J.H. Simpson and artist R.H Kern. Without a word, she aimed and shot the 1849 inscription, murmuring, "This autograph will be the prize of the photo spread."

"Not quite," Darrius said. "I think this will be: Don Juan de Ornate, New Mexico's supposed first governor, though many an Indian ruled this place first. Let's look at his and a few more and then try to get to the pool of water at the bottom for our picnic."

"Is it safe for us to travel down that far?"

He smiled. "No, not the way I go. I come here a lot when I need to think."

If only I were as brave as he thinks I am. "To have sweat lodges or vision quests?"

"No, just to think about life, what's going on and what I need to do to make my people happy despite adversity."

Justine looped her arm through his. "You always seem to think of others first. That's the second thing I like about you."

"And the first?"

"The way you love me. I feel warm and needed when with you."

"I need you too, kid. Come on, my belly is rumbling, and we've got things yet to see."

Justine took a few shots of the inscription Don Juan Ornate and his men made back in 1605. Using her poor Spanish skills, she tried to make out the inscribed words. Finally, she pulled Darrius away from other inscriptions and asked, "What does *Paso por aqui* mean?"

" *'I passed through here.'* He made his arrival on April 16ᵗ 1605. You see where he made his mark, just above a native petroglyph, almost disfiguring its natural beauty."

"That bothers you, doesn't it?"

"Our land should be respected. I, too, am part of the efforts to keep this place intact. I donate money, and sometimes my time when I have it." He faced her. "I love my land, Justine, and anyone who can't doesn't have a place in my life. That's why I'm so taken with you. True, you would like to venture into territory that is off limits, but not to exploit it without seeing the beauty of it. You want to share its beauty with others, not see what you can get out of it."

Not quite knowing how to respond, she took his hand. "Come, let's see the rest of its beauty."

With a lighter heart, Darrius took her to a place that he had sworn he would never take anyone who wasn't Native American—the Pueblo ruins. Atop a large hillside, they stared into the distance and saw the beautiful sandstone city sectioned off into what looked like separate ancient homes. "The Pueblo city, huh? It reminds me of the old Pueblo woman who had this bracelet before I did. Her family probably had many memories of how this place used to look when it was thriving."

"Probably so."

Justine's eyes soon looked beyond him and widened in glory. She was dying to photograph the place, but remembered what Darrius had said about loving her for her non-exploitive ways. She wanted to keep his view of her intact, and that meant not desecrating sacred lands for a mere photograph. It took hundreds of years for the Pueblos to create life there, back in the day, and that's how she wanted it to stay. Yet her zeal to explore was almost getting the best of her.

19

KACHINA SUNSET

Darrius saw the look on Justine's face and knew she was itching to get closer to the Pueblo ruins. No deal. True, she was a part of his heart now, but his ancestors were still his ancestors. He took her by the hand. "Come, we've been here long enough. You never know who might be watching us."

"There's no one here but us."

"I don't mean the physical."

She felt a sudden chill, and looked skyward, as if expecting to see the great kachina rise above the clouds and scold her. "You *are* kidding, right?"

"No, I'm very serious. This world is not simply inhabited by the living but also by spirits who protect us. I think after lunch you and I need to have the kachina talk. I'll let you in on a few things you need to know about me, my people and the land."

"Sounds like *the talk* parents give pre-teens about sex and procreation."

"You know that talk pretty well, Justine. You show me each time we're alone."

"Then maybe we should make love up here."

"Not here. Come on, let's go," he urged, pulling her along. She reluctantly went, but her eyes said that her interest had not diminished. Darrius knew her fixation with the place went way beyond that of getting material for her job. Trying to shift her focus, he suggested another place he thought she would like just as much. "Let's go to the large pool at the base of the cliff. It's a miraculous place, and you can even take pictures."

At the base, large stones of alabaster, basaltic rock and yellow stone surrounded them, blocking the midday sun. The place was quiet, serene and secluded, and had a relaxing effect on Justine's restive mind. She lay next to Darrius on the blanket he had spread on the shady stretch of grass and rested her head on his chest. After a few moments of silence, she said, "I hope you didn't misread my excitement at the ruins and confused it with greed. I would never betray you, Darrius."

"What brought this on?"

"The way you hustled me away from them."

"I'm sorry. I just get a little edgy when non-Indians want to learn more about the ruins. It's not that I don't trust you, Justine, but I know how interested you are. I just want to keep something sacred in this life we have."

"I understand."

"I know you do. Now with that said, are you hungry?"

"Uh . . . no, but a bottled water would be good. Got any?"

"I've got everything in here," he said, reaching into the basket and pulling out a bottle. "It is beautiful here, isn't it?"

"It sure is. Is this where you come to think?"

"One of the places. Another is on the other side of El Morro."

"Near the ruins?"

"Yes, not far from Red Rock. It's a very dangerous place, Justine; not the area where the ceremonials take place, but on the other side, past the rugged strip of road leading to the mountain range. Only people who know what they're doing go up there, and that's only to rescue idiots who dare the terrain and the few Navajos who live nearby. They're used to it, because it's where they live. Still, it's tricky even for them. You're not thinking anything, are you?"

"Why would I do that, Darrius? I already told you I respect the land and the people too much to go there. Besides, it's dangerous." Her panic attack the other day had been warning enough to leave dangerous areas alone. "What did you pack for lunch?"

"Ah, lots of stuff for a late lunch. It's almost two o' clock. We have shrimp salad in tortilla bread, guacamole with blue corn chips, fruit, candy—your favorite, black licorice. We have soda and something special, a bottle of white wine."

"Wow! You were busy after you made love to me last night."

"I did this just before making breakfast. I already had the shrimp salad in the refrigerator. I cheated a bit and bought it from Escro's instead of making it myself."

"I'm sure it's great. After we eat, will you tell me the kachina story? I know I sound like a third grader begging her teacher for story time."

"Beg all you want. You know I'm weak for you and most likely will give in to your demands."

"So if I beg to see more of the ruins, will I get my way?"

He kissed her tenderly on the lips, and then said, "No!"

"I was just kidding, anyway," she said, biting into her shrimp salad tortilla. "You sure you didn't make this?"

"Positive, but I *can* make it. I just ran out of time with getting back into the dance and all."

"One you did quite well, I might say. Very provocative."

"Yeah? I can show you more provocative moves."

Justine looked around cautiously. "In the light of day?"

"We've done worse. Remember the stable, the store, the—"

"I get it, Darrius. No, let's just sit here, watch the water, talk. After the sun sets, who knows where our imagination will lead us? But I want your version of the kachina story."

The sun was setting by the time Darrius finished relating the history of El Morro, and Justine was definitely getting in the mood for a kachina sunset. Looking at the sunset, she swore she could see the old Atsinna Pueblos dancing their dances, praising their gods, looking forward to a bountiful harvest. That was the life she wanted—basic, natural, uncomplicated. Yet the lives of Darrius's ancestors weren't easy and she knew it, but the lifestyle appealed to her.

Darrius poured a glass of wine into plastic goblets, and they settled back against a cottonwood tree. With Justine nestled between his thighs, he was ready to give her exactly what she wanted—her kachina story. "Ready for your story? Is it dark enough for you yet?"

She smiled and looked up at the vastly darkening sky and lazily replied, "Yes, I'm ready now; take me back to ancient times and live there with me for a while."

"Then let's start with where the Hopi originated and why the kachinas are such an important part of their lives. Life for the Hopi, as we know it, began untold centuries ago on mesas in Flagstaff, Arizona. The land was inhospitable, due mainly to scarce rainfall. So, life was hard, but they managed to make a living. They were mostly farmers and grew crops like beans, squash and corn, a mainstay of their diet. And this is where the kachinas come in. The kachina story is basically about religion and exhorting supernatural beings to assist with the harsh land conditions, planting—things like that."

"Sounds like a creation myth."

"No myth here. This was told to me by my father, who had been told by his father and his father before him. It has been passed down by generations of Hopi families, and it's true. How else would people be able to live in inhospitable lands with very little water? Water is the primary motivation for survival everywhere."

"So, what role did the kachinas play here?"

"Prayer for water and other things is the reason kachinas came into the picture. Kachinas are the spiritual lifeline of the Hopi. They are spirits that help the people with the demands of life and they come in countless forms from ancestors to energy: from crops to farm animals. What they really embody is infinite. As I said earlier, there are hundreds of kachinas, and they are ever increasing. They influence everything, helping us in our quest for survival."

"They're not gods, so they must be more like helpers. Right?"

"Exactly. Their mission is to help the world, Indian or non-Indian. The Hopi have always been a giving people, a friendly people, but they have been taken advantage of. Natural disasters, every manner of mayhem have been visited upon our people."

"Right. By Europeans."

"Yes, but also by other Indian tribes searching for food."

Justine was eager for yet more information. "I know a little about kivas, but haven't read much about them. What exactly are they, and what are they for?"

"Kivas are underground chambers in which kachinas dwell. Kivas are seen as portals to another world, and kachinas emerge from them during the kachina season, which begins in late December and ends the summer following. They go about performing rituals and engaging in various ceremonies."

"What do the other kachinas do once the first ones are gone?"

"Many things. Each set of kachinas perform different tasks. The next ceremony takes place soon after the first kachinas leave the kivas. The kachinas associated with this ceremony are always accompanied by guards, warriors and the clowns for many reasons."

"The clowns. I know they have dual roles, that of performer and teacher."

"That's right. You know the major things about the Koshari."

"He's a fun character, and I know you like him, too. Is that why you chose the clowns, because they're multi-faceted?" Justine asked.

"Actually, it was chosen for me. Kachinas are like middlemen in spirit form. People can't physically interact with spirits so a human is chosen to portray them. The method by which the right person is chosen to portray the kachina varies. The Koshari is an educator, but he does it in parody form. They are usually not seen at the powwows. This powwow is a special one. Derrick and some of the elders decided it would be interesting to add a few traditional kachinas for once."

"I'm glad they did. You make a good Koshari, Darrius."

Darrius stroked her inner thighs and chuckled into her ear. "Of course, a little levity always makes my day. It's fun to be a jackass sometimes and poke fun at people—you know, loosen up sometimes. I'm beginning to realize why I love the role so much. It's part of me, both sides of me."

"I know you're glad you came back to dancing."

"I am, but one thing still bothers me. The general public sees our dances as just entertainment. A lot people have no realization that this is part of our religion. That's why I still don't think everything we do should be open to the public."

"They can be taught."

"Yes, those who want to learn. Others take trinkets from our lives and go back to theirs without knowing what the trinket means. That's why our children are initiated into the cult. I know our religion isn't the only one on earth, but it's very important to us and it hurts me to think it's taken lightly by some."

"People make fun of all religions, Darrius. I'm not saying it's right, but it happens."

She rested quietly in his arms, almost afraid to ask her next question, but she had to know. "Darrius, do you see me as one of the trinket takers?"

He took a deep breath and let it out slowly, as if impatient with her. "Justine, you know the answer to that. You came here with knowledge, came wanting to know more. Do you think I could love someone who didn't respect my nation and religion? Don't ask me that anymore."

"Then can I ask you something else?"

"Anything my Justine wants, all she has to do is ask. But make sure it's not about the ruins."

"No. It's about the kachinas. How many can you estimate off the top of your head?"

"That's hard to say. The dolls you see are of major and minor kachinas. Some aren't even kachinas, but supernatural beings nonetheless. You see, these aren't simply dolls.

They are teaching mechanisms, usually given to children, girls mostly, to understand what the kachina is all about. The Crow Mother and most of the other kachinas are not usually seen at powwows, nor are most of the other major kachinas. They are only seen at certain dances and ceremonies. The main event yesterday and last night at the powwow was a good example of the ceremonies some major kachinas attend. Derrick and some of the other organizers thought it would be different to incorporate them into this one, to add to the entertainment—and education of those who are interested in the kachinas."

"Like me."

"Yes. The kachina ceremonial calendar ends in July, with one final ritual soon after that—like last night. It's a great ending to a fabulous season. Don't you agree?"

"I do, and it was even more special to me because of the miraculous man I met here."

"Derrick?"

"Sure. He's the love of my life. I've only been pretending with you."

"Then you're a great actress because I'm completely taken by you."

She playfully nudged him in the ribs. "You know who I'm talking about."

Darrius planted a short, sweet kiss on her lips. "Any other kachinas you want to know about?"

"You've covered a great deal. I'll learn about the rest."

"You already are, darling—you already are. Our culture celebrates abundant life, and when I'm with you, I feel rich."

She lay on her back on the Pueblo-patterned quilt. "Make me feel rich. It's dark enough now."

"Dark enough to take you to my ancestors." He straddled her thighs and pulled his shirt off. He took her, parting her legs wider than ever before and feeling them wrap around him in desperate passion.

Bodies rocked endlessly in the night. In the heat of the moment, Darrius swore he could see the elders smiling down at him as he made love to her. The sky gods opened the heavens, and the most brilliant sunset flooded the area.

20

ADVENTURES IN PARADISE

Justine awakened early and gazed through the picture window near the foot of the bed. She saw that the sun had begun its ascent. Streaks of orange, yellow and dark blue accented the Gallup sky. She smiled. Yes, she could get used to a life like this—rising to beauty, lying in comfort and being serenaded all night by her lover.

Her joints still ached from climbing hills and descending valleys at El Morro. Once they returned to his house, they had barely made it to the bed before making love again. There was probably clothing strewn from the front door to the bedroom. Justine remembered looking up at the Koshari painting as they made love, seeing the 3D movements of a fast and furious clown. Then they both fell into a dead sleep.

Darrius stirred next to her, yawning. He turned and stroked her exposed leg. However, the expression on her face concerned him. "Hey, where's that smile you had a second ago?"

"You saw that?"

"I see everything when it comes to you." He sat up, letting the sheet fall to his hips. "What are you thinking about that's making you so sad suddenly?"

"Tomorrow."

"What about it?"

"Don't you remember what tomorrow is?"

"Yes, Monday."

"I go home day after tomorrow, Darrius, and I don't want to."

"Do you have to?"

She slumped against his shoulder. "Yeah. They're expecting me back now that the powwow is officially over."

He wrapped his arm tightly around her, as if hoping a loving caress would take her mind from going home. "Well, let's not think about it right now. Let's grab some breakfast, get your things shipped off and then go to the golf course for a round or two with the guys. We'll take things from there. You don't mind watching a few rounds of golf, do you? It's the last round after the ceremonies."

"No. I don't mind. I'd love to see you play again."

The look of sadness persisted, and Darrius held her tighter. "I've got a surprise for you after the golf outing."

A smile finally appeared. "What is it, lunch at the El Rancho? You know I've wanted to go there."

"Sure, we'll do that, but it's something else I won't tell you about just yet."

"I love you, you know that?"

"Yes, I know that, and believe me, the feeling is mutual." He pushed the sheets aside and jumped from the bed. "Let's get this day rolling. We've got to go back to your room, pack your goodies and have them all set for Wednesday. I remember now that you're leaving at an ungodly time; 6:50 from the train station."

"If I left any sooner, I'd miss the plane in Albuquerque."

She got up and they held hands in front of the picture window. "Boxing my trinkets and other tokens and sending them on ahead of time is a good idea. Everything goes other than my squash necklace and bracelet." She jingled it, hearing the stones dance against the silver. "This always stays with me no matter what I wear. It'll remind me of you when you're not with me."

"I'll always be with you, Justine."

"I mean in person. When I'm on the train, I won't be able to see you. I don't know when I'll be able to see you after I leave."

"We have today and tomorrow, my love. Today we live life to the fullest, kiss, dance, eat, golf, take more pictures. Whatever you want to do."

"I want to stay in bed all day with you. Well, maybe we could visit your parents and then back to bed. Sound good to you?"

"Maybe tomorrow we can meet them for dinner. Would you like that?"

"Sure. I would love to see everyone before leaving."

"Come on, let's go pack, get breakfast at Michael's and have a good day."

"You're not cooking me more raccoon links!"

"No, but if you like snake, I have some!" He smiled and pulled her arm. "You'll like Michael's. He's got the best blueberry flapjacks imaginable. Let's go shower. Together."

They were at the golf course by 11:45 that morning, and Darrius couldn't wait to get started. He looked so handsome in his white polo and dark blue Dockers.

Like a proud girlfriend, Justine sat on the cart cheering him on, watching him and his friends playing. It was a beautiful day for the golf finale. The golf finale was traditionally the end of the powwow. The air was still, the sun shining and the heat, as sweltering as it was, still felt good. New Mexico felt good, and the idea of leaving it made her sick. She would miss the fun times she had there.

She picked her camera up and took a few shots of Darrius in mid-swing. Several shots caught him with a swirl of long, dark hair circling his face. Beautiful. She shot the rolling greens, the well-manicured landscape and other natives playing their rounds of golf, some on the back nines. Still, there were places in midtown she hadn't had time to photograph. She wondered if she had time before lunch to get in a few more photographs of town. She could take the truck and be back in time to pick him up.

Darrius approached, his hair blowing in the wind. "You're a little bored watching me golf."

"Really, I'm okay."

"Justine, you're bored." He reached into his pocket and took out his keys. "Take the truck and go to some galleries or something. Shoot more things for the paper."

"They have enough."

"Then shoot them for your own photo album. These are your last couple of days here, and who knows when you'll be back? Of course, I'll try to make that as soon as possible."

"Are you sure about the truck? I know how crazy you are about your baby."

"You're my baby. Now go, see something good, but be back by two for a late lunch." He gave her a quick kiss before walking off.

With a casual wave back to him, she heaved her camera and a bottled water into her arms and literally skipped to the truck.

It took a little doing to get comfortable so high up from the pavement in his Ford F150. Her rental car was so small it was almost ground level. Her car at home was the same way. Behind his truck, she felt like the queen of the world.

Traveling down Route 66 with the air conditioning and CD player blasting songs by Jay Z and Nina Sky, she felt free, free to do and explore whatever she wanted. What came to mind were the ruins at El Morro, but if Darrius had an inkling about her going there, he'd blast her but good! Besides, she wouldn't dare break her word to him. Wouldn't dare!

On the way into town, she had to pass the cliffs of Red Rock. She hadn't seen the place in two days, and had thought of the dangerous side only briefly last night. She slowed the truck as she got closer to the main entrance. Her mind was telling her to keep going, forget about the place beyond the jagged hilltop, but she told herself that she had to at least see what was up there. She didn't have to go as far as the sacred lands and rugged terrain. Nothing would happen. Besides, didn't she have the right vehicle to do it now? You bet!

Before she realized exactly what she was doing, she had already turned onto the road that led directly to Red Rock's parking lot. Just beyond it was the road, the infamous road she thought was her demon. She stopped midway up, staring at the hilly, reddish-white road dotted with patches of grass. She put the truck in park and pressed the accelerator, revving the engine as if to tear up that hill and show it who was boss. Yet, she stayed in place. Her mind raced; her palms began to itch and sweat! Words trembled as she spoke. "This is crazy! What am I doing here? Why do I want this so much? Darrius told me to stay away, so why am I going against his word?"

Her other side came into play. *You said you won't go to the sacred place, so what's the problem? Just trek up the damn hill and get 'er done. Easy as pie. Do it!* The thought made her laugh a bit, as if she would stake a victory flag at the top. In a way, she agreed with that terrible, troublemaking idea—she wouldn't go to the part Darrius warned her of.

With that in mind, she took the turtle totem from her purse, held it tightly in her hand and placed the gear in drive. She closed her eyes for a second, as if in contemplation, and then moved further up the mountain, hoping the totem would do what it was supposed to do—give her courage to take things slowly and cautiously.

She was okay, smooth sailing thus far. She moved on. The truck was in the process of climbing, tilting a little. She pressed the brake and looked up. By now, her forehead was beading with sweat. The front of her pink tank dress showed sweat stains, and her eyes darted from side to side of each mountaintop.

She was determined to reach the top with totem in hand! But in the back of her mind, she wondered if Darrius had some inkling of what she was doing. She had deliberately not spoken of Red Rock to him to take his mind away from it. Sure, he knew the place excited her, but hadn't exactly known why. Again, the voice. *Just see the top and come back down.*

Sweat dripped into her eyes, and she felt as if she were crying. Gripping the wheel a little harder now, she pressed on. With hardly any nerve left, she advanced until she got to the fork in the road, the same one she had reached the other day. Now, which way to go? She looked at both roads and chose the one on the left. For some reason, it looked less foreboding. On the other side of it was Red Rock's amphitheatre, only it was near two hundred or more feet down. *That's a heck of a drop, Justine.*

She slowly moved higher. Within seconds, she reached a sort of plateau. The flat surface was a welcome sight. She smiled and wiped sweat from her face. She had passed her previous mark and was at the top of one cliff. After putting the gear in park, she slowly opened the door. Her feet and legs felt like lead as she stepped down from the truck.

The top of the mountain was surprisingly pictur-esque. She thought she would see nothing but arid clumps of earth, barren land. It was lovely. Desert flowers dotted the ground, and there were cacti and trees—some cottonwood. The air was fresh up there, and she could see above most of the state. All around her were the red-dish-brown hills and mountains of Gallup and sur-rounding cities. She put the camera belt around her neck and took a few photographs. Her nerve had returned, and she was eager to see everything. She lowered the camera and looked harder, forced her eyes to see beyond what the normal eye could. She squinted, stepped closer to the drop-off. Everything was the same from cliff to cliff—rows and rows of red hills.

She aimed the camera again, wanting the best angle for more shots. Though she remembered Darrius telling her the terrain was rugged, she didn't see anything dan-gerous. She took a few more shots, and to the right on the next overhang, she thought she saw what could be the ruins of some ancient Navajo dwellings. Was it possible to see the ruins from another city? Was it the dangerous part Darrius spoke of? Whatever the case, she was in too deep now to stop.

With a careful step, Justine reached the next small cliff, stood atop and stared. She thought by now she would be a bunch of rattling bones as she stood near the overhang, but she wasn't. The scenery was beautiful, and that was what had captured her thoughts. There had been two incidents while taking photos for the Arizona powwow where she had fallen down a small hill trying to take shots of distant mountain ranges that she couldn't get to from any other spot. Yet her curiosity was what fueled her, that natural curiosity to see what was beyond. She had definitely been in worse situations—like rescuing one of her brothers from a gang. She had handled herself very well that day with those thugs, and she was going to again today. No dangerous land was going to stop her.

The turtle totem was still clutched tightly in her hand, and it made her think. *Maybe there is something to these totems after all. Maybe this has helped me see that I was scared of nothing.* It wasn't a sudden revelation, more like something she had allowed to manifest in her mind without cause.

She took a few more steps and stopped almost at the edge of the cliff and looked down. Again, it was quite a drop, but there were plateaus below her.

Her weight caused the plate of granite below her feet to crumble, and before she could move, it gave way and she slid onto the next plateau. Fear returned though she hadn't slid but a foot. It made her think about the tumbles she had taken in Arizona. But this was different, not nearly as steep as those hills had been, but still, she knew Darrius was right. The terrain was rocky and it was time to leave. Darrius would be expecting her and she didn't want to give him anything to worry about. As she stepped onto the next plateau to head back, it, too, was unable to hold her slight weight and she could feel it crumbling beneath her feet. Panic returned as the slab gave completely—only this time, there wasn't another one close enough to reach for.

21

MIXED MESSAGES

By 2:25, there was no sign of Justine, and Darrius was pissed off. "I told her to be back by two," he told his golf partner, who had offered him a ride back to the store. No way was he going to leave the area without knowing where she was. He thanked his partner, anyway. "No, she'll be here. She just gets so carried away with her photography. I'm sure time simply got away from her."

Darrius watched everyone leaving the course. Now completely alone, he sat on the pavement of the parking lot, waiting . . . and waiting. Twenty minutes later, his cell phone buzzed. "About damn time she called." The phone had no number listed, but he heard crackling. He called her name into the receiver, but nothing came across, just more crackling. That had never happened on his phone before. He figured it to be mixed messages. The phone rang again and the same crackling noise came across. He practically screamed her name into the phone.

He dialed her cell, hoping to reach her. At that point, he didn't care whether she was late getting back to him or not; he just wanted to know if she was safe. Her cell rang and then cut directly off. He looked at the display in disbelief, mumbling, "Out of calling range! What the hell is going on here?" *Justine, where are you?* In his mind's eye, everything was going wrong. He could see her somewhere injured, unable to reach him. Then again, he knew his imagination was in overdrive, causing him to imagine the worst-case scenario. His intuitions were always right, however, and that's what bothered him.

He looked to the sky in desperation, not knowing what to do. He was stranded there, lost in the middle of a golf course with nowhere to turn. What if she was in trouble? How would he get to her? He looked at the phone in his hand and almost threw it. Then he thought about Derrick. It was a long shot because Derrick was on his way to Roswell to collect more store items. But it was worth a shot.

Within an hour, Derrick drove onto the greens so fast he could hardly stop. He swung open the passenger door and Darrius swept in like a quick flame. "Thank God I got you before leaving for Roswell. Thanks, man."

"What the hell could I do? My brother sends me a 911 call. How many twin brothers do you think I have? Anyway, have you thought about the places she may have gone?"

A distant look crossed Darrius's face. "I can think of a few places, and heaven forbid if she went to one of them."

Derrick stared at his brother's stone-cold face. His voice turned cautious, quiet. "Where?"

"El Morro. I took her there yesterday for a picnic and took her near the ruins."

"You *did* tell her not to go there, didn't you?" he asked, pulling the truck off the grounds and onto the interstate.

"Yes, Derrick. She knows they're sacred grounds, but she was just so fascinated by the idea of them. I know her, though, and I know that pesky inquisitive side she can't help but give in to sometimes. She's a photojournalist, for Christ's sakes! There's something in her that's always hungry for more. I don't fault her, but I don't put looking danger in the face past her, either."

"Come on, man! Give her some credit for having a little sense. I just don't think she'd go against you."

"It's not that she would deliberately go against me, Derrick. Searching and investigating is a part of her."

"I think *you're* in her blood."

"Yeah, and I hope that's all." Darrius stared through the windshield, hoping, praying his intuition was wrong.

Darrius's phone buzzed again as Derrick turned onto the main road leading to El Morro. He quickly flipped it open. "It's another 911, but I can't make out the location. Justine? Is that you, hon? Come on, talk to me if you can." The crackling noise returned and another message flashed across: out of calling range. "Damn it! Where the hell is she?"

"Calm down, dude! Maybe it's not even her."

"Who the hell else would send me an emergency call? Mom and Dad are both in Grants shopping for more tea items. How much danger can they be in doing that? Asinka is in summer school, and Jemez is working at some desk designing Mr. Torrez's summer home. Yeah, that's real dangerous work! No, I know it's her. Come on, keep driving."

"It could be one of your other friends; Donnie, Julius or even—"

"It's not them, Derrick. I'm trying to tell you that!"

They finally pulled into the entrance of El Morro and Darrius's nervous eyes searched the entrance for his white truck. The place was almost barren with the exception of a few campers, a Ford Escort and a Jeep Wrangler. His hands balled into nervous fists. "Drive around a bit, and then let's get to those ruins."

Derrick did as he was told. From what they could see of the grounds from the truck, the place remained barren due to it being a workday. At the entrance to the ruins, Derrick took extra caution in driving around the rugged terrain. Deeper into the ruins, they got out and walked carefully, not trusting the road under the pressure of a Chevy Silverado.

They looked over the landscape, walking as far as safety would allow them. All they saw were jagged cliffs, crumbling stone homes and mountain peaks. There was no sight of a white four-by-four or a silly girl with a camera in hand.

Desperation was now settling into Darrius's heart. He sank to his knees and sifted dirt through his fingers. His voice was so low Derrick could barely hear him. "She's got to be somewhere, man! I'm getting very bad vibes here, and I don't know what to do about it." He looked hopelessly into his brother's concerned eyes. "I know she's somewhere in danger. I can feel it in my spine, and it's melting through me, settling into my heart. I've got to find her."

Derrick knelt beside him, sifting dirt as well. "This is a large state to be looking for one single woman. I say if we don't find her soon we go for help. We know officers who will search before the twenty-four hour waiting period, especially since you're so worried. First, think about where else she may be. We haven't been everywhere, you know."

"She liked town quite a bit, loved the shops on Coal Avenue, but what's the danger in those places?"

"She may not be in danger, Darrius. The calls may have been a mistake or something."

"Will you stop with that? Who is the one who picked up on vibes when Dad fell from that second floor landing at the plant five years ago and couldn't call anyone? He was alone there, but I knew what happened. I felt it! Who is the one who—"

"I get it already! You're psychic! Now will you settle down?"

"No. Something's wrong, Derrick."

A fleeting hush came over the brothers, then Darrius stood to his feet, saying, "God, no! God, no!"

"What?" Derrick asked.

"Red Rock! Why didn't I pick up on this before? She could be dead up there."

"What the hell are you talking about?"

"We've got to get to Red Rock. Justine's there." He pulled Derrick by the arm as he walked towards the truck.

Derrick pulled away and got behind the wheel. "Why would she be there?"

"Because I told her not to. It's just her way. I know and accept this about her. I just hope she hasn't gone where I specifically told her to stay away from."

"The other side?"

"You got it!"

"We'd better go."

The idea of her being on or near the jagged reaches of Red Rock made Darrius both nervous and mad. He hated the fact that she may have gone up there to see the ruins. Yet, fear for her was a much stronger emotion. He knew she was there. He wanted to yell to Derrick to drive faster, but getting upset would only make matters worse.

Derrick glanced at Darrius at times, seeing the worry etched on his face, the stiffness in his body, his mind running a mile a minute. He cleared his throat and tried to take his brother from a temporary hell. "Why would she be there? Would she dare take pictures of the Navajo and the ancient Anasazi lands there?"

"I don't think so. If anything, she would shoot landscape. At the very worst, she would simply view the forbidden places. I think she respects the land and legends too much to take pictures and exploit the place. I know her."

"Yet you love everything about her. Am I right?"

Darrius stared at his brother with a look of fright and desperation. "Yes."

"Then why did you think she would be at El Morro near the ruins when you told her not to?"

"As I have already told you, investigation is a part of her. She wouldn't have taken pictures, and I told you that already. But if she is on those cliffs at Red Rock, I'm mad about it. I told her of the danger, and I hope she listened. Somehow, I don't think she did."

Twenty minutes later, at record speed, they turned onto the entrance of Red Rock. For the first time in Darrius's life, the winding road leading to danger seemed exactly that—danger. And he could feel life draining away up there. He pointed ahead. "Go up there."

Derrick looked at him. "You know the danger all three of us could be in if we do this. We may not be able to save her even if we do make it to the top."

"*When* . . . when we make it up there, now get going."

Derrick shrugged and drove on. "Must be love to make a man want to end his life."

"It's more than that and you know it. If she's up there, I've got to save her."

They soon reached the top and, sure enough, Darrius's four-by-four awaited them. The driver's door was open, and the motor was still running. Darrius quickly ran to the vehicle, shutting the engine off and looking inside for any evidence. Nothing. He and Derrick looked around the immediate area and then ventured to the other side. The pounding of his heart almost deafened him as they both curved along the hills leading to Navajo land.

Moving on, they entered rocky terrain, and Darrius was getting scared—not scared for himself, but scared of what he might see on the other side.

Now leading the way with Derrick behind him, he treaded closer to the flat sections hanging above the steep drop-offs. All along, he shook his head, not being able to believe Justine would go that far—if she had. Then where was she? For the first time in his life, Darrius wanted to be wrong, wanted to prove beyond a shadow of a doubt that it was his mind playing games with him.

They both looked around the cliffs and hills, seeing nothing but brilliant sunshine and reddish-brown giants that were thousands of years old, at least dating back to the Mesozoic. Not a trace of anything. As Derrick turned to go back to the truck, he spotted a black bag on one of the cliffs near old ruins and pointed. "What's that?"

"Where?" Darrius asked, almost with too much enthusiasm.

"To the left of us, but about twenty-five feet up. Don't you see it?"

Darrius recognized it almost immediately. Without saying anything, he took off to the other side, almost sliding down a small hill.

Derrick called after him, hardly able to keep up with his suddenly speedy brother. "What do you see?"

"That's a camera, and it looks like hers from what I can see."

They had to circle one of the larger cliffs just to get to the other side. The ground was terribly rocky, the land unused for centuries. It was no longer fertile; the ground

RED SKY

was barren and lacking nutrients. The land was land wasting away, but for unknown reasons. The place was dangerous. And there was a camera there, a most unwelcome visitor to ancient lands.

Now closer, Darrius now knew for sure it was Justine's camera. He frantically searched around the area, but not being convinced she wasn't there, he moved in closer.

Derrick tried pulling him back but lost grip as Darrius kept walking. Suddenly before them was an overhang that led to a small landing where the bag was. With careful steps, Darrius directed the rescue. "Hold my arm while I reach down and get it."

"No, it's too dangerous. Besides, you don't even see her there."

"Just do it!" He thrust his arm into Derrick's hand. "She wouldn't just leave it here. If I know her, she tried to get it. Besides, where would she go without the truck? Hold on tight or I'm dead!"

Slowly, Darrius lowered himself to the edge and reached over. Just beyond his reach was another landing. On that landing was a ripped sandal, part of a pink dress, and farther to his right, a scarred and bloodied hand with a familiar turquoise and spiny shell bracelet attached. "Justine!"

The sound of Darrius screaming at the top of his lungs almost caused Derrick to let go. Instead, he held on tighter; Darrius had found Justine. "Is she conscious?"

"Oh, my God! Justine!"

"Is she conscious?"

"I can't see her face! Hold me tighter and follow me."

"These rocks are brittle, Darrius. We could both fall."

"I have to get her, Derrick!"

He held Darrius's wrist tighter and slid to the edge. "Damn it! I hadn't planned on dying today. Why is she even here?"

Darrius looked back up. "Look, either you help me or I do this alone. Either way, I'm going down there."

Without another word, Derrick slid as far to the edge as he could, counting on his strength to hold out with possibly two people dangling from him.

The front of Justine's dress was the only thing Darrius could grip with ease. However, it ripped and her lifeless body slumped back against a cracking rock. With determination creasing his face, Darrius stretched, trying to grab her wrist. At the same time, his eyes narrowed in on the slab of sandstone beginning to fracture with each move of Justine's body. He called back to his brother. "Down a little more. This slab is ready to slide, and she'll go with it."

Now with added strength, Derrick held tighter, his boots digging into the crusted sandstone. "I've got you. Just stretch. Get her up, for Christ's sakes, before we all tumble to our deaths."

Darrius again reached for skin, finally grabbing the bracelet, and then the wrist. With a firm grip and a constant eye on the cracking slab, he stretched almost far enough to pull his arm out of socket. His words were silent, but his lips trembled, as if she could hear his nervous mumblings. *Come on, baby, hang in there.*

He slid her closer to him and finally saw her face. Her eyes were closed, forehead bleeding, neck twisted, streaks of tears staining her face.

With sweat rolling into his eyes, he bit down on his lip and pulled. Her body dangled in the air just as the slab of sandstone below her tumbled down, cracking into a million pieces against the bed of the cliffs. Without haste he pulled harder, praying Derrick could hold his grip. His and Justine's fates were literally in Derrick's hands.

Justine's limp body brushed against a jagged cliff, tearing her dress and cutting into her thigh. Blood dripped down her leg as Darrius continued to pull her to safety. The last thing on his mind was a cut thigh; he simply needed to know if his lover was still alive. From the look of her bruised forehead, the chances looked dim.

Darrius soon took her into his arms once they were on steady ground and placed her on a small patch of grass. He brushed the hair and dirt from her face, looking for any sign of life. He felt for a pulse. Nothing. His only recourse was to perform CPR. He breathed as much life as possible into her, watching frantically for even the slightest movement. Derrick was talking in the background, but Darrius could hear nothing, could see nothing and could feel nothing but pain for a love that may now be gone, forever.

Compressions achieved nothing. Darrius pulled Justine into his arms, rocking her, calling to her as he tried to make life return to a hopeless shell. His tears mixed with the sweat on her skin. He looked up at Derrick and said, "Call 911."

22

GONE BUT NOT FORGOTTEN

The gray haze finally lifted, and then there was sight. It hurt to move, hurt to breathe, but Justine had to know where she was. All she could see was white walls. *Am I dead? Is this what it looks like to be dead? Does it hurt to be dead?* Immediately, her right side started to throb. Though it hurt, her hand moved to the pain and rested gently on heavy gauze covering a wound. *There's no gauze in heaven.*

She strained to place her surroundings. Definitely a hospital. She looked over at the open window and saw Darrius sleeping in a chair. His clothes were dirty and torn. His face was covered in streaks of sand and sweat, his hair in disarray. She smiled, realizing Darrius had saved her from an area she had been warned to stay away from. What would he think of her when he awakened, she wondered.

She stared at his profile. He was so relaxed, at peace . . . so handsome. She could see that even though she felt like death itself. With the image of her perfect Darrius burned into her mind, she went back to sleep.

When she awakened hours later, Darrius was staring at her with a less than elated expression. Justine knew what she had done was wrong, and that he had every right to be mad. She spoke first. "Darrius, I'm so sorry. I only wanted to—"

"If you can manage to sit up, drink your tea. I brought a special healing brew. This will help you heal so you can hurry up and leave New Mexico." He sat back, expecting her to defend herself; he knew her well.

His words startled her, but she did what he expected and defended herself. "I know what I did was wrong, Darrius."

He waved his hand. "I don't want to hear it, Justine. I asked you not to go there. The place is dangerous. And besides, the ruins—"

"I didn't go to the ruins, as you already know."

"Your camera was near the ruins, Justine. Don't deny it."

"Near the ruins, Darrius, and that was as far as I went. I wouldn't have gone any farther, and you know it."

"Do I?"

"Yes!"

"But you disobeyed me, anyway. You knew the terrain was treacherous, Justine. Did you go to El Morro, too? You were gone an awfully long time."

"Please, don't be mad at me. I know—"

He moved his chair closer to her. "Don't be mad at you? You've gotta be kidding. I clearly asked you not to go to that part of Red Rock. I know the area, Justine. I almost killed myself up there one day exploring where even I had no business going. You disobeyed me."

Her eyes met his, concern and confusion creasing her forehead. "Disobeyed you! Darrius, I'm not a child. I'm your lover. I'm not someone who is supposed to *obey* you."

"You're right! I *asked*, yet you took it upon yourself to do what you wanted anyway. How can I trust someone like that, Justine?"

She tried her best to sit up and discuss this with him, but pain forced her against the pillow. Still, her weak voice continued. "I would think by now you'd know enough about me that you could still trust me. Sure, what I did was stupid, and I'm sorry. Can't you understand that?"

"Justine, try to get this into your thick skull. It wasn't only yourself you put in jeopardy. *I* rescued you with the help of my brother. All three of us could be dead in some ravine. Your parents could be less one daughter and my own parents would be facing the deaths of two more children. Two more, Justine. Losing a child isn't an easy thing. I saw what losing a child did to my parents years ago when the baby died, and it wasn't a pretty sight."

His words stung like a million bee stings, but they were true. Yet she remained defensive. "I didn't ask you to save me, did I?"

"What? How stupid is that? In case you don't realize this, I care an awful lot about you. Maybe this whole ordeal was only one-sided. Do you even care about me and what you put me through?"

"Of course I do, and don't ever question my love for you. That's why I apologized. I know I was wrong."

"You're damn right you were wrong." He pushed the bed tray closer to her. "Drink the tea. I had Derrick go to my store and bring it here. Even he isn't crazy about seeing you after what you put us through." He saw tears welling in her eyes and suddenly hated himself for being so harsh with her. He sat on the corner of her bed, smoothing the crisp white sheet over her knees, softening his voice. "How do you think it made me feel to see you lying on that slab of cracking sandstone not knowing whether you were dead or not? The minute I moved you, the slab fell. Had I not gotten there in time, you'd be part of the ravine. You wouldn't even be recognizable."

Her eyes widened as she visualized the image he had painted so vividly.

"Once I got you here and they told me you would survive, my heart screamed with joy. Then it hit me what you had done. You went against me, against my people's land. Sometimes you have to know when to not be so adventurous, especially when it could endanger someone. I could have lost you."

He stood and walked over to the door. Before leaving, he turned back to her. "Maybe I already have lost you. Maybe I care just a little bit more about *us* than you do. How do you think it made me feel when you didn't trust *my* words? I felt so worthless and unimportant—like I was nothing more than a New Mexico fling—something to do, something to give you yet one more experience in your career. I know these lands, Justine. Let me tell you what else I think I know—that you would have eventually made it over to the ruins beyond where we found you. You may have even photographed them. Don't say you wouldn't have."

She slowly looked into his eyes. "Well, you are going to hear it. Photographing the ruins was not going to happen. I know they're sacred, Darrius. I may say and do a lot of things I shouldn't, but exploiting native history isn't one of them. I respected what you told me, and I never would have taken pictures. I would hope by now you would trust me."

"Really? Why should I?"

"Because it's true. I swear."

"I don't believe you. What other forbidden places have you gone to? I know there is something else. How am I to not to know you haven't already gone up Red Rock once before? I don't know, Justine. Something tells me there's more to this whole charade than you're letting on."

"Darrius, don't leave. Stay here so we can work this out. Help me to save us. I was wrong and I've admitted it. Don't you love me enough to at least try to get over this?"

He thought about her words for a second, and then walked out. He was as stubborn and bullheaded as she was, an aspect he hated about himself. This time, however, he felt defeated. Defeated by yet another woman, and his heart dragged behind him down the long hospital hall and into the setting sun of another long Gallup evening.

For a long time, Justine stared at the door, hoping, praying, he would come back, but somehow knew he wouldn't. He was a proud man, and his heritage was important to him. Apparently, it was more important to him than she was. In her heart, Justine knew that wasn't true. He loved her and she knew it. She knew she was the one who soiled their relationship. Her investigative side had gotten her in a heap of trouble before, but this was, by far, the worst of her misadventures. Her heart ached as she recalled the words he had spoken. And what made them hurt more was that they were true. He knew her actions, her every move. He apparently also knew of her trip up the hills of Red Rock the other day as well. Only then she was scared to go all the way up. Today had been different.

And then she thought: *Why would she want to be involved with a man who knew so much about her?* Her *other* side answered, the side that craved love and affection and wanted it more than ever now. He was sweet, kind—the best thing that had ever happened to her. Now he was gone. Tears stained her face and bed sheets. With shaking hands, she reached for the cup of hot tea. With each sip she could taste Darrius. She could feel him in every drop. He was in her blood.

Justine sat by the entrance to the hospital waiting for her taxi to arrive. She knew Darrius should have been there, but he hadn't been back to the hospital since their argument. She took total responsibility, but the pain of it was like a jolt of lightning. Everyone was mad at her: her boss, Darrius and probably his entire family. Seemingly, all of the Southwest was ashamed of her. She felt as if she had wandered into a sacred crypt in one of the great pyramids. Crypts, sacred grounds, what did it matter? She had messed up. Now the task at hand was to get to the train station early the next morning and return to reality. Being there with Darrius had been beyond reality, it was more like a dream vacation, and he was the best souvenir of all. That was over now.

She was helped into the taxi by her nurse and driven to the Red Rock Best Western to order room service and sulk the rest of the day and night.

When she entered her room, she realized everything was gone except for her clothing and the bracelet Darrius had given to her. She slipped it on and tried to at least keep a small part of him alive in her.

There was a note on her pillow along with an envelope. Inside, there were $200 dollars and another note. "Have a good meal or two, pay the taxi to take you to the train station. Anyway, have a good life. Darrius."

Direct, impersonal and devoid of feeling—everything the real Darrius wasn't. She read the other note. "I've packed the rest of your things and had them shipped to your home address in San Francisco. I even went back to Red Rock to retrieve your camera. I had a few men on harnesses go down and get it. It's still usable. I also left the bracelet for you. The hospital handed a bag of your belongings to me the day I took you there. The bracelet was inside it. I figured you'd like to have this as a memento of how much I love you. I only wish you had appreciated it. Darrius."

Her heart dropped to the basement of the hotel. From that point on, all she did was curl into a ball in the center of the bed, watch HBO and order food. Periodic tears kept her face wet until she cried herself to sleep around midnight.

Red Sky Jewelers opened up at nine each morning, and she knew she had just enough time to have the taxi run her over there for a few minutes. She was hoping for one more chance to make Darrius believe in her again.

She hesitated before pulling open the heavy oak doors to the store to face Darrius, but she knew she had to if she wanted to prove herself to him. True enough, there he was at the counter doing inventory on a pile of red-oyster necklaces. But as she moved closer, she realized it was Derrick.

Derrick's gaze met hers and his body visibly stiffened. In a cautious monotone, he said, "I see you're feeling better."

"Much. I want to thank you—"

"No need."

Moments of awkward silence passed between them before she continued. She looked around the store as if the surroundings would give her courage. But there was no courage to be had, just facts and truths. "Is . . . Darrius around? I'd like to—"

"Say goodbye to him?"

She stared blankly into his eyes before answering. "Uh . . . no. Actually, I'd like to—never mind. Is he here?"

"No."

"Where is he?"

"He's gone to the mountains."

"Oh, I see. Did he have another vision?" *Of us?*

Derrick flashed an irritated look. "A vision!" He drummed his fingers on the counter. "If you really need to know, he went up there to think! You really messed him up. He can't even sleep at night. He's gone to the mountain to get some peace, think things over—start a new life." He hung several necklaces on a rack, and then turned to her. "I don't think this *new life* will involve you."

A bomb went off inside her, shattering her insides along with any hope for forgiveness. Her words came slowly. "Can . . . you tell him something for me?"

"Maybe."

"Can you tell him I love him?"

"Do you? It seems hard to believe after what you put us through."

"Can you just tell him?" Before she heard his answer, she rushed through the door and into the taxi. Soon, New Mexico would be a blur, and thankfully so.

As the train passed mountains, she wondered which one Darrius was on. To stop herself from having a crying fit, she kissed the bracelet and thanked God for it. She at least had it to remind her that she once had love in her life.

"Ms. Paretti, your packages arrived from New Mexico. I wasn't sure if you would have wanted me to open your loft and put them in, but I took a chance. I left everything else as is. Hope you don't mind."

She smiled thankfully at her landlord. "That's fine. I'm glad someone still cares enough about me. Thanks."

Her landlord looked at her with concern. "Are you okay?"

"Not really, David, but I suppose one day I will be—again."

That was definitely an indication she and Darrius were finished. Something so sweet had suddenly turned so bitter, and just hearing about Darrius sending her things along had made her stomach instantly sick. Yes, this failed relationship was definitely of her own doing.

As a diversion, she unpacked the box labeled 'Kachinas' and pulled out her Koshari, admiring it, touching the tasseled hat. Images of Darrius dancing the clown dance immediately popped up, and her first smile in days appeared when she remembered how well he danced, how he made her feel that night—and the awesome love they made after returning to his home. Then the smile faded and she placed the Koshari on a shelf in her living room. There was another item in the box. Justine reached inside and carefully pulled out the Crow Mother kachina. She definitely did not remember buying it, but remembered Darrius saying he would take her to buy one. She couldn't help but smile as she held the doll, feeling its smooth wood finish. The designs painted onto the doll were so intricate, with long jagged edged ears and a foxtail circling the neck. It was a marvelous piece that easily cost six or seven hundred dollars.

She placed the doll near the Koshari, seeing it as a sign that Darrius still loved her enough to spend that kind of money to make her happy; only she didn't need expensive things to make her feel loved by him.

Knowing she would never feel his arms around her again suddenly made her want to put both dolls away, along with the bracelet, T-shirts and any other part of the Southwest she had collected. They served to remind her of what it had cost her.

She resisted the impulse to hide everything, picking up her camera instead. One corner was damaged, but Darrius had done a great job cleaning and repairing it. She was just thankful he was able to retrieve it. Many a wonderful picture had been taken with that camera, along with her others. Funny thing, she had almost taken her other camera with her to Red Rock that day; the one where film had to be exposed in a dark room. What would Darrius have seen then? Everything he asked her not to photograph because she shouldn't have been on that side of the park anyway. Then she thought about it. He may have downloaded the images inside this camera. He would have seen everything.

That gave her an idea—something that would possibly take her mind off Darrius, at least temporarily. Film was still inside her other camera, and she immediately went to her makeshift darkroom to develop them. Being in the dark reminded her of the first time Darrius kissed her, how his fingers slid up her blouse, caressing her skin. She shook the thought away, not wanting to recall the memory of something that would never happen again.

Minutes later, Justine hung pictures of the desert flowers atop Red Rock, the few cottonwood trees and the red mountain ranges. There was nothing of the ruins. She didn't even know where they were, and hadn't planned to look. Her mission had been to take great photographs and to take her curiosity to new levels by trying to see as much as possible. Whether or not that was accomplished was another story. She had slipped down slabs of sandstone, almost ending her life—all for the sake of a few personal shots. Stupid! Also, she *had* ignored Darrius's warnings, had not trusted his word. Trust was very important to him, as it should be in any relationship.

She stepped back and admired the pictures, letting them take her back to a place where she had been truly happy, at least for a week. She unpacked another box and took out her personal pictures of the powwow, the day and night parade, and the hills behind Darrius's house. Maybe the beauty of the photographs would soften her boss's anger. Yes, her boss knew of her accident, but he was a hard-nose and wanted his stuff in on time. Justine looked at the small calendar hanging on the wall. The timing was still good, because the edition wasn't due to print for another three days. That was the only thing that could possibly save her butt—and her job.

23

MISSING HIM

September 10

The powwow edition of *The Examiner* came out on
Justine's birthday. It had been her only perk since
returning home a month ago. She had tried her best not
to think of Darrius, her trip or anything remotely related
to New Mexico. She buried herself in work, taking on
new assignments no matter how menial. Earlier that day,
she did her usual volunteer work at the boys club.
Working with the children always made her feel better.
However, working with the Native American boys that
day only reminded her of Darrius. One boy, Sanchez,
even looked like a ten-year-old version of Darrius, and
working with him made matters worse. Sanchez had
always been her favorite student; he was so willing to
learn photography and angle shots. He saw the pain in
her eyes that day.

"Are you okay, Ms. Paretti?"

She smiled into his innocent face and mussed his thick,
dark hair. "Just not one of my better days, Sanchez."

He handed her a fabric flower he had been holding
behind his back. "I made this for you in arts and crafts
today. You like it?"

Taking the flower, she smiled and said, "It's beautiful, Sanchez, and guess what? Today is my birthday. A woman loves flowers on her birthday." She kissed the top of his head, and started her lesson as the other children slowly filed in.

When she walked into the office at work, she found the new edition of *The Examiner* on her desk and the memories seemed to flood her, like an awakening. For once, it was refreshing to see a picture of a native sky, the true blueness of it, the richness and serenity of it. Unlike a San Francisco sky and its fog, the photograph she'd taken of an early Gallup morning made her smile. One of her main pictures graced the cover—the banner and entrance of the Day parade.

She thumbed through until she found the reddish-brown cliffs. They were her photographs of Red Rock State Park. It had taken her until now to actually think fondly of the place. What had taken longer was not persecuting herself over what had transpired there. In the back of her mind, Red Rock represented why she and her lover were a no-go, but she had gotten used to the reality of it, had accepted the fact that love was gone. Now it was time to move on, take pride in her work, accept kudos from coworkers on a job well done and make her photos of New Mexico something people would remember. As she looked at the photos, pleased at how good they were, she thought of the man who was probably still somewhere in the mountains, grappling with the betrayal of a lover.

As she put the newspaper down, her boss came in with a bouquet of yellow and desert-sand sprayed flowers. His smile, something that hardly saw the light of day, seemed to brighten the room. Finally, he had gotten over the fact that one of his best photojournalists almost died for the cause. However, she would never reveal what her *true* cause had been after meeting Darrius Red Sky.

"Love the photo spread, Justine. Love it! This is by far our best piece on the Southwest in the paper's history. Sure, you had a little stumble, but we pulled through, right?"

She looked at him. *A little stumble? I almost fell from a damn cliff!* "Yes, I was just looking through it. Quite a beautiful layout, too, if I do say so myself. I really captured the flavor of the area, those beautiful hills, mountains in the distance, the quietness of the early mornings. What did you like most about the photographs, the pow-wows?"

"Actually, I like the pictures of you helping out at the mission schools. Never knew you liked kids so much."

"You never asked. I've always loved children, and when I can help them, I do. I always donate money to mission schools, St. Jude's Hospital—any institution or program that helps children. You should know that about me by now. I've only worked for you for three years."

"Yeah, whatever. I love the photos of the day parade and how you got right in the middle of the action. That's one thing I've always liked about you, Justine; you're never afraid to take a chance."

"Yeah, brave ol' me." *A curse.*

He held his arm up in a half salute. "For the cause, do or die, right?"

"You don't know how true those words really were when I fell from the cliff."

"And one of the local natives rescued you, you say?"

Local natives! He's a little more than that! "You could safely say that. And it was two men—brothers."

"We need to send them their own edition. Did you get their names?"

All too well. "Yes, Darrius Red Sky and his brother Derrick."

A smile wrinkled his red, aging face. "Red Sky, huh? Well, make sure you send them both a copy." He walked to the door, but paused. "Ready for the Western Voices interview in a few weeks?"

"Sure. Can't wait." *I just wish it wasn't on Darrius's birthday, October 31.*

"Oh, by the way, thanks for the invite to your party tonight. A few of us may decide to drop by and meet the parents of such a fine photographer."

"Sure, come on by."

Once alone, she thought of her boss's words. *Send him an edition.* Would Darrius even open mail from her address or *The Examiner's?* She looked through her edition again, knowing he'd love to see his people represented so well, so proudly. A spread on his homeland across the pages of a national newspaper would make him happy. That is what she wanted—a way to somehow make Darrius happy, to think better of her, even if they never got back together again. Being known as a good person by others had always been important to her, even more so with him.

At that, she decided to take a chance and mail a copy to him and Derrick. She would include a note; not just one hoping for forgiveness, but one of apology, thanking him for the experience of showing her, for the first time, what love was, and that it didn't have to take months or years to establish. Her parents dated for a year before deciding to take it to the next level. That had been impossible for her and Darrius. They knew right off that they were supposed to be together.

Her hand shook as she wrote the note. She started to ball the paper up and forget the whole thing, but she knew it was worth a shot for Darrius to have kinder thoughts of her:

Darrius, I hope you don't mind me contacting you, but I wanted you to see just how serious I was about making Albuquerque, Gallup and the native culture something to be cherished and respected. I know I did terrible things to break us apart, and there is not a day that goes by when I'm not thinking about you and what we had. I miss you, love you and will always cherish the brief time we had together. Always know that you are in my heart, and will always be. You're my soul mate, and if I never see you again, it is truly my loss. Please enjoy the photographs. I think I've captured some very valuable scenes that people around the world will remember. I've included photos taken the day of my fall. I hope this will prove to you my true intention, which was solely to take great photographs. I would never desecrate something so valuable to you and your people. I love you so much, Darrius.

Justine.

Overnight, Justine had become one of the most sought-after photographers on the West Coast. She looked forward to seeing her family and friends all together to celebrate two special occasions—her birthday and the photo spread. So, it was a double celebration. Her office had been flooded with calls from other publications trying to lure her to their team. Her email inbox was clogged with good wishes.

Just before leaving the office for the party, she took a call from *Western Voices News Magazine* asking for an interview to be aired nationally. She was enjoying the attention, having fun with the notoriety, but there was still a huge part of her missing, and she could feel his presence in the aching in her heart. *He should be here.*

After the party wound down, the only guest was her girlfriend since eighth grade, Fara, half Native American, half African American, the best friend a girl could have.

Fara took Justine's hand and said, "I didn't give you the other gift I have for you."

"What other gift?"

"I gave you turquoise earrings to match the bracelet Darrius gave you, but there is something else."

"I told you not to get me anything. You being here with me tonight is gift enough, Fara."

"One more little thing." She took out an envelope from her purse and handed it to Justine. "This may be just the thing you need to soothe your mind, if not your heart. I know you miss Darrius. For God's sakes, you cried on my shoulder the first three days you returned from New Mexico and you would hold on tightly to that fetish his sister gave you as you cried. I'm surprised you don't have it with you tonight."

"The fetish is my totem. It protects me. I had it in my hand the day I fell from the cliff and I never dropped it, even though I was unconscious. Go figure, huh?"

"If you say so. Now open my other gift. This will help."

Justine opened the envelope and took out two tickets. "Two tickets to the San Francisco Autumn Native American Festival. Wow! I didn't know it was coming up so soon."

"It's in early November, as usual. Time always gets away from you. Will you go with me?"

Justine did not relish the prospect of going to another powwow. She knew just the sight of the vibrant colors, the decorative dress and the talented dancers would take her right back to where she wanted to be but couldn't be—in Darrius's world. But she didn't want to make Fara feel bad, so she graciously accepted the invitation. "I'll wear my new earrings, my Koshari shirt and the squash necklace."

Fara reminded her, "Don't forget to wear Darrius's bracelet."

"It is his bracelet, isn't it? I see him all over it and I never leave home without it."

"You hadn't better dare."

Justine eyed her friend suspiciously. "Do you know something I don't?"

"What would I know?"

"You have always been a sneaky little thing. Something's up and I'd better keep an eye on you, my dear."

"Nothing is going on. I just want you to have fun, live your life despite any setbacks. You're beautiful, young and smart. You can have any man you want."

But I want Darrius. She hoped she wouldn't receive Darrius's newspaper back with the letter inscribed *Return to Sender.*

Would her wound ever heal?

24

MISSING HER

Two copies of Justine's newspaper with photo spread lay in front of Darrius as he sipped a cup of Warrior's Brew tea before opening his store. One he had purchased, and the other was the one she had sent. No way on earth could he have sent it back to her. It was like a present from a distant friend . . . too distant. Though he was still mad at her for going against his word, he couldn't keep his mind off her. His every thought was of what she was doing, what she was wearing, her smile, her intelligence. Yet he remained too stubborn to pick up the phone and call her.

Several times during the past month he had reached for the phone, wanting to hear her voice, but would suddenly change his mind. Once he had even dialed, but hung up before she could answer. He had written emails about how he missed her, but would neglect to press the "send" button. Darrius knew his cold feet were related to his feeling that maybe he'd been too hard on her. He knew how inquisitive she was. Now, he was unsure as to whether she would even want to talk to him after weeks of no contact. Whatever the case, he had to have a piece of her, even if it was simply through reading her newspaper spread.

The television played softly in the background. It was the day of Justine's interview, so he closed the newspaper, drank the last of his tea and settled in to watch the only woman he had ever loved.

The bells on the door jingled, and Derrick came in the store with a bag of bagels and honey cream cheese. "Is she on yet?"

"Hush! They haven't mentioned anything yet." Then he looked at his brother with surprise. "How did you know about her interview? I haven't told you anything."

"I read newspapers, too, like the one she sent me. Did you think the wind told me?"

"Max out! Only I have that power."

"You should by now. God only knows you stayed on that mountain long enough after she left to have gained more power."

"I was asking our relatives what to do about Justine."

"And what did they say?" Derrick plopped the bag of bagels and cream on the table.

"Go to her."

"Then why are you still here after weeks of missing her? I see how depressed you've been since she left. I've seen it before with what's-her-name? Ma Barker?"

"Cute! Kid all you like, but it's never been like this before. The day Justine left town I had a tantrum. Remember?"

"Who couldn't? You tore your house up, broke furniture, busted some pots and ripped the Koshari picture off your wall. Your bed was turned upside down. When I walked in and saw you, you were huddled in a corner, drunk and crying. Funny thing. I haven't seen you cry since we were kids, the day I broke that stupid toy airplane Uncle Pete bought you."

Darrius quickly opened one bagel and smeared the light brown cream cheese on it. "No one has taken my heart away before—not like this."

"Then again I'm asking, what are you still doing here when you should be hightailing it to San Francisco? What are you afraid of?"

"Rejection."

"Bull! You're not afraid of anything—well, other than facing Justine. Look, man, I was mad at her, too, but I'm not her lover. You are. She does still want you, you know?"

"Yeah? How do you know?"

"The wolves told me."

Darrius waved his hand in front of his brother's face. "Whatever. Be quiet, I think Justine is due up next."

Darrius sat quietly, determined not to get excited over seeing Justine. After all, she was the one who went against his wishes and almost got three people killed. Then why was he still in love? Having no answer to that, he decided he couldn't change fate. He'd also decided never to be hurt by another woman again—even if she was the reason he smiled. He waited expectantly for her face to appear on the screen. She had good things to say, and he wanted to hear them. He knew that was an excuse. He just plain wanted to see her, and that was all there was to it!

Next to the host was a vision of loveliness. She wore the Koshari T-shirt and a pair of white jeans. He slowly stood without knowing it.

"Thought you weren't going to get bent out of shape over her," Derrick said in a rather sarcastic tone.

Darrius's only response was, "Hush!" Indeed, absence did make the heart grow fonder. Suddenly, any thought of staying away from her seemed to evaporate. Now more than ever he missed how she held him tight in her arms, how she kissed him, how they made love. It was something powerful, something he'd had with no other woman before Justine. They made magic together. He missed it.

"Sit down already! You're blocking the TV."

Derrick's voice brought Darrius back to reality. He slowly sat, but turned the volume up and tried his best to listen to her words instead of wallowing in the need to touch her.

"From the look of you, Ms. Paretti," the host said, "you've really gotten into the spirit of the way of life of the Native Americans in the region."

"It's been my experience that you have to live the life in order to capture it. I think that can be seen in a lot of my photographs. This time it is a little different, I admit. I just want readers and viewers to appreciate the lives of these remarkable people. In some ways, how they celebrate life is more like poetry. How they honor their ancestors and respect the earth and its living things is an approach to life I think all of us can benefit from."

"And bringing this to life by way of a powwow is very enlightening, Ms. Paretti. Can you tell us a little about the photographs we have here?"

In the background, Darrius saw enlarged photos of native dancers, the cliffs of Red Rock and of his store. Never had he thought his own store would be featured on television.

"The first photo is of the grass dance at the main powwow the weekend of the Intertribal Ceremonial, one of the few dances I was allowed to photograph. It's a religious dance, as are most of their dances. To the Hopi nation, and probably others, when they dance, they pray; when they pray they fix things, people. It's all for the well-being of the community and beyond. These dances are beautiful metaphors to celebrate life. The grass dance is one of the oldest dances from the warrior society. Briefly, a warrior is in search of a ceremonial place. The dancer portrays tall, swaying prairie grass. The red cliffs you see are those of Red Rock State Park, where the main powwow takes place. As you can see, the area is very scenic. Anyone who has been to New Mexico has seen how picturesque it is."

"And the store? Is there something special about it? Many stores throughout the Southwest sell native artifacts. What makes this one special enough to photograph?"

Darrius moved closer to the TV in the small kitchenette in back of the store anxiously awaiting her comments on him, if she had any. But, maybe she would only speak of the store. After the way he had ended things with her, he would understand if his name didn't come up at all.

"This store is owned by a very wonderful man I met—Darrius Red Sky. He was my host and guide, and showed me many of the area's wonders. Besides that, his store is filled with the most exquisite works of art from all Indian nations, not just those of the Southwest." She held her bracelet to the camera. "This piece is turquoise and spiny oyster hearts, one of many specially hand-crafted items you'll find here. The store carries all kinds of pots, baskets, rugs, Navajo and Hopi kachinas, and even the Koshari clown, one of which is resting happily on my T-shirt. So if you're interested in native art, Darrius Red Sky is the man to see. He also makes a ter-rific brew of Teepee Dreams tea. I should add that won-derful stores can be found throughout the Southwest, so buyers can't go wrong."

Darrius was smiling so hard his cheeks hurt. Finally, "That was me she was talking about, Derrick. Me! I can't believe she still thinks so highly of me after the way I acted with her."

"You had every right to treat her the way you did, Darrius. Don't second-guess yourself. You were pro-tecting the ruins, the past lives of our people, and you didn't want them desecrated."

"That's the thing. She didn't desecrate anything. She never took pictures of the ruins, just surrounding trees and flowers. I know she wouldn't have wanted to dese-crate anything. I should have understood her inquisitive nature. It's part of her, like me knowing aspects of the future is a part of me. I know what else is a part of me."

"What?"

"Justine Roberts-Paretti, if she'll have me."

"What are you going to do about it?"

"I don't know. Suppose she rejects me. She would have every right, and I can't risk wanting her and not being able to have her, Derrick. I don't know what to do."

Derrick turned the television off. "I would think the answer is simple. Use your intuition; see what the wind tells you."

"This time I think it's my heart I need to have a sit-down talk with."

"Just go to her and get it over with, man. You heard the wonderful things she said about you. Words like that can mean only one thing—that girl is still in love with you. It doesn't take a genius or shaman to figure that out."

"Maybe, but there's more to it than that. After I make the jewelry run to Santa Fe, perhaps I'll know what to do. That'll give me time to think, gather some nerves, and then maybe I can convince her I'm not the animal who bit into her jugular at the hospital."

"She already knows that. Didn't she explain anything to you in her letter?"

"Yes, but seeing each other face to face could be another matter altogether."

"You'll never know unless you try. Right? Do you love her enough to try?"

"Look at my face and tell me."

Derrick stood and grabbed his brother's shoulder. "Yep! Looks like love to me. The thing to do now is con-fess it again to her—if you still have the nerve."

25

POWWOW PANDEMONIUM

November 8

After a grueling Saturday of photo shoots, Justine did not feel like going anywhere. But it was the powwow and she knew she would enjoy it once there, even though it would remind her of Darrius. She hadn't heard from him since that awful day at the hospital. He hadn't even responded to the newspaper she sent. Did he even like it? There had been no call, no postcard, not even a simple email. Days after she *knew* he'd received the paper and she still hadn't heard from him, she knew they were through!

She no longer cried in Fara's arms, but she never removed the bracelet he had given her. She seemed to need a reason to remember him, as if her aching heart wasn't reminder enough! And now she had to go to the powwow. Had it been a gift from anyone but Fara, she would have cancelled.

Fara was to pick her up at seven and she wanted to be ready, physically and emotionally. Emotionally was the hard part. Justine looked at her face in the mirror and saw way more than a young woman tired from a hectic day at work. There were lines around her eyes, worry creases on her forehead. They had been there since leaving New Mexico, and the only remedy for them was being in Darrius's arms.

As the water drenched her body and awakened her senses to the lovely April Rains shower gel, her hand traveled over her naked body, touching places she had forgotten she had. And there Darrius was, as if he was actually standing there naked and wet. She could see him, smell his natural aroma, feel him touching delicate and aroused parts of her body. Her own hands traveled to her breasts, squeezing them, heightening the sensitive buds. She hadn't allowed herself to become excited over the idea of Darrius since New Mexico, but there he was, and again she was his slave.

Her nipples swelled even more in her hands as she imagined they were his. She was no longer in a shower, in her loft in the middle of downtown San Francisco—she had leapt straight into Indian country and landed in the arms of her past lover.

Velvety April-scented hands encircled her breasts, and then slid down her sides and slender hips as his had done back when she was alive. She was alive now, and yearned to become supernatural with one touch to her sex. No, she couldn't go there, wouldn't go there! Sure, she had already entered his world, but for some reason, touching her sex, one he had toyed, browsed, claimed, she felt it would take her over the edge and into a realm of continuous tears.

She went there, anyway, slowly touching wet, warm feminine folds dying to be pleasured by the touch of one man. Slowly, her fingers traveled to the secret place, rubbing, stroking, seeing Darrius's excited, sensuous face kissing her. The friction peaked with each stroke and brought her to an enormous orgasm. She hadn't had one since kissing Darrius the night before the accident at Red Rock.

It was hard to determine whether the wetness on her face was from the shower, or a mixture of tears from pleasure and sadness. Sadness. She leaned against the shower wall and let go, crying, almost out of control, sinking to her knees. Then suddenly, she looked around and saw herself in the most pitiful state she'd ever been in. Almost immediately, she rose, reached for her towel and dried her tears.

Justine eagerly jumped into Fara's Saturn as if she hadn't had the most awful crying spell of her life. But, her tears had faded away, and suddenly she was ready for the powwow.

Fara looked at Justine's perfectly made-up face and asked, "Okay, what's the problem?"

That took her by surprise, having thought she had done an excellent job of covering up pain. "What are you talking about?"

"I see something in your eyes. You don't want to go, do you?"

"Yes, I do, and I know what you're thinking, that the powwow will make me sad."

"Am I right?"

"You would have been earlier, but I'm fine now. I'm actually excited about seeing the dances and buying more things. They have the most incredible—"

"Justine! Really, are you going to be okay? It won't hurt me if we don't go."

Justine settled against the seat, looking straight ahead with a dreamy, far-away look. "I should go, help myself get over him, and maybe this is the way to do it."

For the first time since she started going to area pow-wows a few years ago, the dancing would be the main event to watch. When she and her mother had gone, their first order of business was to check out the native wears, take whatever photos she could, and then, as an afterthought, sit and watch the ceremonies. The colors and dance steps fascinated her so she stayed, took in the festivities. As the years passed, she found other reasons to attend the smaller powwows.

Justine took a seat in one of the upper bleachers in the expo center near the drums and waited for the Grand Entry to start. Fara had gone to fetch buffalo burgers— something they had both come to love. After standing for the veteran tribute, she tried to concentrate on the beating drums as the men pounded a ceremonial tribute. But she kept seeing Darrius among the drummers. She knew this would happen. Every man she saw would resemble her lover. That, she expected, and was almost the reason she didn't attend.

Fara returned and handed her a paper cup of tea and the burger. "Hey, don't you want to walk around and see the goodies first? I saw The Mountain T-shirts on the other side, and they have more great designs this year."

Justine's voice was listless, a hint of despair choking her words. "No, I basically came to watch the dances more than anything. Maybe after the Grand Entry we can look around."

Fara pulled out the schedule of events. "Yeah, that's good timing because the storytelling is next, and we can hear that from anywhere in here."

She stared at Justine's profile, feeling sorry for her lovesick friend. Trying to ease her woes, she nudged her shoulder and asked, "So, have you seen his look-alike yet?"

Justine turned to her. "Whose?"

"You know who I'm talking about. I see you scanning the area as if searching for him. I knew you'd do this, Justine, and you need to stop."

"I'm not looking for him, okay? Believe me, I know better than anyone that Darrius isn't here. He'll never be here, and we both know it."

"I don't think you believe that."

"Come on, Fara, don't do this. It's bad enough that I'm not over him. I don't need anyone forcing the issue, okay?"

Fara shrugged. "Fine, but I just want you to have a good time." She pulled out a wrapped item from her bag. "Here, I bought you something before I got the food." She unwrapped a single eagle feather with a clip on the end. "Here, wear this. It'll look good with your attire." She clipped it to some of Justine's long strands.

"Where did this come from? It looks awfully real."

"It is. Actually, I found it lying on the ground, dusted it off and—"

Justine was appalled. "You didn't! Tell me you didn't see it laying there and—"

"I'm kidding. I know you never pick up an eagle feather. I know you always get a tribe member to retrieve it instead. Come on, I'm aware of all the myths and sayings of my people—well, half of my people. Look, I'm just trying to lighten your burden by making you think of something else. Darrius told you about the feather, didn't he?"

"Good guess, Tonto."

The Grand Entry began and everyone stood as the first dancers entered the arena. It took her back to where she wanted to be, the main arena at Red Rock. But, Fara's words had hit home, and she realized she had to get a grip, enjoy the powwow and try to forget Darrius.

The drums started again, and out came the dancers into the middle of the arena floor. Several of the male dancers were tall, and their headdresses made them seem even more towering. They were handsome men, and Justine could see that through their highly decorated faces. Suddenly, she was in a better mood and she smiled at Fara. "Thanks for bringing me here. I think this is what I needed to take my mind away from my problems."

"It'll all get better with time."

Justine finished her drink and burger just as the grass dance started. One of the men who came out to perform was tall and had a complexion much like Darrius's. But his face was covered with war markings and other designs so she really couldn't see his features. Then her mind went to work to combat anything she subconsciously may have been doing. *No, he is not Darrius. You are seeing things that you want to see. He's not here. Enjoy the show, stupid!*

Still, the more she watched this man and his style of dance, the more she couldn't take her eyes off him. *No, he's not here.* She knew that, but the way the dancer's hair whipped across his face and shoulders did nothing but remind her of Darrius's Koshari dance. This was no Koshari tonight because this dancer had on bright yellow with stripes of cobalt blue throughout his headdress and costume. His moccasin-clad feet were bright yellow as well, matching the tassels of his pants. Besides, as far as she knew, Darrius never did the grass dance. He was strictly Koshari at its best. *No, this definitely isn't Darrius.* And there was no way Darrius would be in San Francisco and not find her.

The dancer seemed to have spotted her, and Justine picked up on it. But maybe he was fixed on something beyond her. She kept her eyes on him until he left the area after the dance.

Justine said nothing to Fara about her encounter with a strange dancer. It was for the best because she'd have been called psychotic by her best friend. She forced her mind to go elsewhere, like shopping, the part Fara liked the most anyway. It was fun trailing behind Fara as they stopped at booth after booth to see and partake of the wares.

Something made her turn around. At the T-shirt counter, several rows away was her grass dancer, still in his yellow and blue attire. The dancers hardly ever walked around in their outfits and makeup while browsing, but this guy did. What made it more interesting to Justine was that the dancer was looking at her. His face was still hidden by the makeup, but he was good looking—very good-looking.

This time she had to get Fara's attention. "Look at the dancer behind us. He looks like Darrius from what I can see of him."

With T-shirt in hand, Fara turned, saying, "Don't start."

"I'm serious. Look at him."

"How would I know what Darrius looks like?"

"I showed you his picture."

"Right. Forgot. But the guy is wearing makeup, and besides, every man is going to be Darrius to you tonight."

"I realize that, but—"

"Here. Isn't this the shirt you saw online and wanted to order?"

Justine looked at the shirt Fara was shoving into her chest. It was of a shaman conjuring a buffalo hunt. "Yeah, and the dark brown will look good on me, but—" She turned in the direction of where the dancer had been. He was gone. She scanned the area, but he was nowhere. "Fara, he was here and he looked so much like Darrius."

"It wasn't him, but if that guy looks like your Darrius, then he's a hottie, isn't he?"

Justine twisted her face into an arrogant frown. "People are beginning not to use 'hottie' anymore, Fara. Besides—"

"Besides nothing. Come on, let's shop before the jingle dance starts. You gonna buy that shirt or not?"

Justine threw it onto the table and pulled out a twenty. "Yeah, I'm buying it, okay?"

Before the transaction was completed, she looked in the area of the dancer, wondering where he went, if it were Darrius, and if he was really looking at her. So many questions, but in the back of her mind, she knew there was no way it was her Darrius. He was a lost cause.

26

LOVING HER

The powwow ended late, and all Justine wanted was a good long sleep and to spend Sunday alone. It had been a good powwow and also a good respite, and she wanted to thank Fara before saying goodbye.

At home in her bedroom, she took her shaman T-shirt from the bag and tried it on. It was a little large on her, fitting more like a nightshirt, so she kept it on. She plopped into her bed, never wanting to take the shirt off. Having something else that reminded her of Darrius so close to her heart made her calm. She retrieved the cottonwood carving of the Koshari from her nightstand and rested it on her chest in the quiet room.

The small nightlight by her bed softly illuminated her surroundings. Shadows danced slowly across the walls, propelled by a swift breeze outside. Drafty windows. Justine returned the doll back to its resting place, deciding the only way not to think of Darrius was simply to go to sleep.

But sleep did not come. What came instead were thoughts of the powwow. Her eyes popped open. Shadows still danced across the ceiling and walls, but they were beginning to lull her and she was thankful. One shadow by her bedroom door held her attention more than the others. She lingered on it for a second or two, knowing what she was seeing was a figment of her imagination. Extreme fatigue could easily have produced any kind of imaginary figure. Her mind saw Darrius dressed as the Koshari, and she quickly looked at the doll on the nightstand, hoping the vision at the door would be gone before looking back. Squinting, she then looked at the bedroom door again. It was still there.

Justine sat up. She was so frightened of what her mind *had* to be producing to say anything, let alone scream.

"Justine."

She jumped at the sound of his voice. *God, no! Is this a figment of my lunatic mind talking to me? I'm not that crazy yet, am I?*

"Justine. It's me, Darrius." He moved from the shadows and approached the bed. His hands hovered above her feet—feet too frightened to kick, too scared to even move. "Don't be scared, baby. It's me." He touched her, feeling the soft sheet covering frozen-in-place feet.

One touch from Darrius and she knew he was no figment. He was there, but how? Why? "Darrius?" She leaned forward, her voice cracking as she called to him once more. "Are you real, or am I a nutcase bound for the nearest ward?"

"You're no nutcase, my love. I know I look pretty damn odd coming to you in the middle of the night wearing the Koshari getup, but I had to come, baby."

Now, if I put my hands on this guy and make love to him all night, and he's not here in the morning—I'll commit myself to San Francisco General's nut ward immediately. She touched him. God, yes! He *was* real. Her mind danced with joy, her body trembled with want. She reached up to him, cradling him in her arms. "Darrius! Oh, my goodness! This *is* you."

She rested on her knees in the middle of the bed, keeping him in a tight embrace. Her Darrius was there, in her arms, and she touched him as if he'd break. Her fingers traveled over his features—draping across his nose, brow, jaw line, neck. She could feel the smoothness of the body paint on him. The striking black and white stripes glowed in the moonlight, peering in through her window. The only other light came from her nightlight.

Darrius reached to turn off the lamp, and Justine caught his hand. "No! Don't you dare turn off the light. I . . . need to see you, talk to you and convince myself you *really* are here. If you're not, Darrius, then I'm really losing it, and the thought scares me."

He pressed his forefinger against her lips. "I'm here, baby, and you're not crazy. I just want to see you, touch you, make you completely aware I am in this room with you. Love me, Justine, and let me love you back. Let me show you that I was a jackass. I never should have—"

Instantly, her lips engulfed his. Her wild tongue traveled within him, coiling around his until they both gave out and lay across the bed, never parting for one second. Her hands traveled up and down his taut body, smearing the paint, making it turn into slate-gray streaks across his almost-nude frame. Her man was in her arms, and no feeling in the world could compare.

Her heated kisses drowned him, and she tasted sugar-coated body paint as it mixed with his heat and sweat. He tasted of black licorice and white chocolate, one hundred percent male—one thousand percent Darrius Red Sky.

Justine briefly pulled back from him. "You taste like—"

"Yes, your favorites—black licorice and white chocolate, two powerful flavors created in body paint just for you. One of the dancers tonight helped me put it on after the dances."

"Then you were at the powwow tonight—"

He tenderly kissed her forehead. "Yes. I left the powwow the same time you did, wearing my paint, but with an overcoat on. I followed you and your friend here and made up my face once I parked in your lot."

"But how did you get in here? I know my lock is frail and David is fixing it on Monday, but—"

"Simple. It being a frail lock worked for me. I picked it and then gently closed it back behind me. I've picked locks before—the one to my Zuni store about a year ago after leaving my keys at home. Jemez showed me how to get into locks since he builds homes and installs that kind of stuff. It was easy."

She caressed his face. "Remind me to talk to David again about my lock."

"So I can stay out?"

"No, so I can keep you inside—silly. In this case, I'm glad the lock was easy to pick. I'm in the arms of a man I thought I would never see again. I'm so sorry for what I did, Darrius."

"Don't be. It's your nature to be curious and I should have known that. I'm the one who should be sorry—and I am. I was miserable there without you. I know we haven't known one another too long, but I need you, Justine. I have never said that about a woman before, never really had the opportunity because no one has struck me the way you have." He sat next to her, taking her hand. "I want to know everything about you, meet your family, friends, do what you do, like what you like—see what you see."

"That much, Darrius?"

"That and more. I want to learn more about your culture, be a part of it and of my own. I don't want this to be just about me, Justine. There's so much about African and Italian cultures that I haven't had the opportunity to want to know about until now."

"But you could have before meeting me."

"I know, but I never really had a reason until it hit home with me by being with you. There are *some* things I do know, like about Italian chefs—since I cook as well. I know about the African storytelling that is so much like my own. What you're made up of is so rich, but besides that, it's *you* I want to learn about more than anything. Just you, Justine, and I won't rest until I have you back in my life again. I—I was so stupid to let you go."

"I went against your word, Darrius."

"You haven't been the first, probably won't be the last when it comes to that, but that's not what I care about." He kissed her cheek. "We can talk later; there is so much to talk about. I loved the newspaper layout, by the way. You really showed us up."

He lay on his side, facing her. "But for now, I want what I've been missing for weeks. Lick the sweetness from me, enjoy your flavors, baby. Make me wild and truly native the way you did in Gallup."

Justine remembered exactly how native and wild they both had been. That was the truly terrible part about their separation. She had missed his closeness, the physical and emotional contact.

Justine kissed his lips once more before trailing down his chin, neck and collarbone. He was a magnificent flavor, all sex, man and candy—three heavenly delights in one. The most incredible part of it all was that he was there!

Darrius lay on his back against the cool sheets, awaiting his lover. Once her thighs were on either side of his, he noticed her shirt and traced the buffalo paintings on it. "I saw you when you bought this, and it made me so happy to see how much you love items from my culture."

"It's a beautiful shirt, Darrius. Now, take it off and let me show you just how much we belong together."

He uncovered her naked beauty and tenderly squeezed her breasts. His fingertips played at the hardened nipples, stroking them, rubbing them against the pad of his thumb. "God, I've missed you, Justine. I've missed how you talk, smell, feel. I've missed how you make my body do any and all things you want it to. Each day I wasn't inside you was like living in hell."

"Then surrender to heaven and let me tell you how much I've missed you, too."

His hands slowly traveled down her body, relishing just how much she felt like satin—she was a pure satin doll, his toy, and he wanted to play, all night, all the next morning and for the rest of their lives.

He toyed at her navel, watching her stomach muscles respond to his feathery touch. Her sensual giggle was music to his ears; he had missed it desperately. As he touched the soft brush of her sexual hair, he simply couldn't believe the time he had wasted being a stubborn jackass, being mad at her for something that was in her nature. Her inquisitive side was what he wanted to bring out again that night, because he had the urgent need to be explored, giving her the gifts of his body and love.

His fingers rubbed against her sexual folds. He felt her body tighten to him, yet he probed more, needing to enter her and experience her nectar and let it cover him completely. His desire to taste her was overwhelming, so he slid further down on the bed and looked straight into a core so soaking and ready for him.

With his hands placed firmly against her buttocks for support, he positioned her sex directly above his lips, licking the tender core in swirls, flicking his tongue around her. The feel of her pressing against him almost made him lose it, but he knew he had to hang on to give her the ultimate satisfaction. At that, his tongue licked harder in deep, rugged strokes from front to back. She felt so exquisite against him, and he could feel her hips gently moving back and forth, pressing down on him. He knew she needed deep satisfaction, the kind she could feel within her soul, and he gave it to her.

Never had she experienced the sensations he was now arousing in her. Not even their lovemaking in New Mexico had been this furious. The more he saturated her sex with his fervent tongue, the tighter her body became, rocking with him. She held her breasts in place, rubbing the hardened points until they were almost raw. And then, with a combination of his magic and her own hands, she came hard, shivering and arching her back to the point where she felt she would break.

Once her orgasm subsided, Darrius's hands slid up and down her moist body, rubbing her back and breasts. He needed to kiss her. Now.

Their lips met in wild, sweet sweeps, and Justine's tongue strokes continued down his body, tasting the sweet delights painted on him. Love had never really crossed her path before, and now had come with a vengeance. She felt the need to succumb to any and all things this man wanted her to. She would love him in ways that had never crossed her mind before. Her quest to please beyond reality began.

His nipples tasted like velvety dark chocolate as her tongue glided across one, and then the other. The feel of the hardened peaks brought the intense winding within her core again, but she knew she had to control it. Her mission was to save her feelings for the ultimate orgasm—with Darrius filling her endlessly. But no, with a man like him, one simple touch anywhere on her body would set her off, and it did.

Needing to taste more of this outstanding man, she licked further down his chest, creasing each square of his six-pack abdomen, and watched him stretch to the pleasure. His stomach tightened and she fell into a quick, tasty release, again, moaning to the intense pleasure of it.

The pressure of his taut erection began to purge against the suede of the handmade jockstrap. He knew release was but moments away, yet he let Justine's wicked tongue torment him. The feel of her hair against his chest as she licked around the parameter of the cloth drove him to distraction.

Justine's fingers struggled with the ties at either side of his breechcloth, and he helped her by pulling hard on the knots. The material released, and he felt her eyes feasting on an engorged, clothed erection. Darrius rested his head on the pillow, knowing what was sure to happen next, to be totally taken by the only woman he wanted to be submissive to. However, there was one catch, and he couldn't wait to be witness to her response.

Justine wrapped her hand around the suede erection and pulled in a milking fashion. His muscles flexed to her prowess and she smiled, being so proud to make a man as powerful as Darrius react to her every whim. When her hand moved forcefully to the tip of his manhood, something stopped her. A hard surface graced her fingers. She questioned, "What are you wearing?"

"A stiff erection and nothing more."

She felt the hard surface at the base of his tip again. "Come on! I'm worked up enough already. Don't tease me beyond my limits."

"That I love doing, and your face is so beautiful in the process of it. But since you're certain something other than my flesh is down there, look for yourself."

Not knowing what to expect, Justine slowly pulled the suede sleeve from his swelling rod. Sparkling and dangling from a thin silver chain attached to his breechcloth was a gold engagement band encircled with chips of turquoise and rubies. Hardly able to speak or breathe, she stared at it.

Darrius lifted her chin, drawing her face close to his. "I just have a few things to say to you, darling. Marry me. Be the reason I get out of bed each morning and the reason I get into it at night." He watched her throat bob up and down in a mixture of emotions. "Just say yes to me, Justine, and I promise to be the best husband a woman can have."

Still speechless, she stared into his loving eyes. She slowly retrieved the band from the chain and slipped it onto her finger. "It fits perfectly."

"Like we do." He sat up on the bed as best he could, and took her hand. "What's your answer? Are you going to be mine, or will you let my stupid mistake cost us?"

"Your behavior wasn't a mistake and you know it, Darrius. I never should have gone beyond the main road at Red Rock. I knew it was dangerous, and I should have listened to you."

"I was awfully harsh with you and I regret it."

"You did what had to be done. Maybe things had to happen this way, Darrius. How else would we know there is no one else for either of us? Love *and* absence make the heart grow fonder. We both experienced these things." She moved back on top of him. "I was so miserable without you, Darrius. I cried every day, and sometimes all night."

"Then why didn't you call me?"

"Fear of rejection."

"Like me. I missed you, too, Justine, probably more than any man could miss a woman. When I saw you on television, I knew I had to have you, but didn't know how to get you back. So," he kissed her ringed finger, "I had this ring made."

"You did?"

He placed her hand over his heart, waiting for the right answer to his question. "What are you going to do, be my wife or the proverbial one who got away?"

"I don't run as fast as I used to, but if I ran, it would be straight into your arms. I love you, Darrius, and I would be honored to be your wife—as soon as possible." She looked at the stunning ring again. "I love my ring, and I love my man, but do you know what I love most— at the moment?"

He smiled and lay back. "I do, and it's still waiting for you."

"Smart man."

Darrius took what he needed by raising her upper leg, and guiding himself deeply into her moist and hungry femininity. The deeper he moved into her, the more he could feel every part of her. He was a snug, delicious fit, and the more he moved inside her, the more he felt himself losing control of the situation. His willpower was gone, governed by Justine Roberts-Paretti, soon to be Justine Red Sky. She had awakened everything in him that was purely male, and for the first time in ages, he was glad a woman had been able to break through his hard exterior. He had a heart once again—and it all belonged to her now.

Both rocked against one another, side by side in a frenzied explosion. He wrapped Justine's leg around his hip for better advantage and kissed her, matching his kisses with each thrust. Their tongues coiled, danced, serenaded until their bodies could take no more, and they both tumbled into heated convulsions that shook their existence.

Wet, satisfied bodies lay together, still attached and not daring to disengage. Justine looked into Darrius' sleepy eyes and smiled. "How did I manage to get so blessed to have a man like you for a husband?"

"It was destiny. I know it was for me." He kissed her again. "There will never be another woman for me, Justine, and I'll do anything in my power to keep you."

"You have me, baby, and it is forever."

"That's what I love hearing."

Darrius saw a sudden quizzical look on her face and asked, "What is it?"

"How did you get this beautiful ring to stay attached to your strap without losing it?"

"I have my ways, but just know it was meant never to be removed unless by you."

"You must have walked in here with an erection in order to keep the chain in place."

He kissed her ringed finger. "My love, all I need is to think of you, and the erection is sure to come. I plan to have a lot of them for the next hundred years or so."

"That long?"

"That long."

They pulled the sheet up to their necks and made love again in the approaching dawn.

The aroma of brewed coffee filled Justine's nostrils as she watched it percolate on the stove. She had awakened with the sun to get a nice breakfast prepared. Darrius was usually the cook but he was still asleep, still tired from the quick trip to San Francisco on the red-eye, the powwow and, oh yes, making love until four that morning.

Justine had watched him until he fell asleep in her arms, hardly believing he was the one in her life as opposed to someone she would have to learn to love. She loved Darrius from the moment she had laid eyes on him that fateful Monday in early August—she just didn't want to admit to falling for someone again.

She sat at her kitchen table facing a large picture window, waiting for the coffee to finish brewing and the bacon to turn crisp. San Francisco had delivered another beautiful, lazy Sunday. The sun cast reflections against her engagement ring, and she stared at it in awe. She had never seen such a beautiful ring. She studied the delicate inlay pattern, the huge chunk of turquoise with rubies surrounding it, and she didn't quite know if it was, indeed, the loveliest ring on the planet, or if it was the idea of Darrius giving it to her that made it so priceless to her. Nonetheless, she would wear it forever.

Darrius crept up behind her and began massaging her shoulders. He bent to kiss her cheeks and neck, and she rose to him. Now face to face, the lovers kissed good morning and held one another. Darrius broke the kiss. "I took a quick shower to rid my body of the candied paint you hadn't kissed off."

"You were a delicious meal last night, Darrius Red Sky."

"Indeed! Hey, do you know this is the first day of *our* life together."

"I tend not to agree. I think the first day of our life together began with the first words you spoke to me."

"Which were?"

"You said, 'Ma'am, is there anything I can show you?' And you've been *showing* me ever since, probably in ways you hadn't planned on."

"Oh, I planned on it, all right!"

"And you don't regret it?"

"My stock response: I'm still here, aren't I? And the ring looks incredible on you, darling."

Justine hugged him around his bare hips. "I just can't wait to become Mrs. Darrius Red Sky."

He kissed the top of her head. "Me, too, Justine. Me, too!"

Darrius and Justine became husband and wife on January first in an outdoor celebration in Shiprock, New Mexico. They married in traditional Hopi wedding attire, consisting of a large woven belt, white robes with red and white strips of fabric at the top and bottom, buckskin leggings and moccasins, and their hair was bound in colorful, rainbow string.

As Justine looked into Darrius's handsome face, she still couldn't believe he was the one she was marrying. She always thought it would be Horton Johansen, of all names and people. He was a Swedish boy who lived across from her as a child and had a perpetual crush on her since sixth grade. He still tried to keep in touch with Justine—useless efforts on his part. However, destiny had put the man before her into her life, and for that she was grateful.

To bless them into a lasting love affair were her parents, siblings and best friend, Fara. Darrius's family and friends were scattered about the campgrounds as well. The ceremony was set to native drums conducted by Derrick and other tribe members.

Both Darrius and Justine held their totems in hand and awaited the rings. They could hardly keep their eyes off one another, anticipating the start of their enchanting new life together. In the audience, Justine saw Fara smiling at her and giving her a thumbs-up. She then returned to the loving smile of her new husband, knowing he was her best achievement, and the love she had for him was timeless, limitless.

27

MANY MOONS

Three years later

Justine gazed through the large kitchen window that faced the reddish-brown peaks of the outskirts of Gallup. That was her ritual every morning: to rise before everyone else, capture a few secluded moments of peace and admire the miraculous landscape.

She had taken many a picture of the red cliffs all over New Mexico before, but the mornings were always so special, so quiet—hers. The mountains looked surreal, enchanting, and she always saw something different each time she looked at them. It calmed her even more than Darrius's unyielding love had.

Now a full-time photographer with *New Mexico Magazine*, she could set her hours, plan her photography sessions, work with children at the orphanages and continue to bring the beauty of New Mexico and surrounding states to the rest of the world. It was her dream job, and she was living her dream life. She looked around the spacious kitchen with its hints of western and Italian modern tiles and designs, and smiled. She remembered the first time she saw the house, but at the time, it was simply Darrius's house. It had nothing but Native

American flavor. Now it was decorated in a mix of African face masks, her Italian kitchen tile and the Native American culture. Now it was an expression of both of them—and their family.

The new day brought with it a kind of serenity, and she was enjoying it while she could because she knew shortly there would be the sound of little feet everywhere and a hungry man about to rush off to check on the new tea plant he and his family were opening. The plant would bring many jobs to the many impoverished Native Americans in the area, which was one of the main reasons he and Derrick had decided to expand the family business. Darrius was the overseer and part-time manager. Though he still owned his jewelry stores, being involved with providing jobs appealed to him.

Justine smiled and drank the rest of her Good Morning Medicine tea. She loved her life and wouldn't trade it for anything, though juggling a career and a household could be hectic at times. Minutes later, she heard gentle laughter coming from the deck on the side of the house. She knew that warm, giddy laugh, and couldn't wait to see the source.

Justine looked out her back patio and saw a breath-taking sunrise and mountain backdrop. The air was crisp and fresh, but what truly caught her attention was Darrius teaching their two-year old son, Honovi, the traditional dance so he could follow in his dad's footsteps. The little dark-haired second joy of her life was named after his uncle, who had died shortly after birth many years ago due to weak lungs. Her son was a strong baby, however, and looked just like his father, but was darker in complexion and with deeply set eyes.

She smiled as she watched them dance without a clue of being watched. "You two are up awfully early today."

Honovi smiled upon seeing his mother, and twisted in his father's clutches until released. He ran directly into her outstretched arms, and the two cooed together until Darrius entered, wanting a piece of the action.

Justine quickly put the wiggling child back on the grass and gave her husband a warm good morning hug. She quickly kissed his warm lips, and then briefly parted. "Hungry? I can make you something before you go off to conquer the world."

He nuzzled her nose against his. "The only thing I'm hungry for is a little more bed action with my first lady. Possible before I head off?"

"And what do we do with our little miracle playing in the grass? He's not exactly the patient type who will let Mom and Dad have a little alone time. Am I right?"

"Yes, you are, but he did sleep long enough to let us do this." He ran his hand over her growing stomach.

Seeing joy spread across Darrius's face, she asked, "So, what do you think he wants, a sister or a brother?"

"At this age, I don't think he cares."

"Then what about you, papa? Boy or girl?"

"I don't care either, so long as my first lady comes through with flying colors."

She smiled, stroking his handsome face. "I'm gonna be just fine, Darrius. After all, don't I have to live up to my word?"

"Which is?"

"To live happily ever after in your arms. I can't do that without you."

"And you won't have to."

He kissed her in a long, delicious drag, and pulled away with a look of total happiness on his face. "Umm, that's my plan, girl—to have a long, happy life with you in my arms."

He looked at the gorgeous red mountains in the distance, his baby playing gleefully on the grass and his beautiful wife in his arms, and smiled. "We certainly have a great start to this 'long life' of ours, don't we?"

"A perfect start, Darrius Red Sky, absolutely perfect."

ABOUT THE AUTHOR

Born and raised in Detroit, Michigan, Reneé has always loved the arts. She began her writing career very young with short stories for school newspaper contests. Now the author of several published short stories and single-title books, she is always on the lookout for a new writing adventure. Please contact her at *www.reneealexis.net* or at *reneealexis@yahoo.com*.

2009 Reprint Mass Market Titles

January

I'm Gonna Make You Love Me
Gwyneth Bolton
ISBN-13: 978-1-58571-294-6
$6.99

Shades of Desire
Monica White
ISBN-13: 978-1-58571-292-2
$6.99

February

A Love of Her Own
Cheris Hodges
ISBN-13: 978-1-58571-293-9
$6.99

Color of Trouble
Dyanne Davis
ISBN-13: 978-1-58571-294-6
$6.99

March

Twist of Fate
Beverly Clark
ISBN-13: 978-1-58571-295-3
$6.99

Chances
Pamela Leigh Starr
ISBN-13: 978-1-58571-296-0
$6.99

April

Sinful Intentions
Crystal Rhodes
ISBN-13: 978-1-585712-297-7
$6.99

Rock Star
Roslyn Hardy Holcomb
ISBN-13: 978-1-58571-298-4
$6.99

May

Paths of Fire
T.T. Henderson
ISBN-13: 978-1-58571-343-1
$6.99

Caught Up in the Rapture
Lisa Riley
ISBN-13: 978-1-58571-344-8
$6.99

June

Reckless Surrender
Rochelle Alers
ISBN-13: 978-1-58571-345-5
$6.99

No Ordinary Love
Angela Weaver
ISBN-13: 978-1-58571-346-2
$6.99

2009 Reprint Mass Market Titles (continued)

July

Intentional Mistakes
Michele Sudler
ISBN-13: 978-1-58571-347-9
$6.99

It's In His Kiss
Reon Carter
ISBN-13: 978-1-58571-348-6
$6.99

August

Unfinished Love Affair
Barbara Keaton
ISBN-13: 978-1-58571-349-3
$6.99

A Perfect Place to Pray
I.L Goodwin
ISBN-13: 978-1-58571-299-1
$6.99

September

Love in High Gear
Charlotte Roy
ISBN-13: 978-1-58571-355-4
$6.99

Ebony Eyes
Kei Swanson
ISBN-13: 978-1-58571-356-1
$6.99

October

Midnight Clear, Part I
Leslie Esdale/Carmen Green
ISBN-13: 978-1-58571-357-8
$6.99

Midnight Clear, Part II
Gwynne Forster/Monica
    Jackson
ISBN-13: 978-1-58571-358-5
$6.99

November

Midnight Peril
Vicki Andrews
ISBN-13: 978-1-58571-359-2
$6.99

One Day At A Time
Bella McFarland
ISBN-13: 978-1-58571-360-8
$6.99

December

Just An Affair
Eugenia O'Neal
ISBN-13: 978-1-58571-361-5
$6.99

Shades of Brown
Denise Becker
ISBN-13: 978-1-58571-362-2
$6.99

2009 New Mass Market Titles

January

Singing A Song…
Crystal Rhodes
ISBN-13: 978-1-58571-283-0
$6.99

Look Both Ways
Joan Early
ISBN-13: 978-1-58571-284-7
$6.99

February

Six O'Clock
Katrina Spencer
ISBN-13: 978-1-58571-285-4
$6.99

Red Sky
Renee Alexis
ISBN-13: 978-1-58571-286-1
$6.99

March

Anything But Love
Celya Bowers
ISBN-13: 978-1-58571-287-8
$6.99

Tempting Faith
Crystal Hubbard
ISBN-13: 978-1-58571-288-5
$6.99

April

If I Were Your Woman
La Connie Taylor-Jones
ISBN-13: 978-1-58571-289-2
$6.99

Best Of Luck Elsewhere
Trisha Haddad
ISBN-13: 978-1-58571-290-8
$6.99

May

All I'll Ever Need
Mildred Riley
ISBN-13: 978-1-58571-335-6
$6.99

A Place Like Home
Alicia Wiggins
ISBN-13: 978-1-58571-336-3
$6.99

June

Best Foot Forward
Michele Sudler
ISBN-13: 978-1-58571-337-0
$6.99

It's In the Rhythm
Sammie Ward
ISBN-13: 978-1-58571-338-7
$6.99

2009 New Mass Market Titles (continued)

July

Checks and Balances
Elaine Sims
ISBN-13: 978-1-58571-339-4
$6.99

Save Me
Africa Fine
ISBN-13: 978-1-58571-340-0
$6.99

August

When Lightening Strikes
Michele Cameron
ISBN-13: 978-1-58571-369-1
$6.99

Blindsided
Tammy Williams
ISBN-13: 978-1-58571-342-4
$6.99

September

2 Good
Celya Bowers
ISBN-13: 978-1-58571-350-9
$6.99

Waiting for Mr. Darcy
Chamein Canton
ISBN-13: 978-1-58571-351-6
$6.99

October

Fireflies
Joan Early
ISBN-13: 978-1-58571-352-3
$6.99

Frost On My Window
Angela Weaver
ISBN-13: 978-1-58571-353-0
$6.99

November

Waiting in the Shadows
Michele Sudler
ISBN-13: 978-1-58571-364-6
$6.99

Fixin' Tyrone
Keith Walker
ISBN-13: 978-1-58571-365-3
$6.99

December

Dream Keeper
Gail McFarland
ISBN-13: 978-1-58571-366-0
$6.99

Another Memory
Pamela Ridley
ISBN-13: 978-1-58571-367-7
$6.99

Other Genesis Press, Inc. Titles

A Dangerous Deception	J.M. Jeffries	$8.95
A Dangerous Love	J.M. Jeffries	$8.95
A Dangerous Obsession	J.M. Jeffries	$8.95
A Drummer's Beat to Mend	Kei Swanson	$9.95
A Happy Life	Charlotte Harris	$9.95
A Heart's Awakening	Veronica Parker	$9.95
A Lark on the Wing	Phyliss Hamilton	$9.95
A Love of Her Own	Cheris F. Hodges	$9.95
A Love to Cherish	Beverly Clark	$8.95
A Risk of Rain	Dar Tomlinson	$8.95
A Taste of Temptation	Reneé Alexis	$9.95
A Twist of Fate	Beverly Clark	$8.95
A Voice Behind Thunder	Carrie Elizabeth Greene	$6.99
A Will to Love	Angie Daniels	$9.95
Acquisitions	Kimberley White	$8.95
Across	Carol Payne	$12.95
After the Vows	Leslie Esdaile	$10.95
(Summer Anthology)	T.T. Henderson	
	Jacqueline Thomas	
Again My Love	Kayla Perrin	$10.95
Against the Wind	Gwynne Forster	$8.95
All I Ask	Barbara Keaton	$8.95
Always You	Crystal Hubbard	$6.99
Ambrosia	T.T. Henderson	$8.95
An Unfinished Love Affair	Barbara Keaton	$8.95
And Then Came You	Dorothy Elizabeth Love	$8.95
Angel's Paradise	Janice Angelique	$9.95
At Last	Lisa G. Riley	$8.95
Best of Friends	Natalie Dunbar	$8.95
Beyond the Rapture	Beverly Clark	$9.95
Blame It On Paradise	Crystal Hubbard	$6.99
Blaze	Barbara Keaton	$9.95
Bliss, Inc.	Chamein Canton	$6.99
Blood Lust	J. M. Jeffries	$9.95
Blood Seduction	J.M. Jeffries	$9.95

Other Genesis Press, Inc. Titles (continued)

Bodyguard	Andrea Jackson	$9.95
Boss of Me	Diana Nyad	$8.95
Bound by Love	Beverly Clark	$8.95
Breeze	Robin Hampton Allen	$10.95
Broken	Dar Tomlinson	$24.95
By Design	Barbara Keaton	$8.95
Cajun Heat	Charlene Berry	$8.95
Careless Whispers	Rochelle Alers	$8.95
Cats & Other Tales	Marilyn Wagner	$8.95
Caught in a Trap	Andre Michelle	$8.95
Caught Up In the Rapture	Lisa G. Riley	$9.95
Cautious Heart	Cheris F Hodges	$8.95
Chances	Pamela Leigh Starr	$8.95
Cherish the Flame	Beverly Clark	$8.95
Choices	Tammy Williams	$6.99
Class Reunion	Irma Jenkins/ John Brown	$12.95
Code Name: Diva	J.M. Jeffries	$9.95
Conquering Dr. Wexler's Heart	Kimberley White	$9.95
Corporate Seduction	A.C. Arthur	$9.95
Crossing Paths, Tempting Memories	Dorothy Elizabeth Love	$9.95
Crush	Crystal Hubbard	$9.95
Cypress Whisperings	Phyllis Hamilton	$8.95
Dark Embrace	Crystal Wilson Harris	$8.95
Dark Storm Rising	Chinelu Moore	$10.95
Daughter of the Wind	Joan Xian	$8.95
Dawn's Harbor	Kymberly Hunt	$6.99
Deadly Sacrifice	Jack Kean	$22.95
Designer Passion	Dar Tomlinson Diana Richeaux	$8.95
Do Over	Celya Bowers	$9.95
Dream Runner	Gail McFarland	$6.99
Dreamtective	Liz Swados	$5.95

Other Genesis Press, Inc. Titles (continued)

Ebony Angel	Deatri King-Bey	$9.95
Ebony Butterfly II	Delilah Dawson	$14.95
Echoes of Yesterday	Beverly Clark	$9.95
Eden's Garden	Elizabeth Rose	$8.95
Eve's Prescription	Edwina Martin Arnold	$8.95
Everlastin' Love	Gay G. Gunn	$8.95
Everlasting Moments	Dorothy Elizabeth Love	$8.95
Everything and More	Sinclair Lebeau	$8.95
Everything but Love	Natalie Dunbar	$8.95
Falling	Natalie Dunbar	$9.95
Fate	Pamela Leigh Starr	$8.95
Finding Isabella	A.J. Garrotto	$8.95
Forbidden Quest	Dar Tomlinson	$10.95
Forever Love	Wanda Y. Thomas	$8.95
From the Ashes	Kathleen Suzanne	$8.95
	Jeanne Sumerix	
Gentle Yearning	Rochelle Alers	$10.95
Glory of Love	Sinclair LeBeau	$10.95
Go Gentle into that	Malcom Boyd	$12.95
Good Night		
Goldengroove	Mary Beth Craft	$16.95
Groove, Bang, and Jive	Steve Cannon	$8.99
Hand in Glove	Andrea Jackson	$9.95
Hard to Love	Kimberley White	$9.95
Hart & Soul	Angie Daniels	$8.95
Heart of the Phoenix	A.C. Arthur	$9.95
Heartbeat	Stephanie Bedwell-Grime	$8.95
Hearts Remember	M. Loui Quezada	$8.95
Hidden Memories	Robin Allen	$10.95
Higher Ground	Leah Latimer	$19.95
Hitler, the War, and the Pope	Ronald Rychiak	$26.95
How to Write a Romance	Kathryn Falk	$18.95
I Married a Reclining Chair	Lisa M. Fuhs	$8.95
I'll Be Your Shelter	Giselle Carmichael	$8.95
I'll Paint a Sun	A.J. Garrotto	$9.95

Other Genesis Press, Inc. Titles (continued)

Icie	Pamela Leigh Starr	$8.95
Illusions	Pamela Leigh Starr	$8.95
Indigo After Dark Vol. I	Nia Dixon/Angelique	$10.95
Indigo After Dark Vol. II	Dolores Bundy/	$10.95
	Cole Riley	
Indigo After Dark Vol. III	Montana Blue/	$10.95
	Coco Morena	
Indigo After Dark Vol. IV	Cassandra Colt/	$14.95
Indigo After Dark Vol. V	Delilah Dawson	$14.95
Indiscretions	Donna Hill	$8.95
Intentional Mistakes	Michele Sudler	$9.95
Interlude	Donna Hill	$8.95
Intimate Intentions	Angie Daniels	$8.95
It's Not Over Yet	J.J. Michael	$9.95
Jolie's Surrender	Edwina Martin-Arnold	$8.95
Kiss or Keep	Debra Phillips	$8.95
Lace	Giselle Carmichael	$9.95
Lady Preacher	K.T. Richey	$6.99
Last Train to Memphis	Elsa Cook	$12.95
Lasting Valor	Ken Olsen	$24.95
Let Us Prey	Hunter Lundy	$25.95
Lies Too Long	Pamela Ridley	$13.95
Life Is Never As It Seems	J.J. Michael	$12.95
Lighter Shade of Brown	Vicki Andrews	$8.95
Looking for Lily	Africa Fine	$6.99
Love Always	Mildred E. Riley	$10.95
Love Doesn't Come Easy	Charlyne Dickerson	$8.95
Love Unveiled	Gloria Greene	$10.95
Love's Deception	Charlene Berry	$10.95
Love's Destiny	M. Loui Quezada	$8.95
Love's Secrets	Yolanda McVey	$6.99
Mae's Promise	Melody Walcott	$8.95
Magnolia Sunset	Giselle Carmichael	$8.95
Many Shades of Gray	Dyanne Davis	$6.99
Matters of Life and Death	Lesego Malepe, Ph.D.	$15.95

Other Genesis Press, Inc. Titles (continued)

Meant to Be	Jeanne Sumerix	$8.95
Midnight Clear (Anthology)	Leslie Esdaile Gwynne Forster Carmen Green Monica Jackson	$10.95
Midnight Magic	Gwynne Forster	$8.95
Midnight Peril	Vicki Andrews	$10.95
Misconceptions	Pamela Leigh Starr	$9.95
Moments of Clarity	Michele Cameron	$6.99
Montgomery's Children	Richard Perry	$14.95
Mr Fix-It	Crystal Hubbard	$6.99
My Buffalo Soldier	Barbara B. K. Reeves	$8.95
Naked Soul	Gwynne Forster	$8.95
Never Say Never	Michele Cameron	$6.99
Next to Last Chance	Louisa Dixon	$24.95
No Apologies	Seressia Glass	$8.95
No Commitment Required	Seressia Glass	$8.95
No Regrets	Mildred E. Riley	$8.95
Not His Type	Chamein Canton	$6.99
Nowhere to Run	Gay G. Gunn	$10.95
O Bed! O Breakfast!	Rob Kuehnle	$14.95
Object of His Desire	A. C. Arthur	$8.95
Office Policy	A. C. Arthur	$9.95
Once in a Blue Moon	Dorianne Cole	$9.95
One Day at a Time	Bella McFarland	$8.95
One in A Million	Barbara Keaton	$6.99
One of These Days	Michele Sudler	$9.95
Outside Chance	Louisa Dixon	$24.95
Passion	T.T. Henderson	$10.95
Passion's Blood	Cherif Fortin	$22.95
Passion's Furies	AlTonya Washington	$6.99
Passion's Journey	Wanda Y. Thomas	$8.95
Past Promises	Jahmel West	$8.95
Path of Fire	T.T. Henderson	$8.95
Path of Thorns	Annetta P. Lee	$9.95

Other Genesis Press, Inc. Titles (continued)

Peace Be Still	Colette Haywood	$12.95
Picture Perfect	Reon Carter	$8.95
Playing for Keeps	Stephanie Salinas	$8.95
Pride & Joi	Gay G. Gunn	$8.95
Promises Made	Bernice Layton	$6.99
Promises to Keep	Alicia Wiggins	$8.95
Quiet Storm	Donna Hill	$10.95
Reckless Surrender	Rochelle Alers	$6.95
Red Polka Dot in a World of Plaid	Varian Johnson	$12.95
Reluctant Captive	Joyce Jackson	$8.95
Rendezvous with Fate	Jeanne Sumerix	$8.95
Revelations	Cheris F. Hodges	$8.95
Rivers of the Soul	Leslie Esdaile	$8.95
Rocky Mountain Romance	Kathleen Suzanne	$8.95
Rooms of the Heart	Donna Hill	$8.95
Rough on Rats and Tough on Cats	Chris Parker	$12.95
Secret Library Vol. 1	Nina Sheridan	$18.95
Secret Library Vol. 2	Cassandra Colt	$8.95
Secret Thunder	Annetta P. Lee	$9.95
Shades of Brown	Denise Becker	$8.95
Shades of Desire	Monica White	$8.95
Shadows in the Moonlight	Jeanne Sumerix	$8.95
Sin	Crystal Rhodes	$8.95
Small Whispers	Annetta P. Lee	$6.99
So Amazing	Sinclair LeBeau	$8.95
Somebody's Someone	Sinclair LeBeau	$8.95
Someone to Love	Alicia Wiggins	$8.95
Song in the Park	Martin Brant	$15.95
Soul Eyes	Wayne L. Wilson	$12.95
Soul to Soul	Donna Hill	$8.95
Southern Comfort	J.M. Jeffries	$8.95
Southern Fried Standards	S.R. Maddox	$6.99
Still the Storm	Sharon Robinson	$8.95

Other Genesis Press, Inc. Titles (continued)

Still Waters Run Deep	Leslie Esdaile	$8.95
Stolen Kisses	Dominiqua Douglas	$9.95
Stolen Memories	Michele Sudler	$6.99
Stories to Excite You	Anna Forrest/Divine	$14.95
Storm	Pamela Leigh Starr	$6.99
Subtle Secrets	Wanda Y. Thomas	$8.95
Suddenly You	Crystal Hubbard	$9.95
Sweet Repercussions	Kimberley White	$9.95
Sweet Sensations	Gwyneth Bolton	$9.95
Sweet Tomorrows	Kimberly White	$8.95
Taken by You	Dorothy Elizabeth Love	$9.95
Tattooed Tears	T. T. Henderson	$8.95
The Color Line	Lizzette Grayson Carter	$9.95
The Color of Trouble	Dyanne Davis	$8.95
The Disappearance of Allison Jones	Kayla Perrin	$5.95
The Fires Within	Beverly Clark	$9.95
The Foursome	Celya Bowers	$6.99
The Honey Dipper's Legacy	Pannell-Allen	$14.95
The Joker's Love Tune	Sidney Rickman	$15.95
The Little Pretender	Barbara Cartland	$10.95
The Love We Had	Natalie Dunbar	$8.95
The Man Who Could Fly	Bob & Milana Beamon	$18.95
The Missing Link	Charlyne Dickerson	$8.95
The Mission	Pamela Leigh Starr	$6.99
The More Things Change	Chamein Canton	$6.99
The Perfect Frame	Beverly Clark	$9.95
The Price of Love	Sinclair LeBeau	$8.95
The Smoking Life	Ilene Barth	$29.95
The Words of the Pitcher	Kei Swanson	$8.95
Things Forbidden	Maryam Diaab	$6.99
This Life Isn't Perfect Holla	Sandra Foy	$6.99
Three Doors Down	Michele Sudler	$6.99
Three Wishes	Seressia Glass	$8.95
Ties That Bind	Kathleen Suzanne	$8.95

Other Genesis Press, Inc. Titles (continued)

Tiger Woods	Libby Hughes	$5.95
Time is of the Essence	Angie Daniels	$9.95
Timeless Devotion	Bella McFarland	$9.95
Tomorrow's Promise	Leslie Esdaile	$8.95
Truly Inseparable	Wanda Y. Thomas	$8.95
Two Sides to Every Story	Dyanne Davis	$9.95
Unbreak My Heart	Dar Tomlinson	$8.95
Uncommon Prayer	Kenneth Swanson	$9.95
Unconditional Love	Alicia Wiggins	$8.95
Unconditional	A.C. Arthur	$9.95
Undying Love	Renee Alexis	$6.99
Until Death Do Us Part	Susan Paul	$8.95
Vows of Passion	Bella McFarland	$9.95
Wedding Gown	Dyanne Davis	$8.95
What's Under Benjamin's Bed	Sandra Schaffer	$8.95
When A Man Loves A Woman	La Connie Taylor-Jones	$6.99
When Dreams Float	Dorothy Elizabeth Love	$8.95
When I'm With You	LaConnie Taylor-Jones	$6.99
Where I Want To Be	Maryam Diaab	$6.99
Whispers in the Night	Dorothy Elizabeth Love	$8.95
Whispers in the Sand	LaFlorya Gauthier	$10.95
Who's That Lady?	Andrea Jackson	$9.95
Wild Ravens	Altonya Washington	$9.95
Yesterday Is Gone	Beverly Clark	$10.95
Yesterday's Dreams, Tomorrow's Promises	Reon Laudat	$8.95
Your Precious Love	Sinclair LeBeau	$8.95

Order Form

Mail to: Genesis Press, Inc.
P.O. Box 101
Columbus, MS 39703

Name _____
Address _____
City/State _____ Zip _____
Telephone _____

Ship to (if different from above)
Name _____
Address _____
City/State _____ Zip _____
Telephone _____

Credit Card Information
Credit Card # _____ ☐ Visa ☐ Mastercard
Expiration Date (mm/yy) _____ ☐ AmEx ☐ Discover

Qty.	Author	Title	Price	Total

Use this order

form, or call

1-888-INDIGO-1

Total for books _____
Shipping and handling:
  $5 first two books,
  $1 each additional book _____
Total S & H _____
Total amount enclosed _____
Mississippi residents add 7% sales tax